Razzle Dazzle Unicorn

Another Phoebe and Her Unicorn Adventure

Dana Simpson

2584

Andrews McMeel
PUBLISHING®

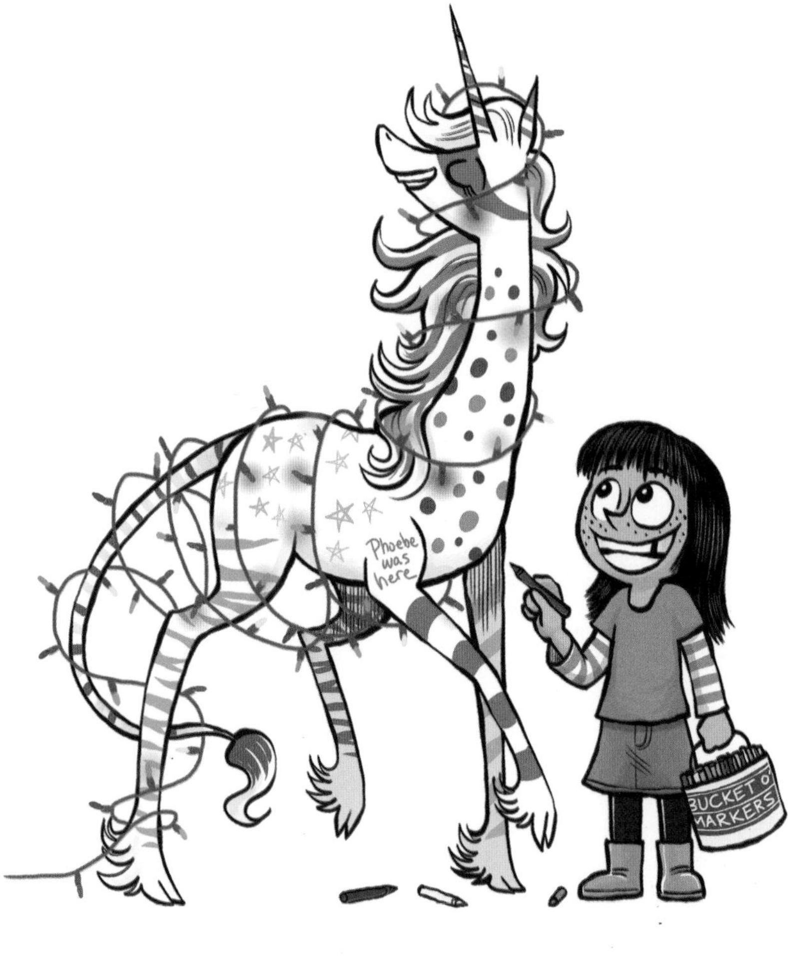
Phoebe was here
BUCKET O' MARKERS

INTRODUCTION

Sometimes a unicorn shows up in your life and makes everything better.

I wasn't really expecting one. A few years ago, I had nearly realized an ambition I've had since age twelve: I had scored a contract to develop a comic strip for newspaper syndication. I won that contract in the Comic Strip Superstar contest, which was sort of an *American Idol* for aspiring comic strip artists (without the surrounding glamour). I won with a comic strip called *Girl*, which starred a little girl who would eventually acquire the name Phoebe Howell. She ran around in the woods behind her house and hung out with talking animals.

I thought I'd just draw a bunch of *Girl* strips, and that would be that, and I'd be syndicated and happy forever. What happened instead was, I sent my required thirty strips in every month, and I got back a lot of notes explaining to me why the work I was doing wasn't good enough to launch in syndication.

My editor at the time, John Glynn, was blunt. "The work you're doing is better than some currently syndicated strips," he told me, "but in a market this tight, your work needs to be transcendent."

I was, as far as I could tell, doing my best. If it wasn't transcendent already, I didn't have the faintest idea how to make it transcendent. I wasn't even sure what I was being asked to do.

A year of my two-year development contract had passed. Despair began to set in. And that's when the unicorn made her appearance.

One day I wrote a strip with a unicorn in it. It was a one-off joke, riffing on a theme that was looming large in my life at the time: knowing what counts as a reasonable expectation. Phoebe was conversing with a voice off camera about whether her ideas about her life were realistic. Final panel: pan out, and look, she's talking about this to a unicorn.

And then the unicorn wouldn't leave. Once she was there, she was there. She more or less announced herself as the second main character in the strip.

Being a unicorn, she wanted attention. She needed to shine in front of an admiring audience. This dovetailed nicely with my own goals. I named her Marigold Heavenly Nostrils, a name I got by typing my own name into an online unicorn-name generator.

The strip must, at last, have transcended, because it launched in over a hundred newspapers. The books have done pretty well, too, as evidenced by the fact that this one is the fourth.

Every year I've spent in the company of Marigold Heavenly Nostrils has had more magic in it than the last.

Unicorns are around. The one I found was the best thing that ever happened to me.

— Dana Simpson
September 2016

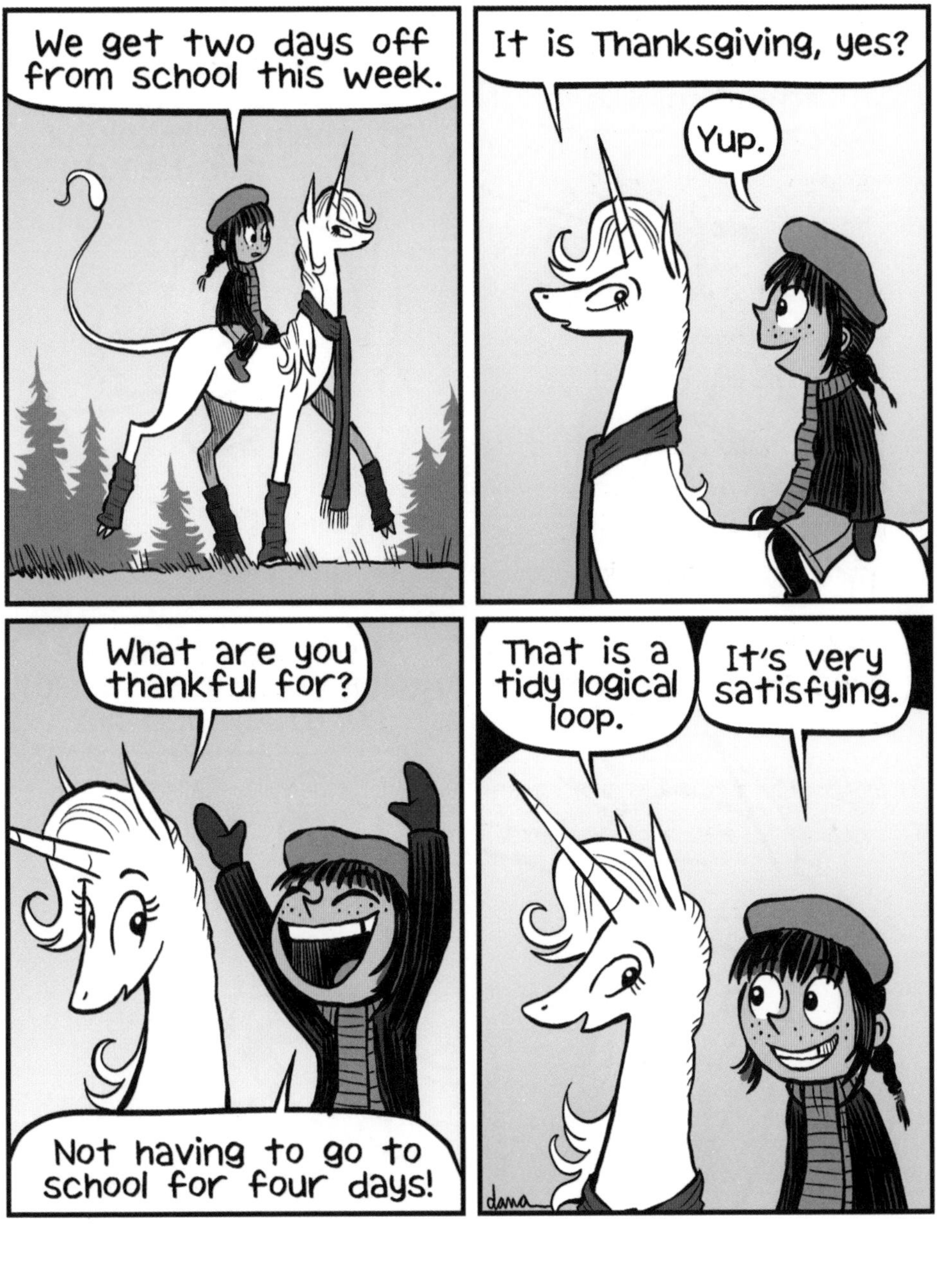
We get two days off from school this week.
It is Thanksgiving, yes?
Yup.
What are you thankful for?
Not having to go to school for four days!
That is a tidy logical loop.
It's very satisfying.
dana

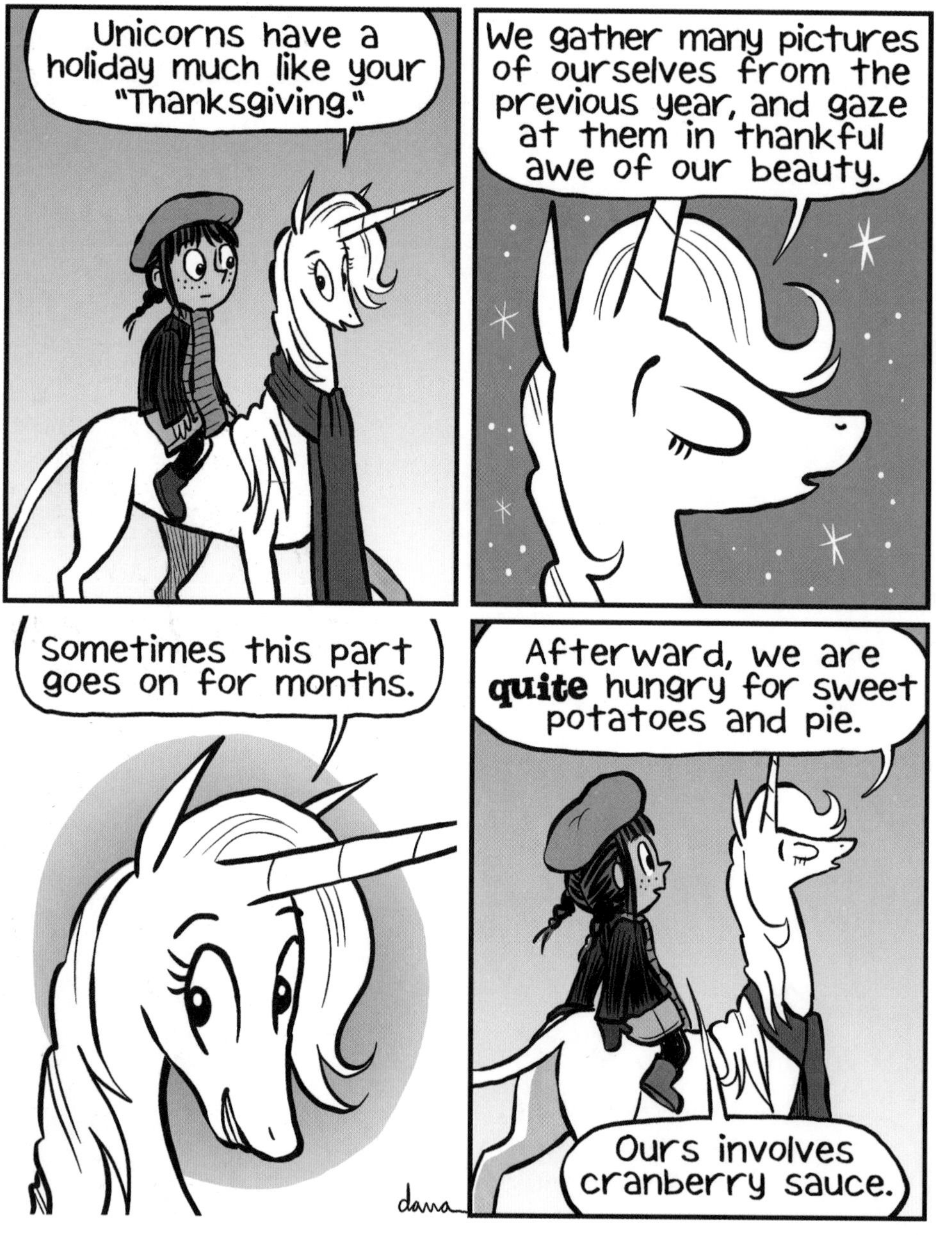
Unicorns have a holiday much like your "Thanksgiving."
We gather many pictures of ourselves from the previous year, and gaze at them in thankful awe of our beauty.
Sometimes this part goes on for months.
Afterward, we are **quite** hungry for sweet potatoes and pie.
Ours involves cranberry sauce.
dana

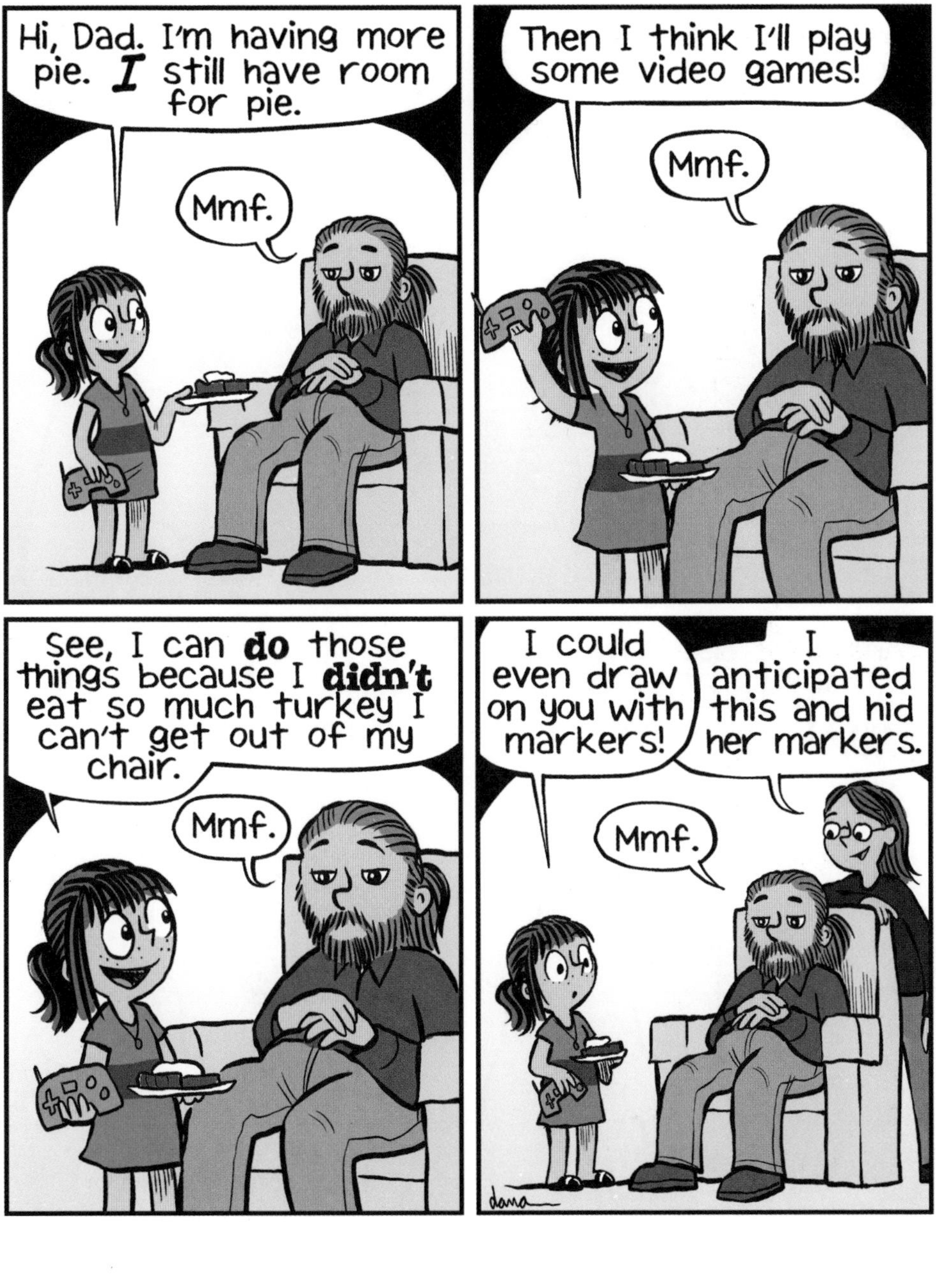
Hi, Dad. I'm having more pie. I still have room for pie.
Mmf.
Then I think I'll play some video games!
Mmf.
See, I can do those things because I didn't eat so much turkey I can't get out of my chair.
Mmf.
I could even draw on you with markers!
I anticipated this and hid her markers.
Mmf.
dana

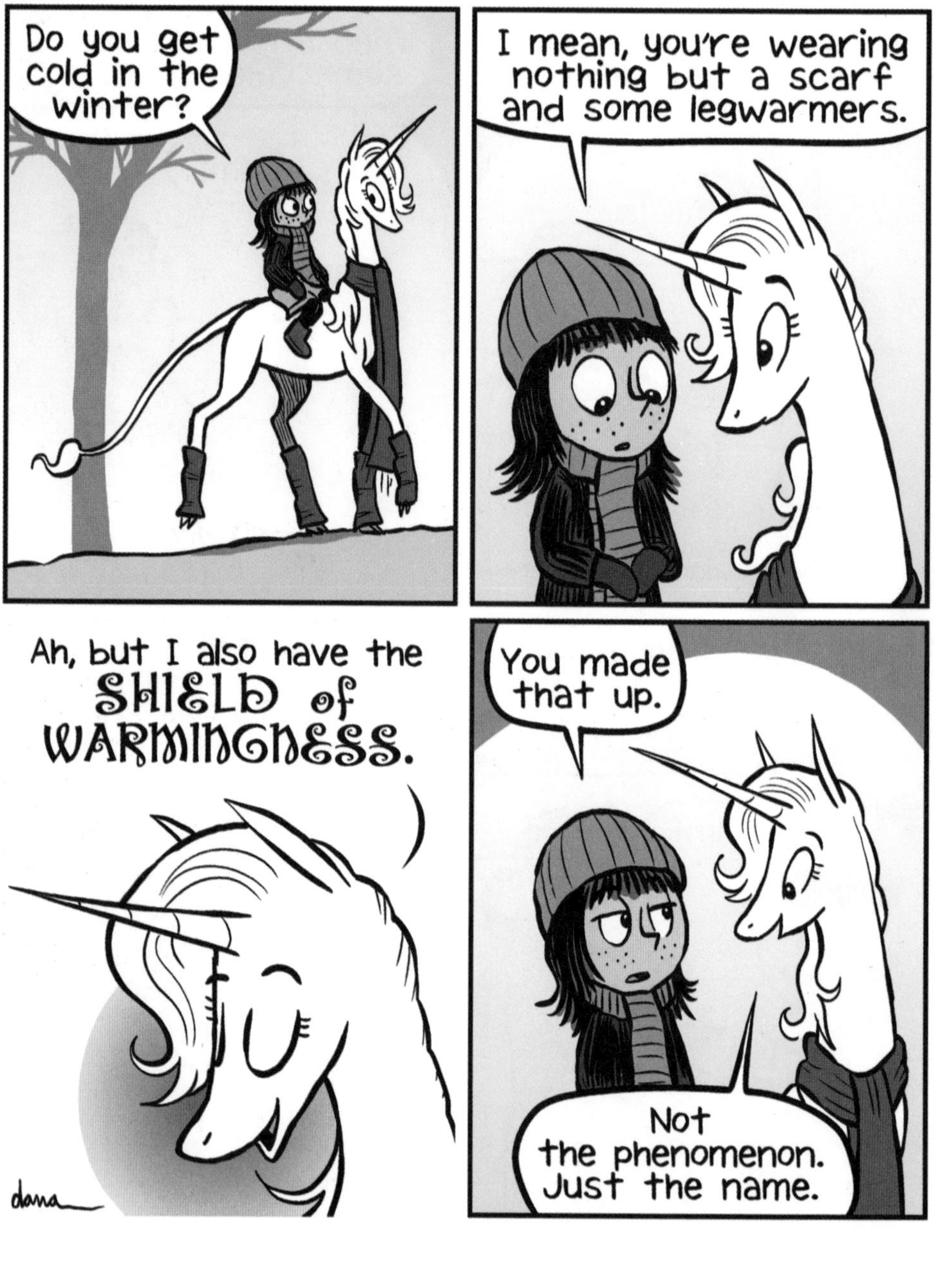
Do you get cold in the winter?
I mean, you're wearing nothing but a scarf and some legwarmers.
Ah, but I also have the SHIELD of WARMINGNESS.
You made that up.
Not the phenomenon. Just the name.
dana

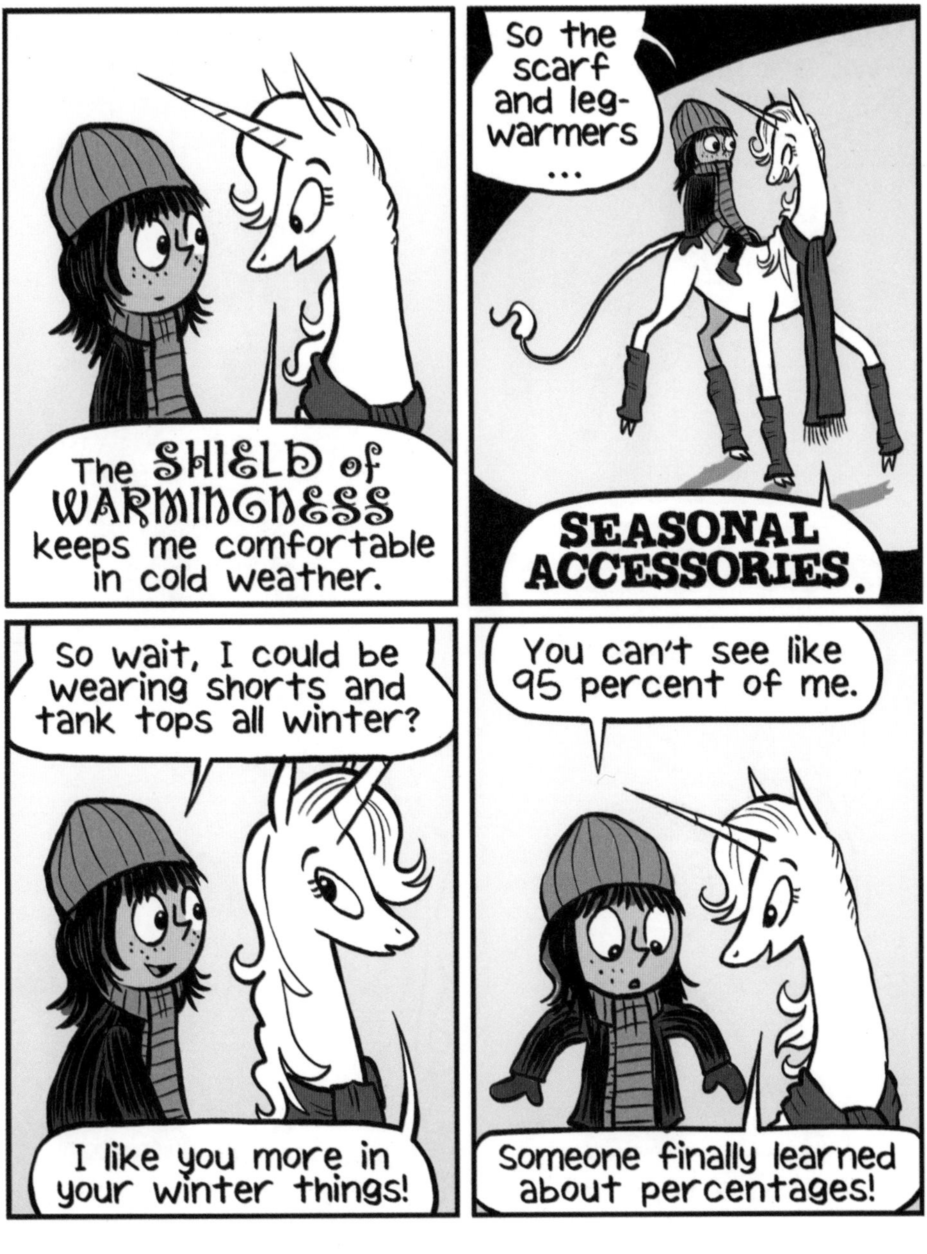
The SHIELD of WARMINGNESS keeps me comfortable in cold weather.
So the scarf and leg-warmers ...
SEASONAL ACCESSORIES.
So wait, I could be wearing shorts and tank tops all winter?
I like you more in your winter things!
You can't see like 95 percent of me.
Someone finally learned about percentages!

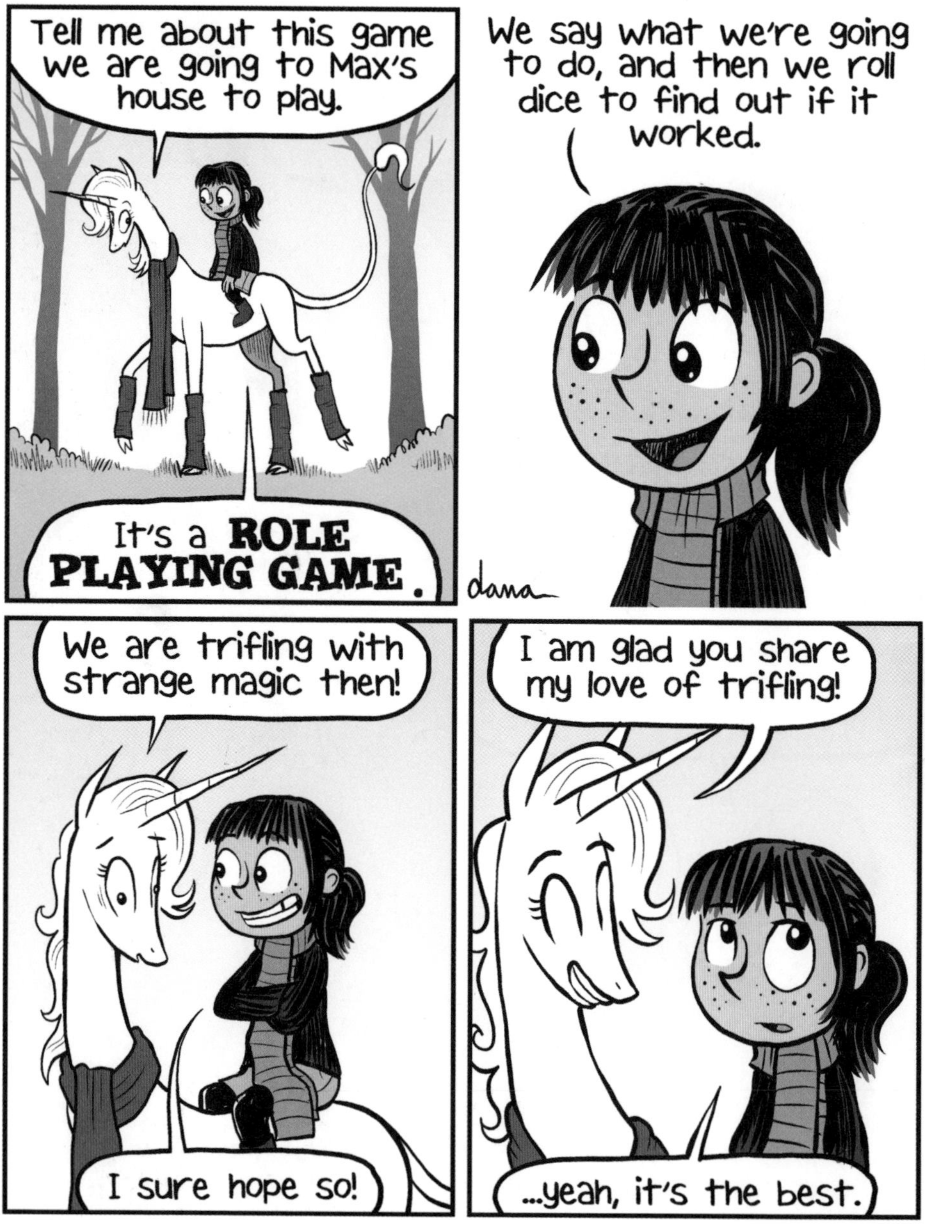
Tell me about this game we are going to Max's house to play.
It's a **ROLE PLAYING GAME**.
We say what we're going to do, and then we roll dice to find out if it worked.
dana
We are trifling with strange magic then!
I sure hope so!
I am glad you share my love of trifling!
...yeah, it's the best.

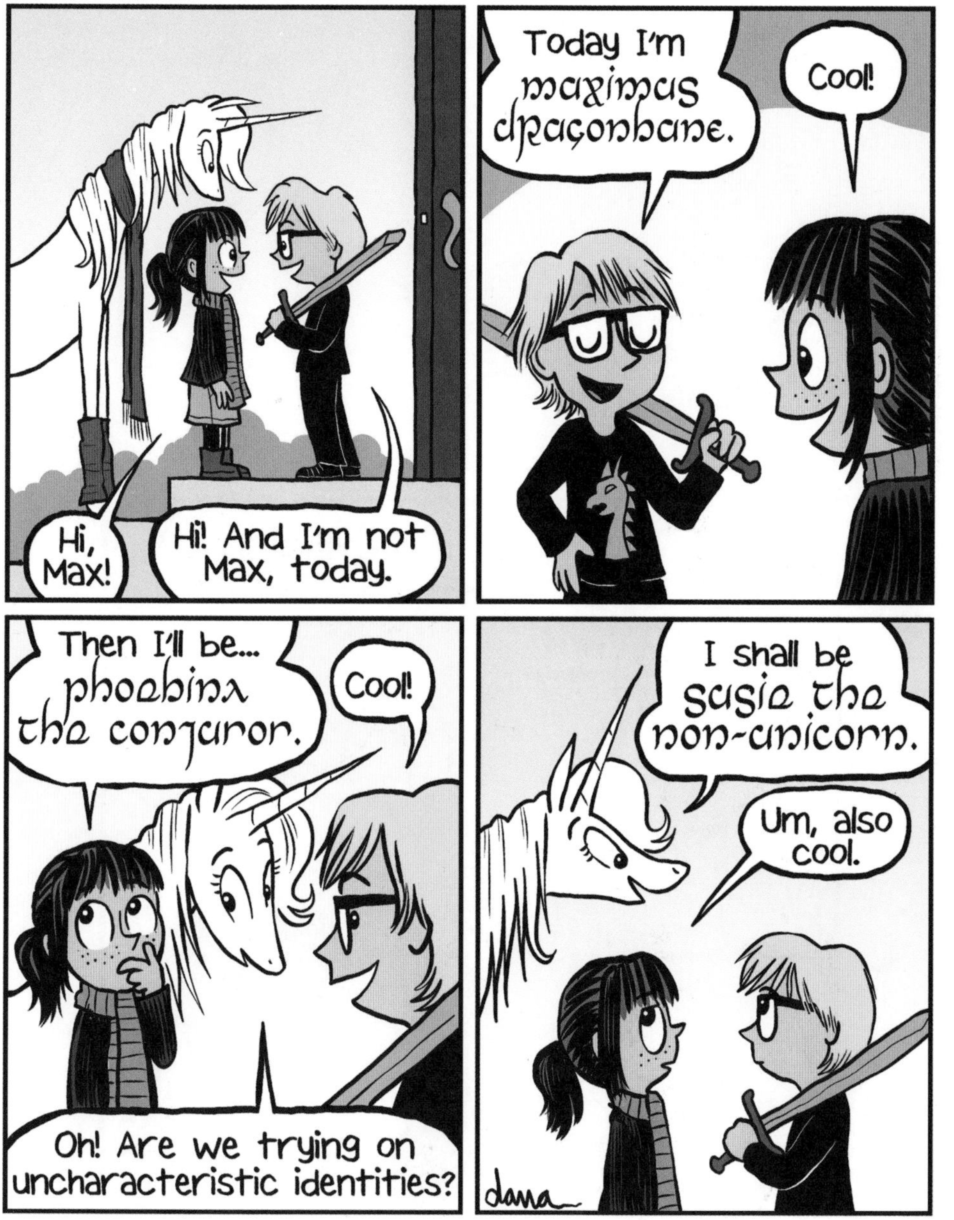
Hi, Max!
Hi! And I'm not Max, today.
Today I'm maximus dragonbane.
Cool!
Then I'll be... phoebina the conjuror.
Cool!
Oh! Are we trying on uncharacteristic identities?
I shall be susie the non-unicorn.
Um, also cool.
dana

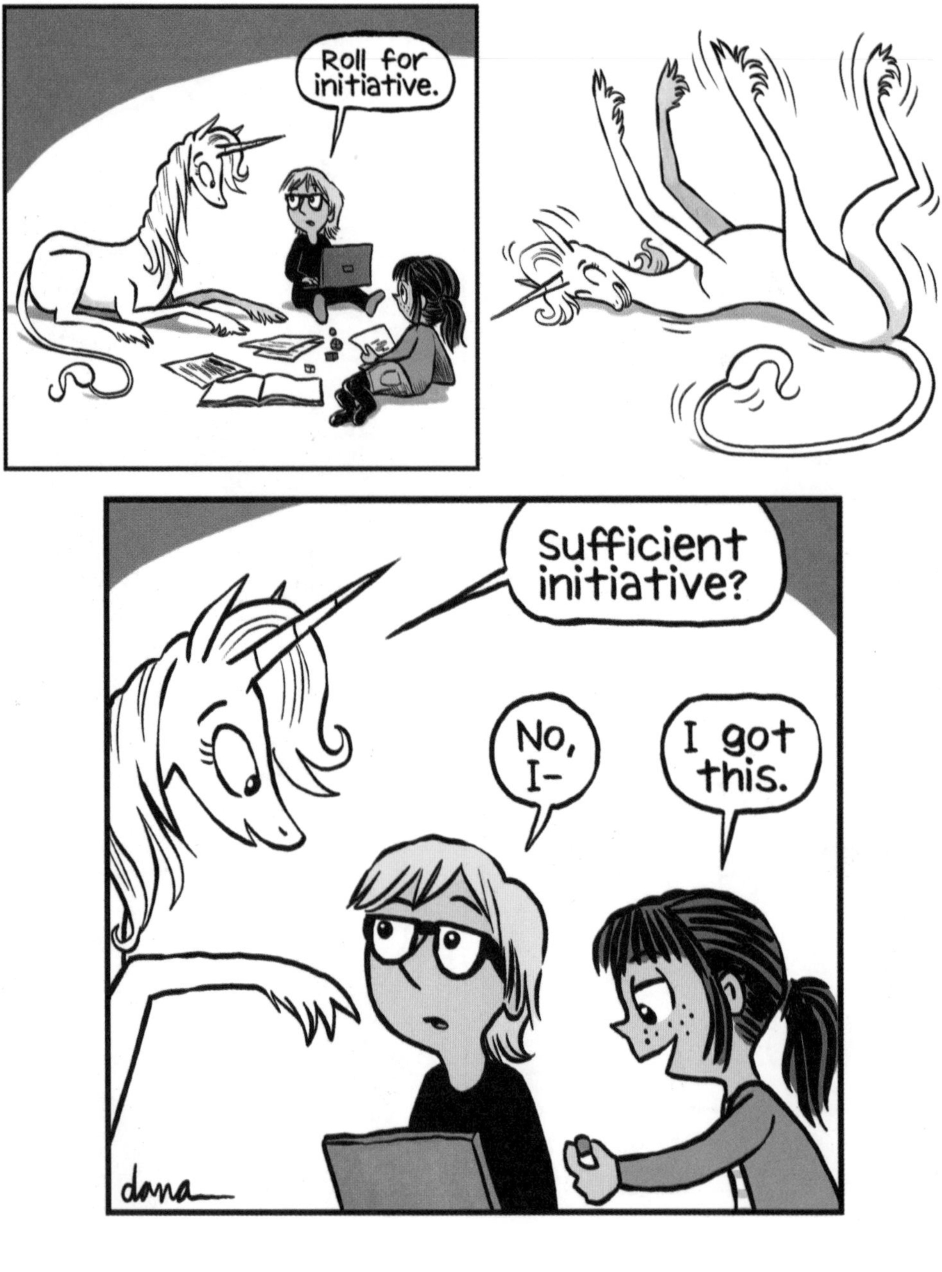
Roll for initiative.
Sufficient initiative?
No, I-
I got this.
dana

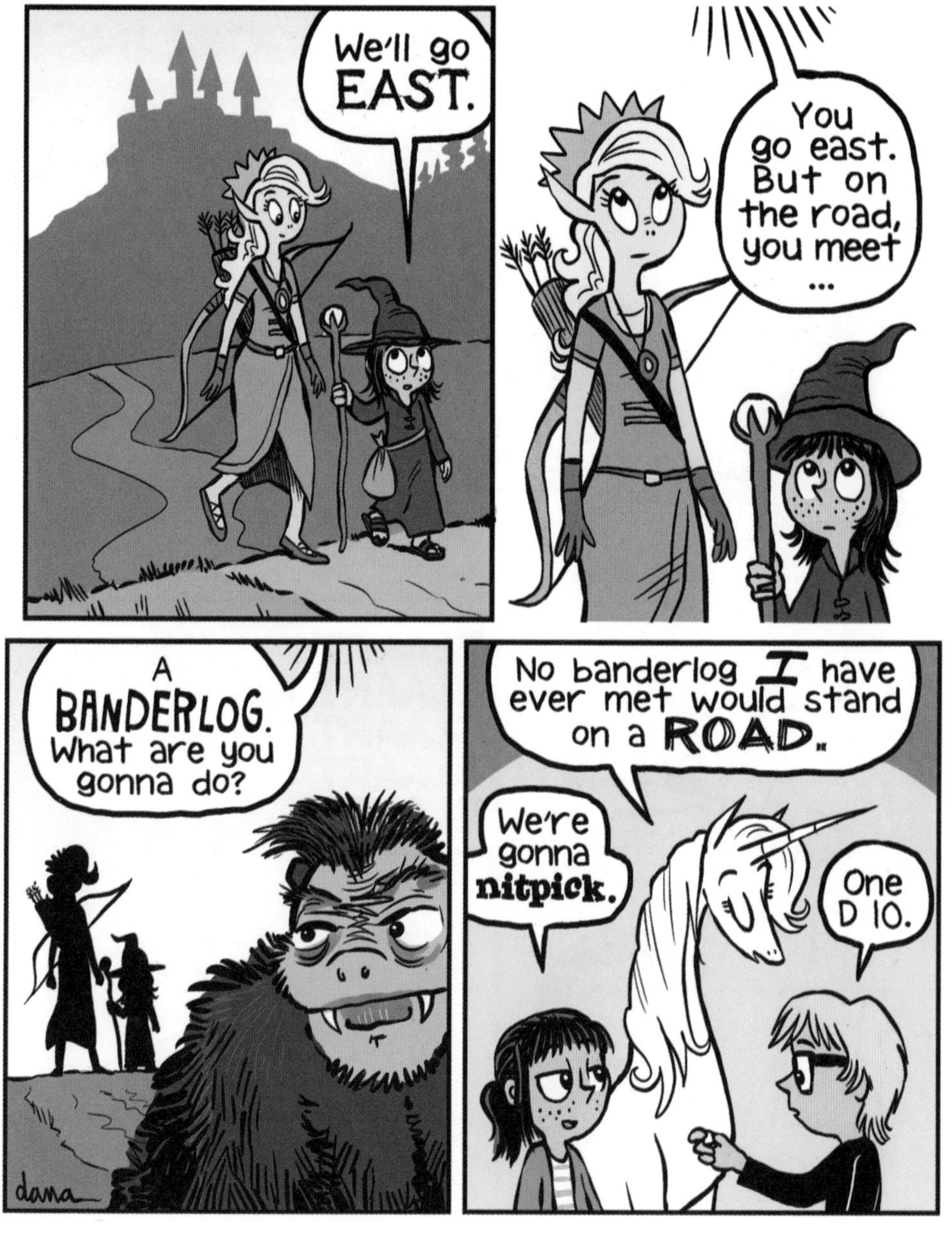

We'll go EAST.
You go east. But on the road, you meet ...
A BANDERLOG. What are you gonna do?
dana
No banderlog I have ever met would stand on a ROAD.
We're gonna nitpick.
One D 10.

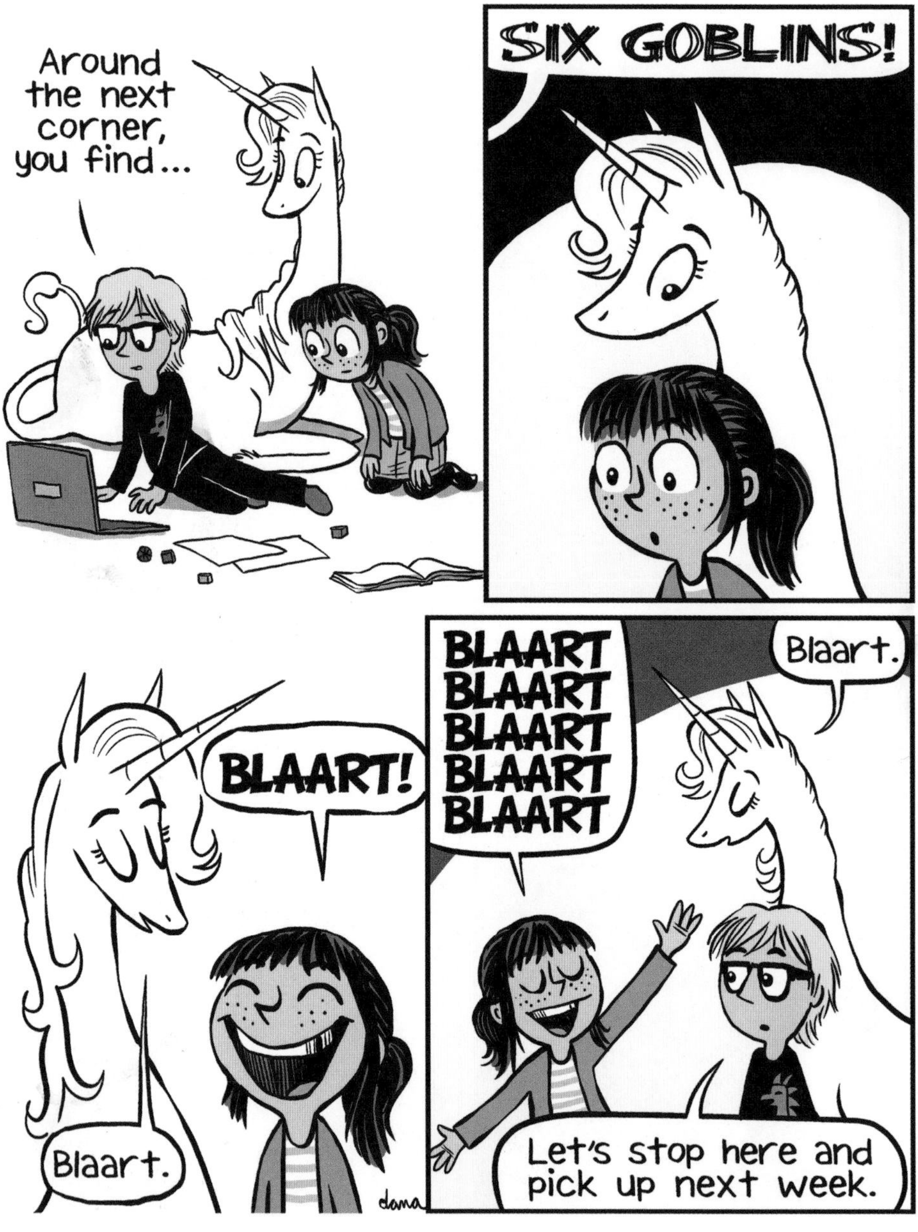
Around the next corner, you find...
SIX GOBLINS!
BLAART!
Blaart.
BLAART BLAART BLAART BLAART BLAART
Blaart.
Let's stop here and pick up next week.
dana

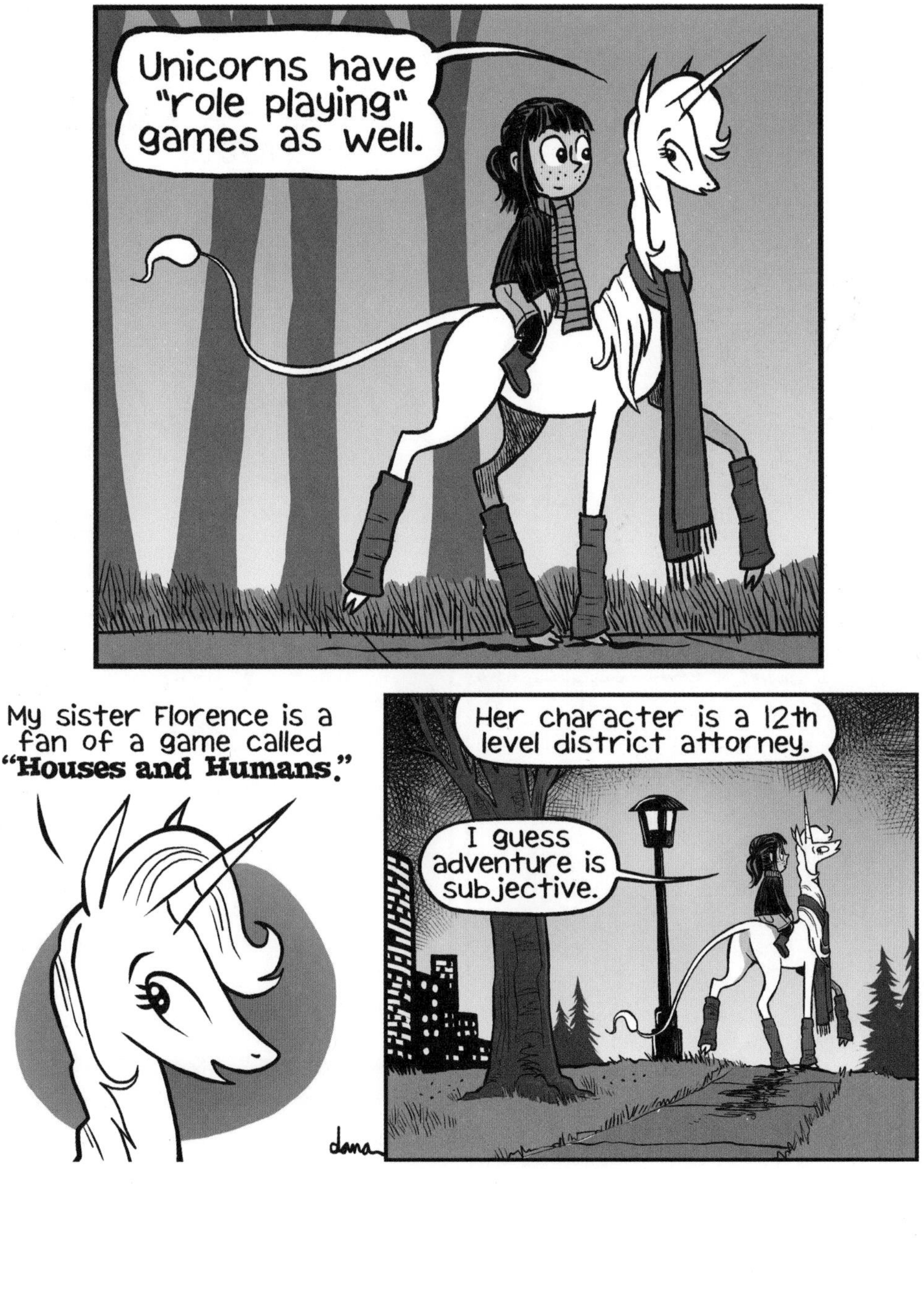
Unicorns have "role playing" games as well.
My sister Florence is a fan of a game called "**Houses and Humans**."
Her character is a 12th level district attorney.
I guess adventure is subjective.

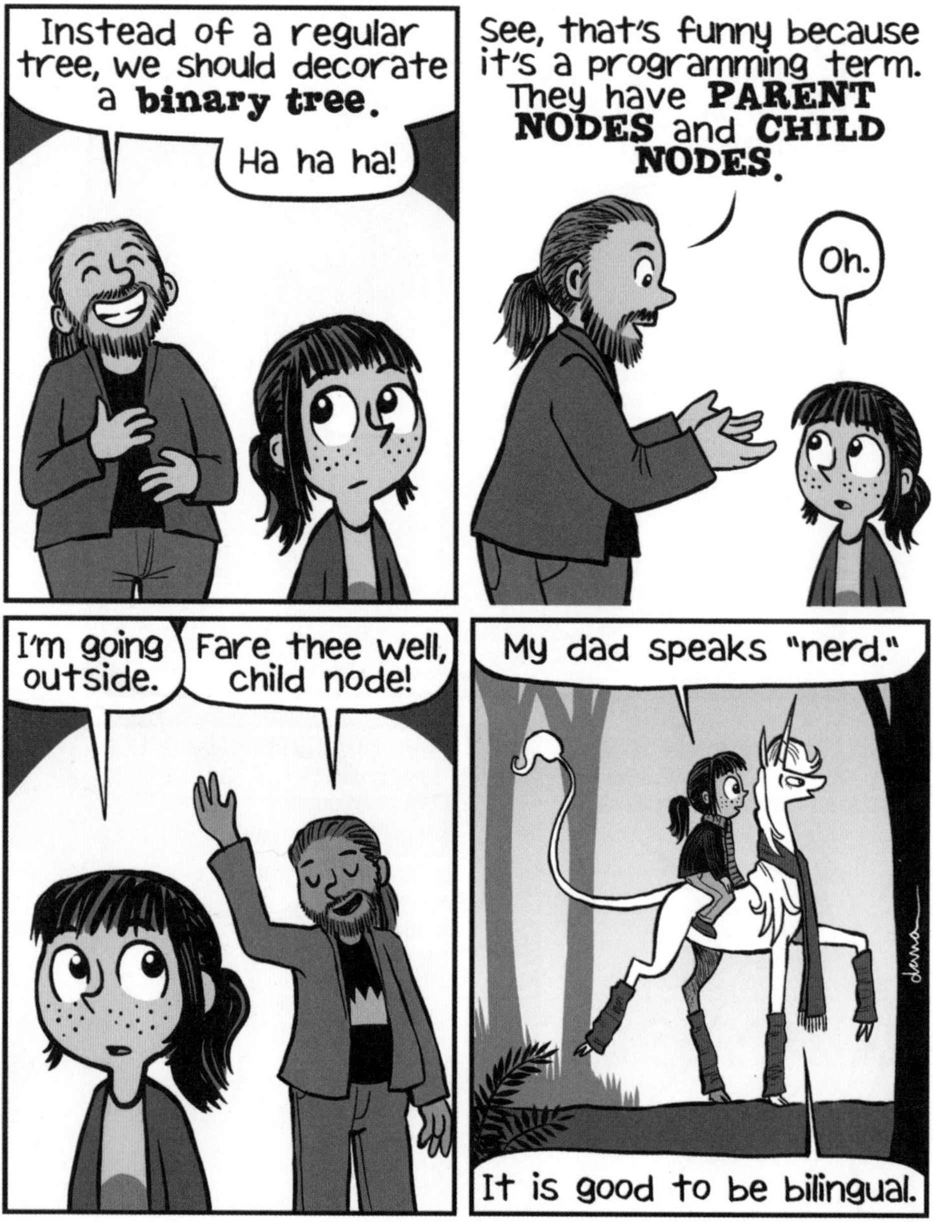

Instead of a regular tree, we should decorate a **binary tree**.
Ha ha ha!
See, that's funny because it's a programming term. They have **PARENT NODES** and **CHILD NODES**.
Oh.
I'm going outside.
Fare thee well, child node!
My dad speaks "nerd."
It is good to be bilingual.

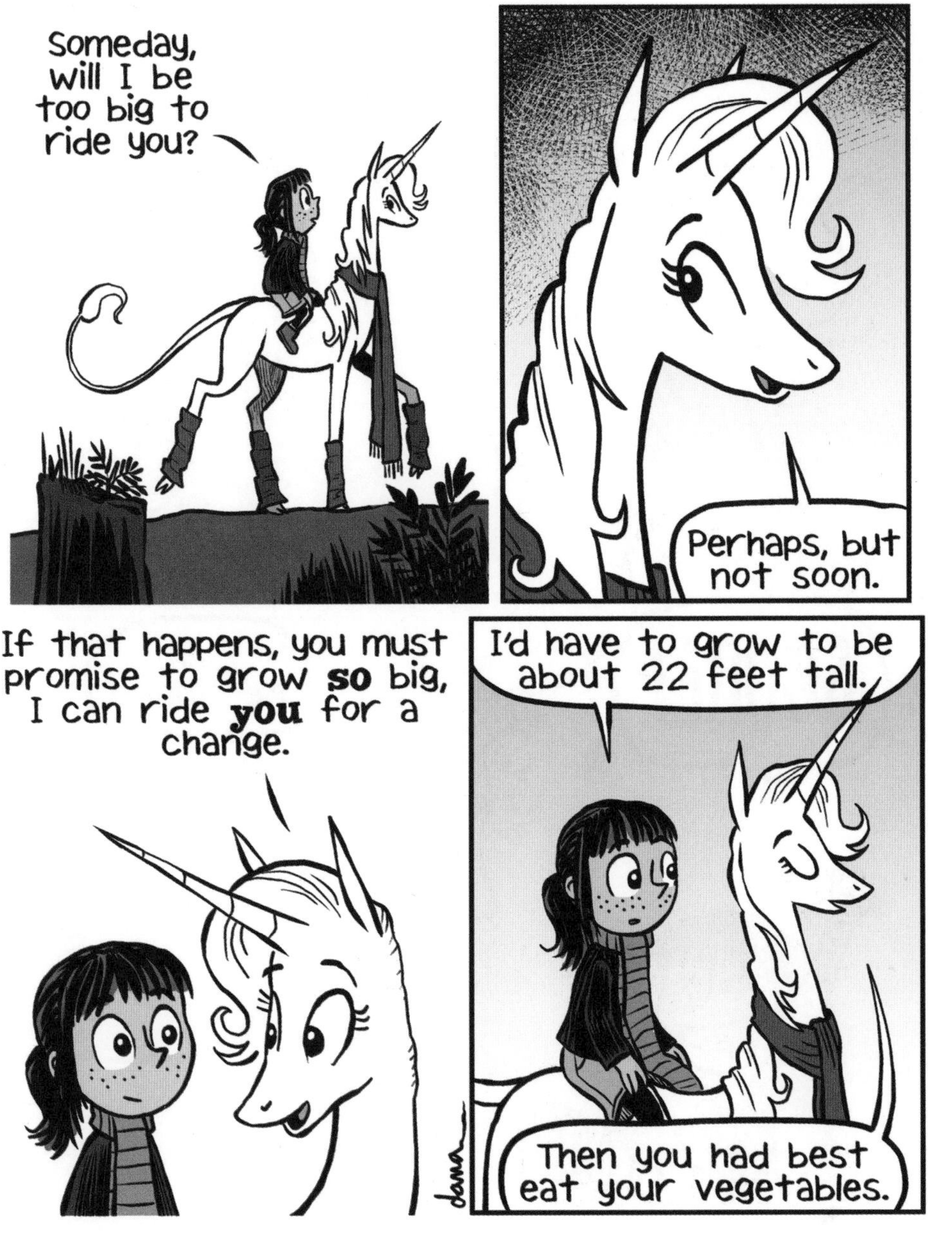
Someday, will I be too big to ride you?
Perhaps, but not soon.
If that happens, you must promise to grow **so** big, I can ride **you** for a change.
I'd have to grow to be about 22 feet tall.
Then you had best eat your vegetables.
dana

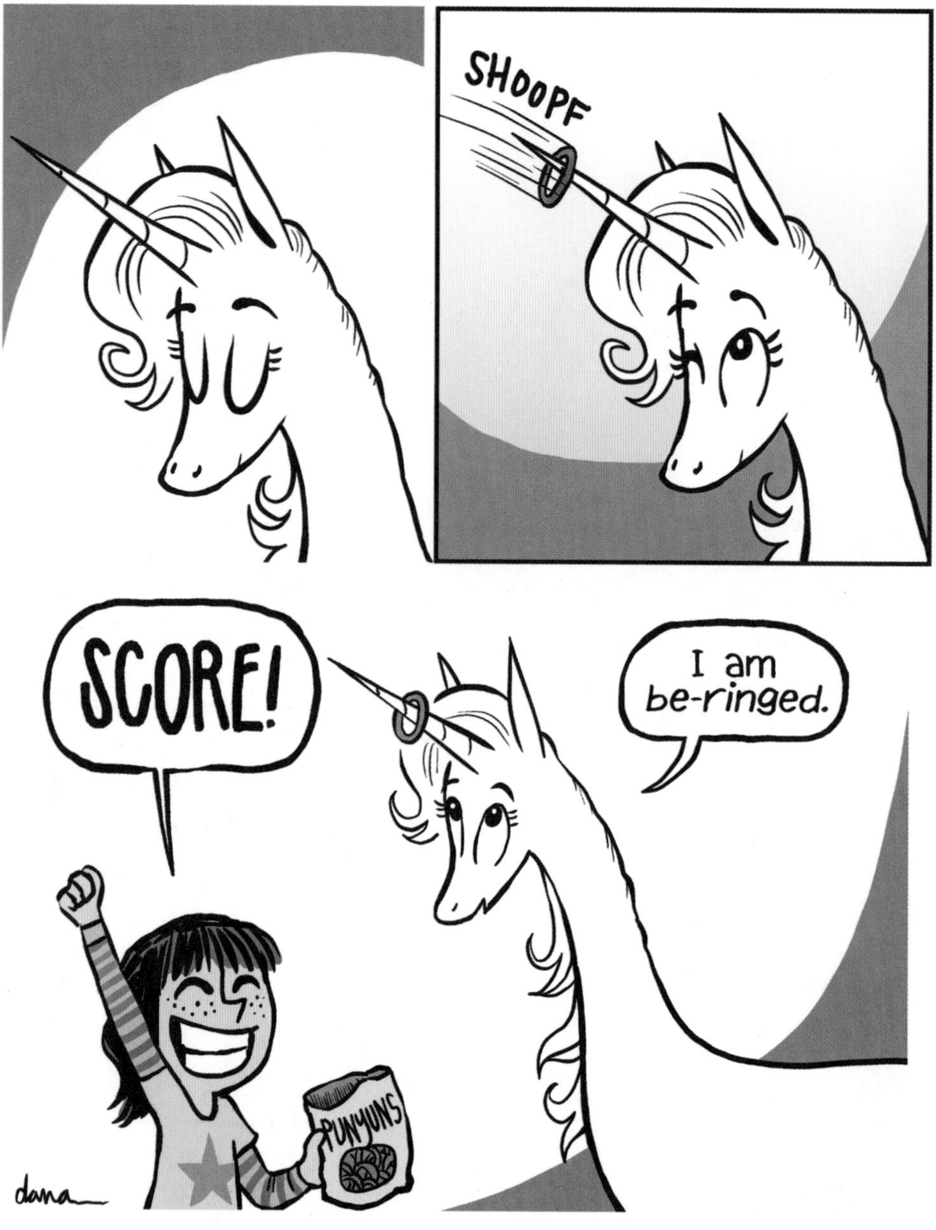
SHOOPF
SCORE!
I am be-ringed.
PUNYUNS
dana

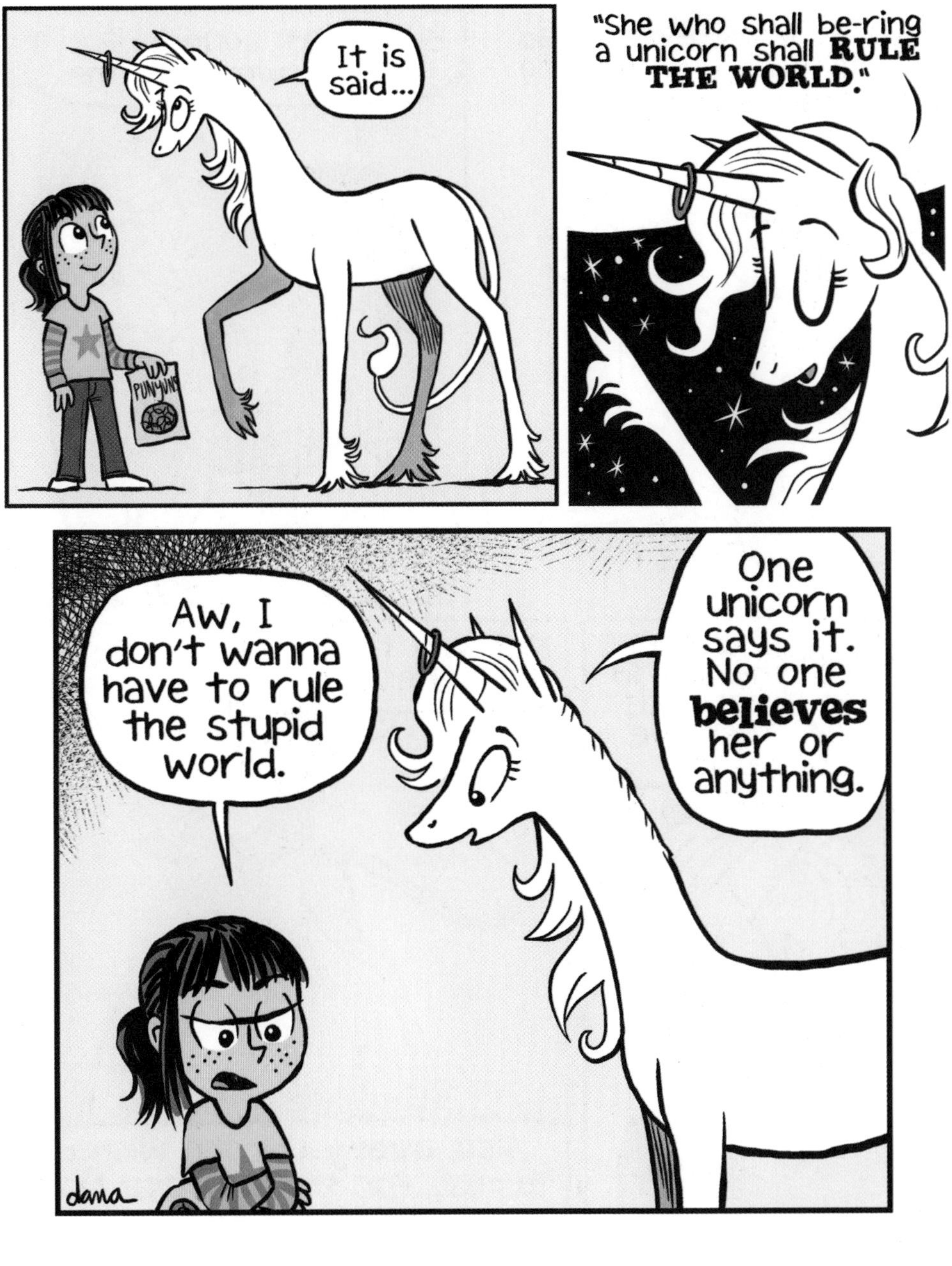
It is said...
"She who shall be-ring a unicorn shall **RULE THE WORLD**."
Aw, I don't wanna have to rule the stupid world.
One unicorn says it. No one **believes** her or anything.
PUNYUNS
dana

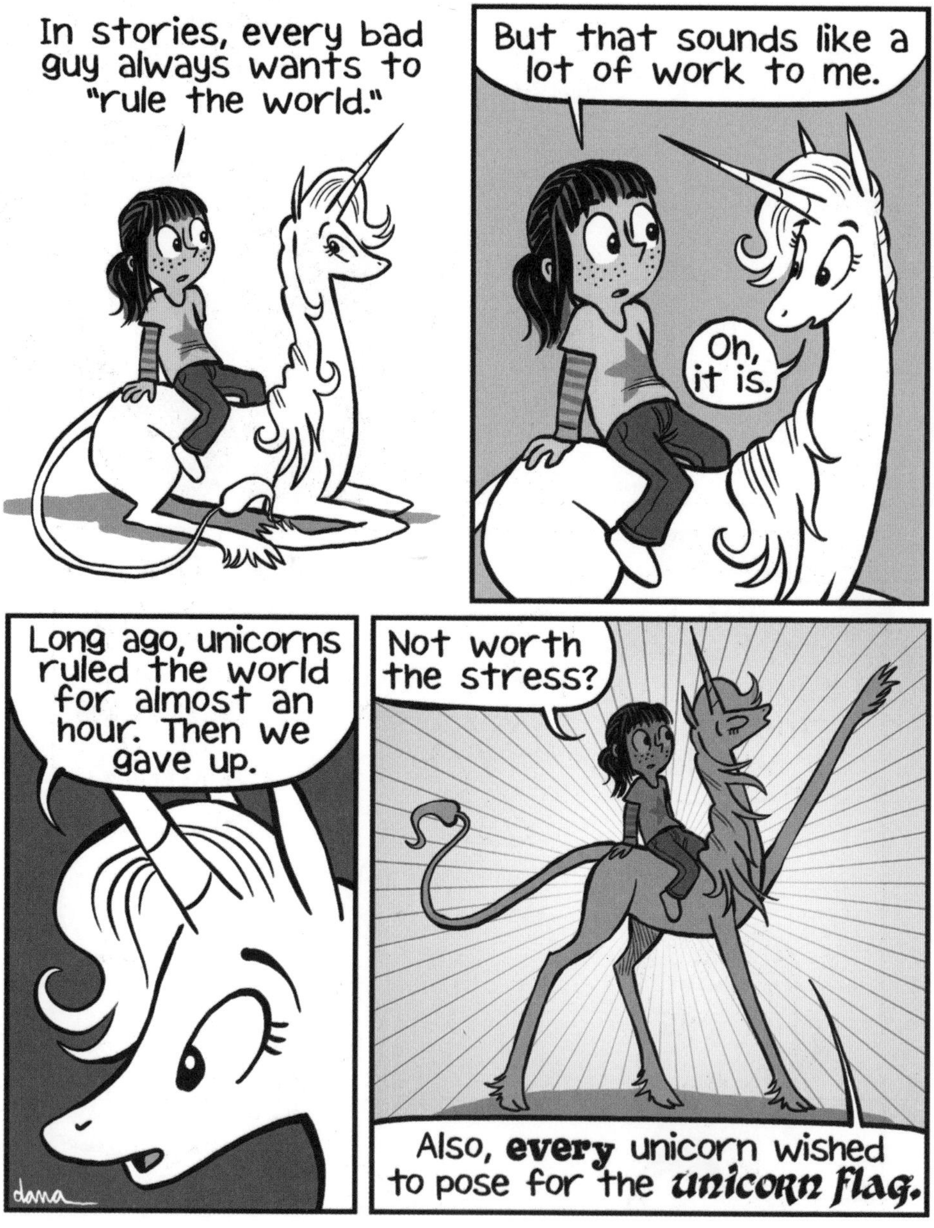
In stories, every bad guy always wants to "rule the world."
But that sounds like a lot of work to me.
Oh, it is.
Long ago, unicorns ruled the world for almost an hour. Then we gave up.
Not worth the stress?
Also, **every** unicorn wished to pose for the *unicorn flag.*
dana

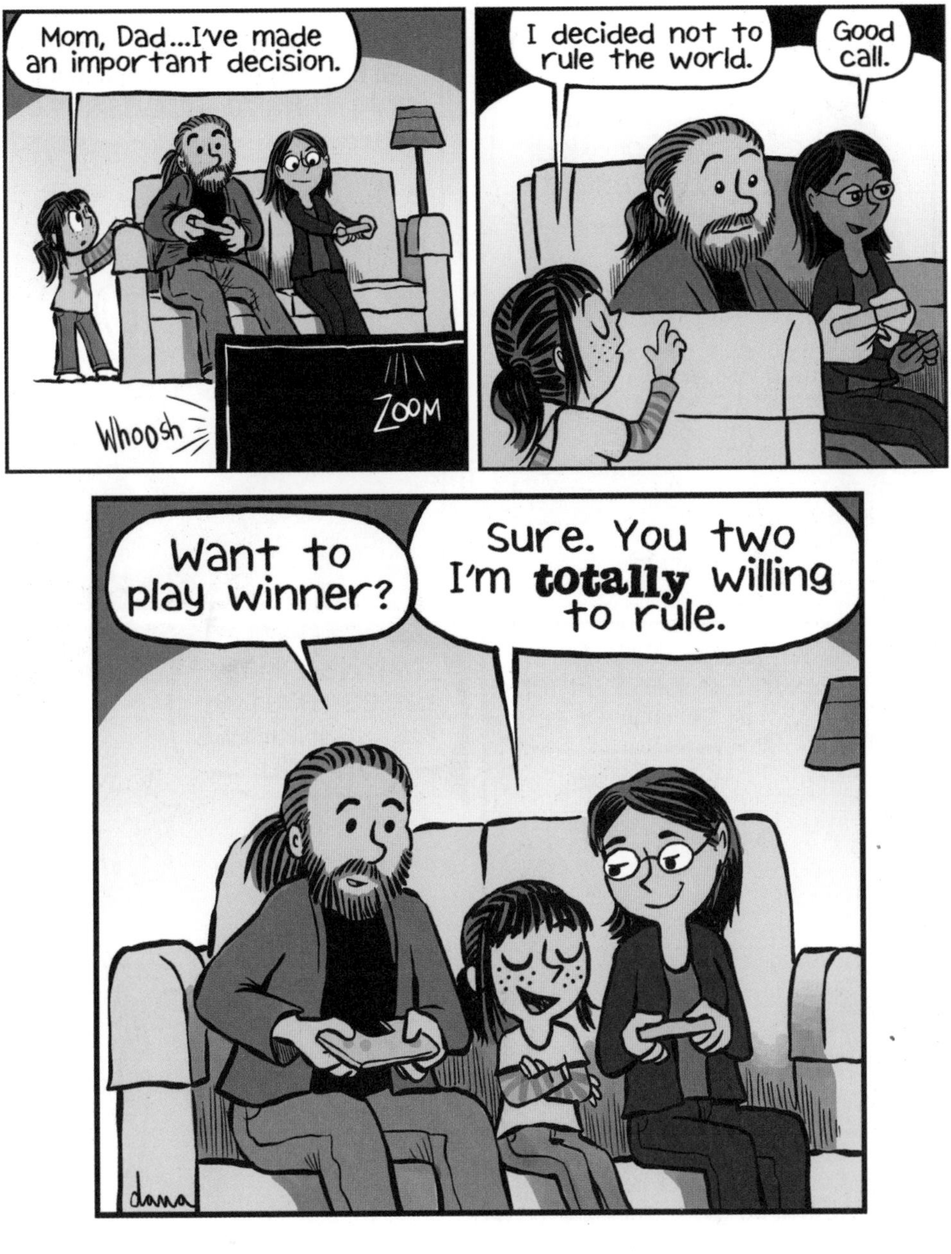
Mom, Dad...I've made an important decision.
Whoosh
ZOOM
I decided not to rule the world.
Good call.
Want to play winner?
Sure. You two I'm **totally** willing to rule.
dana

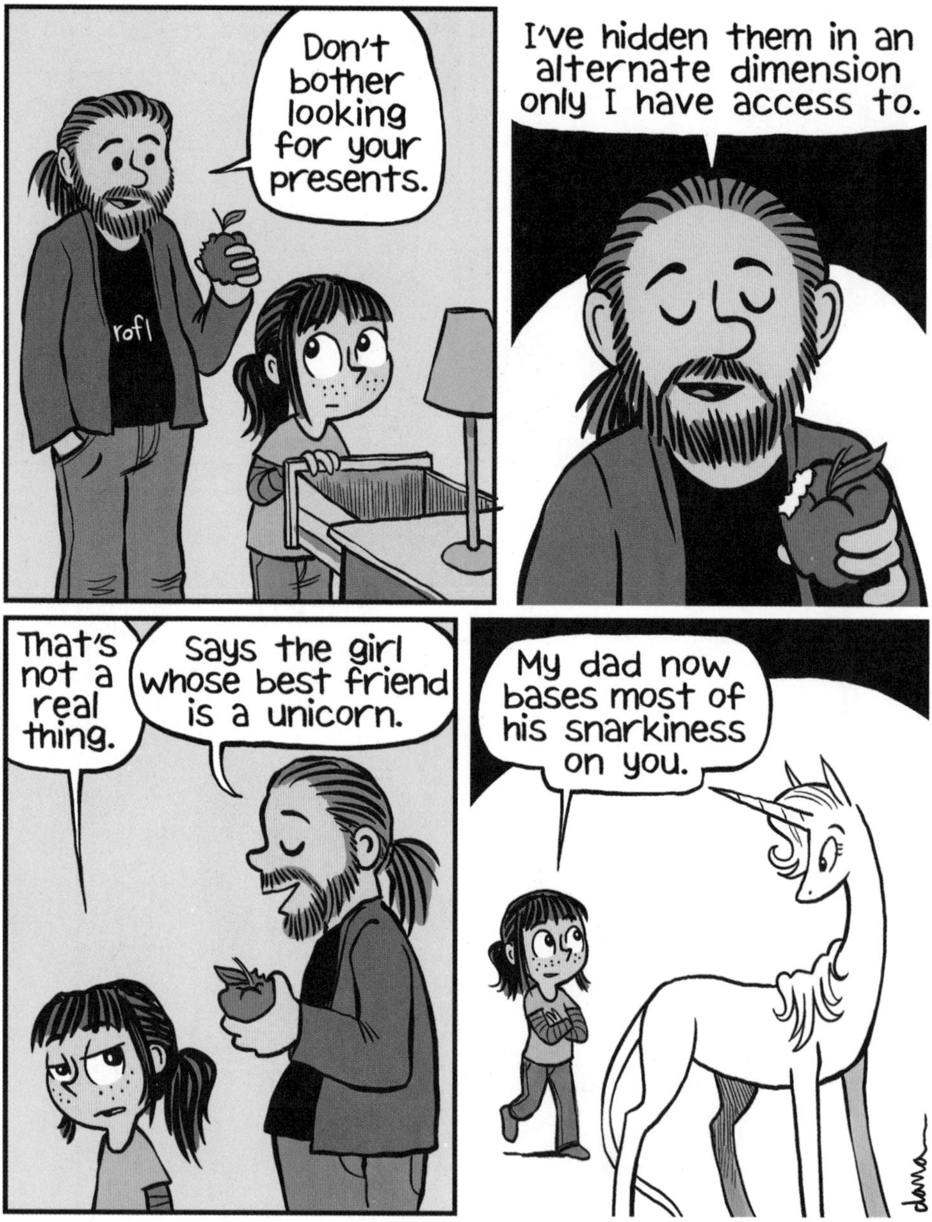
Don't bother looking for your presents.
rofl
I've hidden them in an alternate dimension only I have access to.
That's not a real thing.
Says the girl whose best friend is a unicorn.
My dad now bases most of his snarkiness on you.
dana

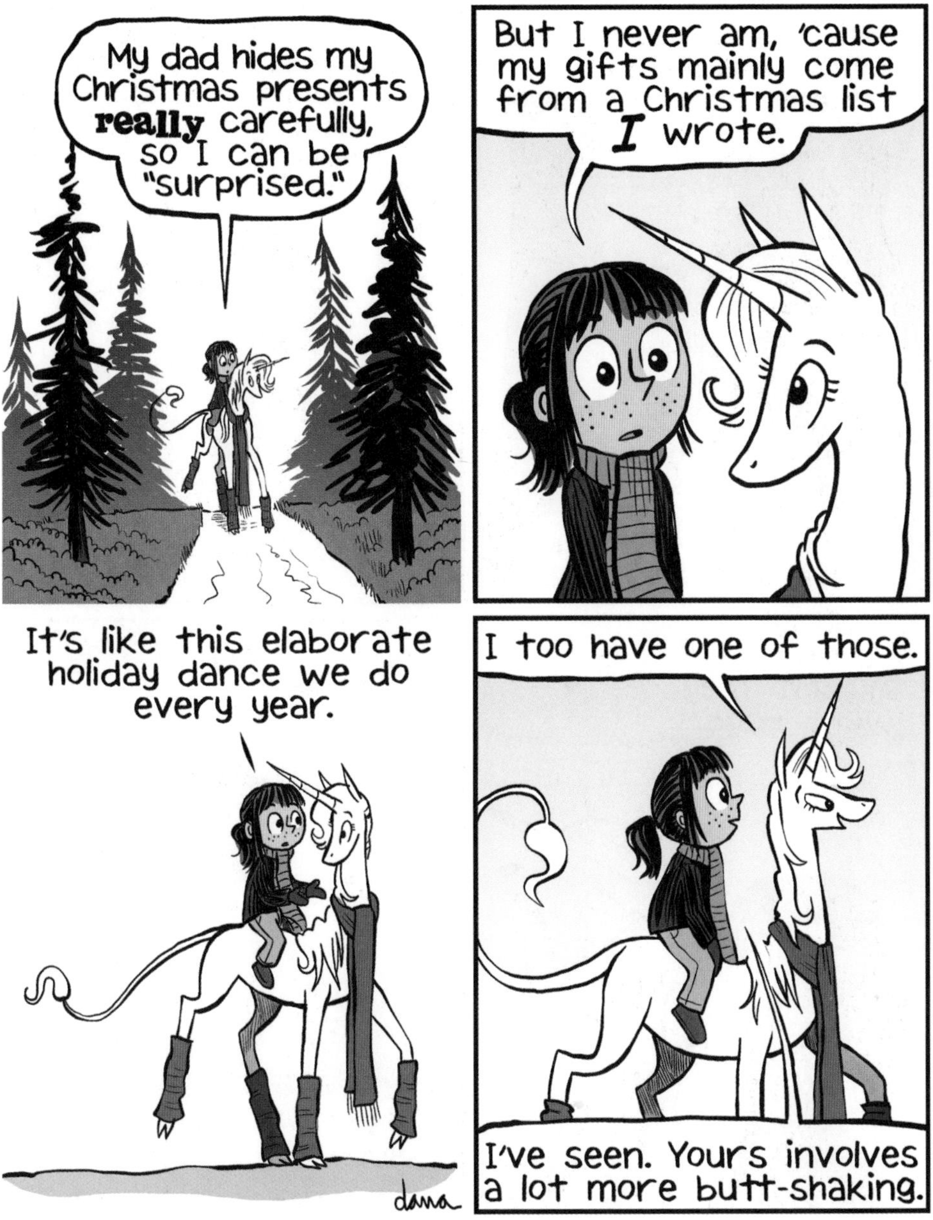
My dad hides my Christmas presents **really** carefully, so I can be "surprised."
But I never am, 'cause my gifts mainly come from a Christmas list *I* wrote.
It's like this elaborate holiday dance we do every year.
I too have one of those.
I've seen. Yours involves a lot more butt-shaking.
dana

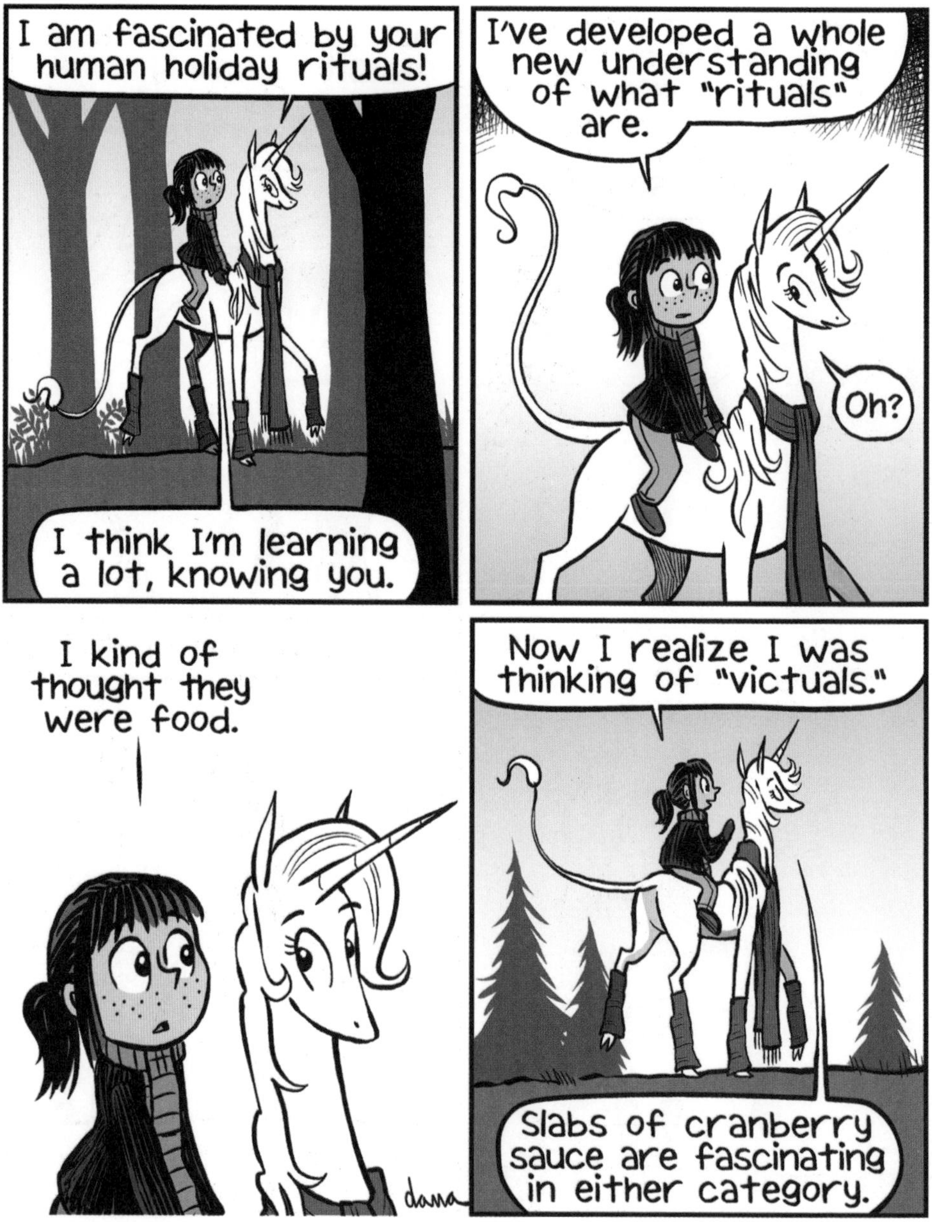
I am fascinated by your human holiday rituals!
I think I'm learning a lot, knowing you.
I've developed a whole new understanding of what "rituals" are.
Oh?
I kind of thought they were food.
Now I realize I was thinking of "victuals."
Slabs of cranberry sauce are fascinating in either category.
dana

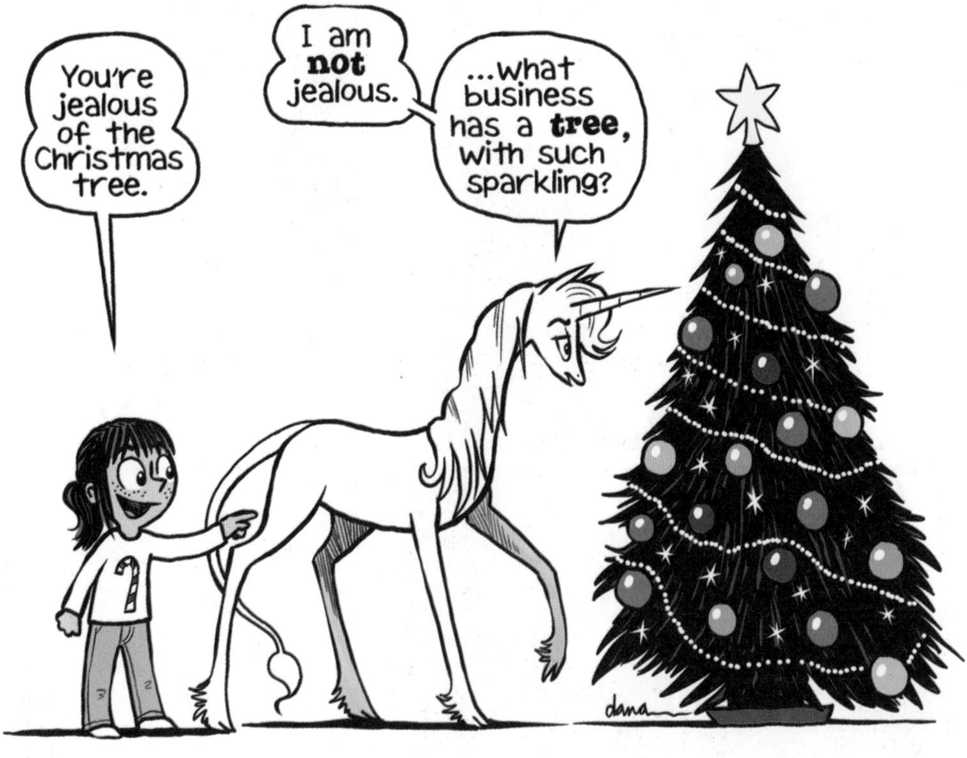
You're jealous of the Christmas tree.
I am **not** jealous.
...what business has a **tree**, with such sparkling?
dana

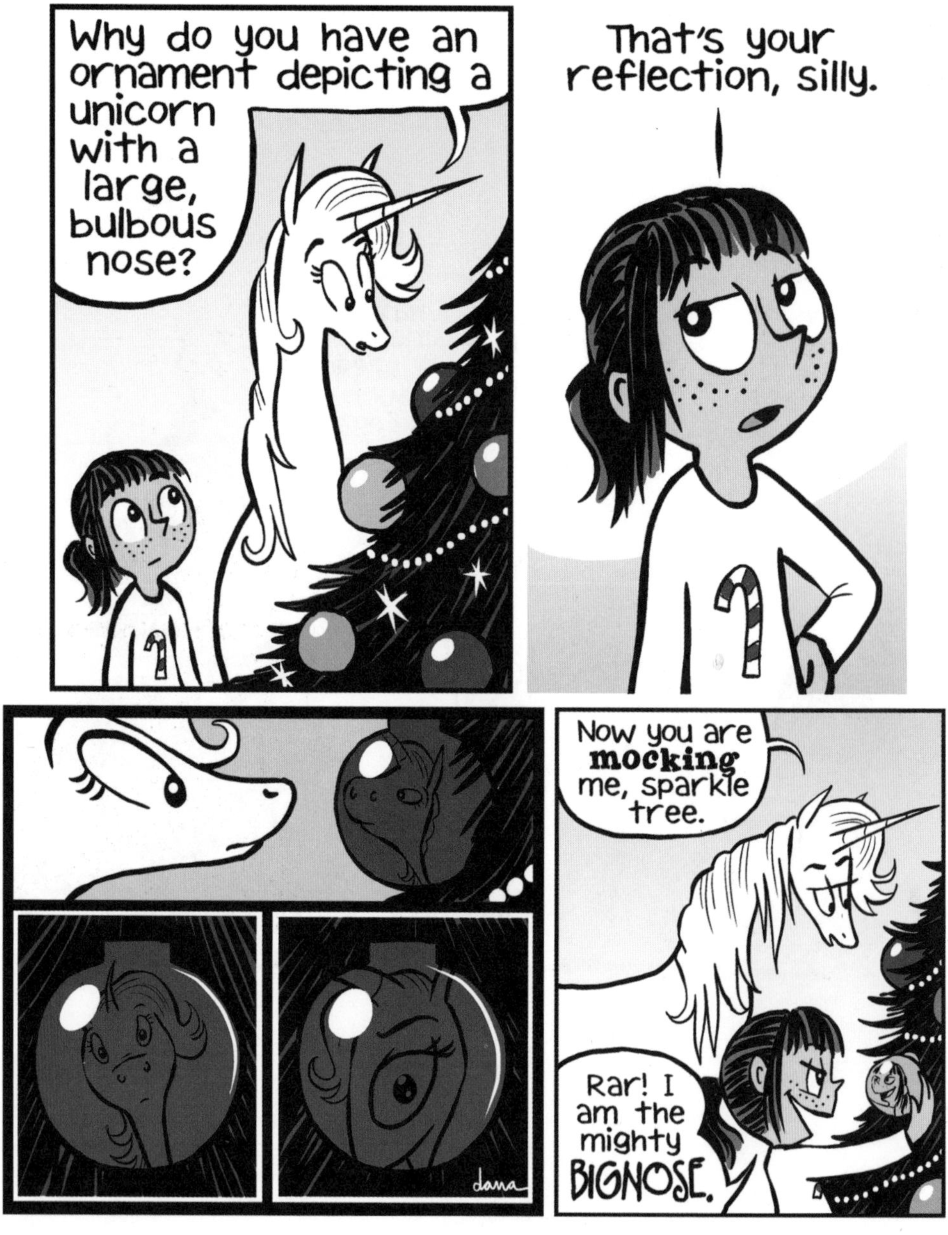
Why do you have an ornament depicting a unicorn with a large, bulbous nose?
That's your reflection, silly.
Now you are **mocking** me, sparkle tree.
Rar! I am the mighty BIGNOSE.
dana

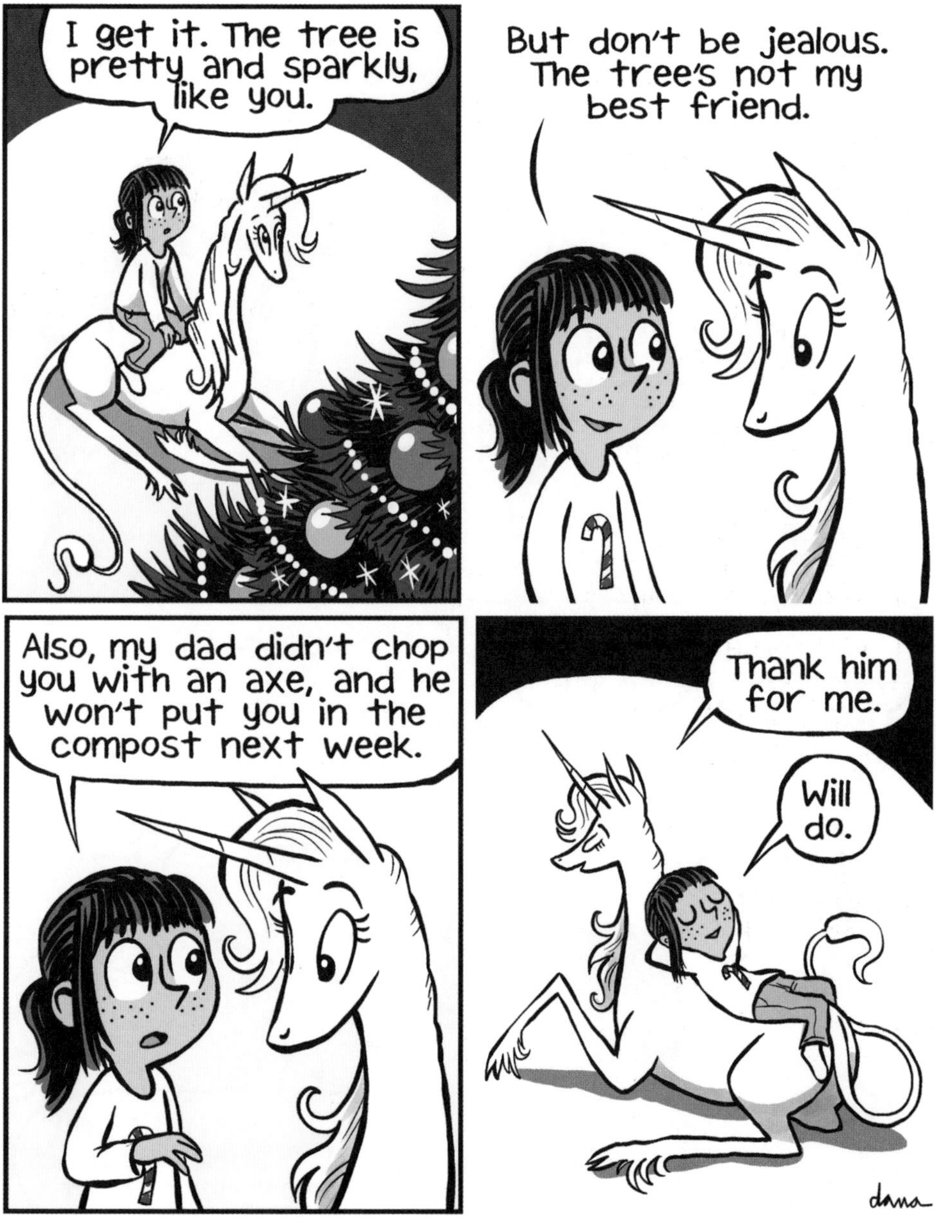
I get it. The tree is pretty and sparkly, like you.
But don't be jealous. The tree's not my best friend.
Also, my dad didn't chop you with an axe, and he won't put you in the compost next week.
Thank him for me.
Will do.
dana

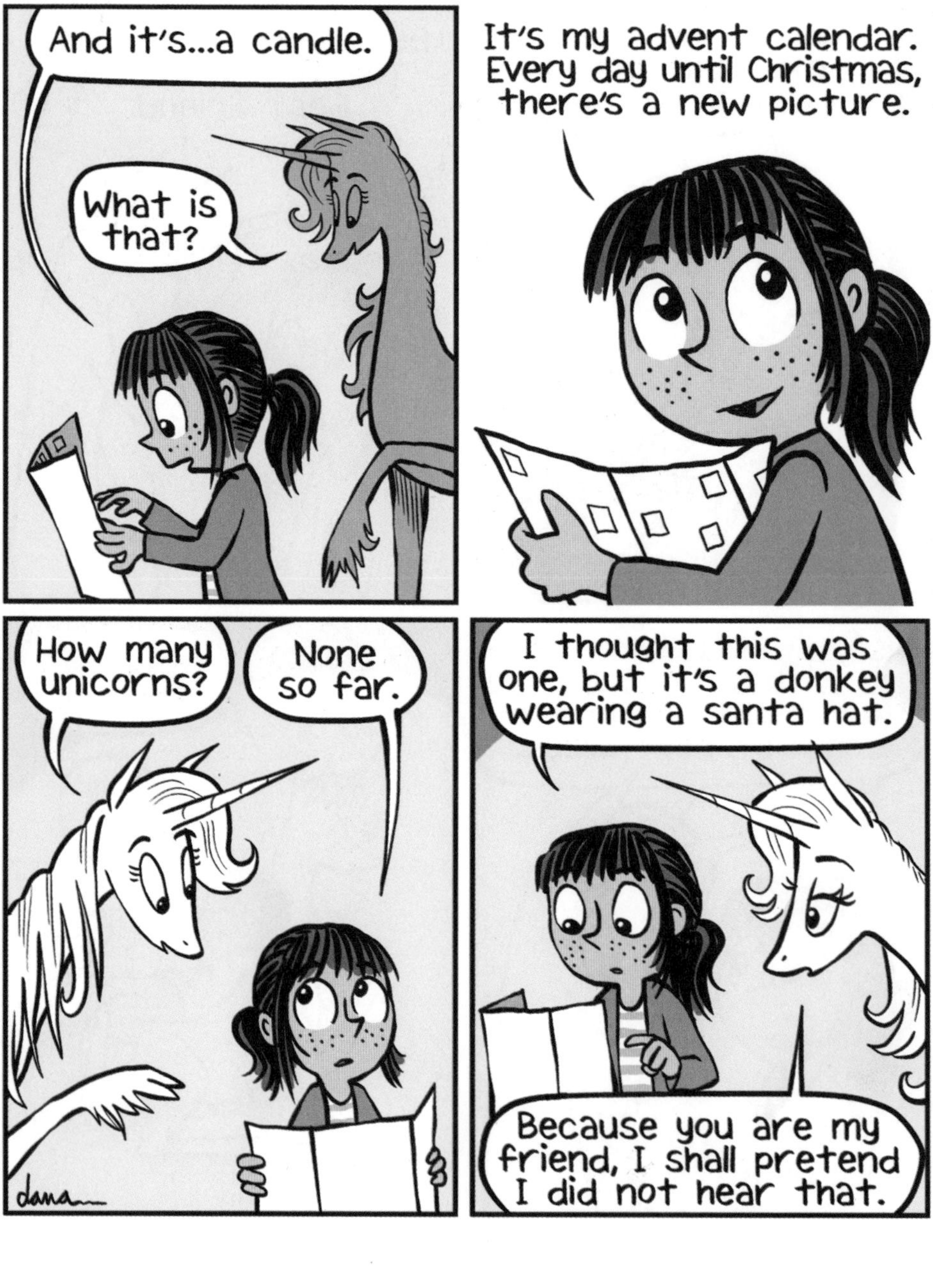
And it's...a candle.
What is that?
It's my advent calendar. Every day until Christmas, there's a new picture.
How many unicorns?
None so far.
I thought this was one, but it's a donkey wearing a santa hat.
Because you are my friend, I shall pretend I did not hear that.
dana

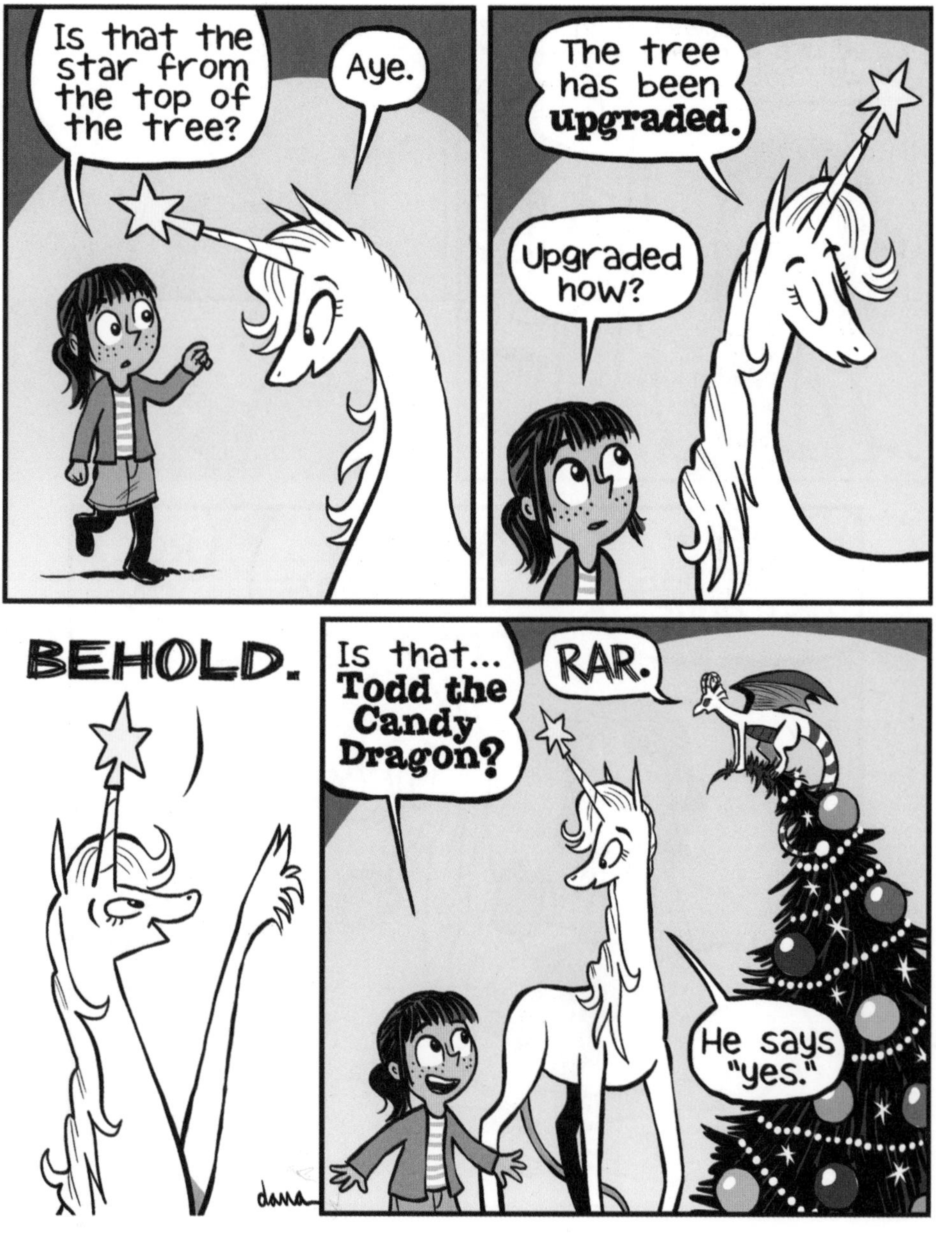
Is that the star from the top of the tree?
Aye.
The tree has been **upgraded.**
Upgraded how?
BEHOLD.
Is that... **Todd the Candy Dragon?**
RAR.
He says "yes."
dana

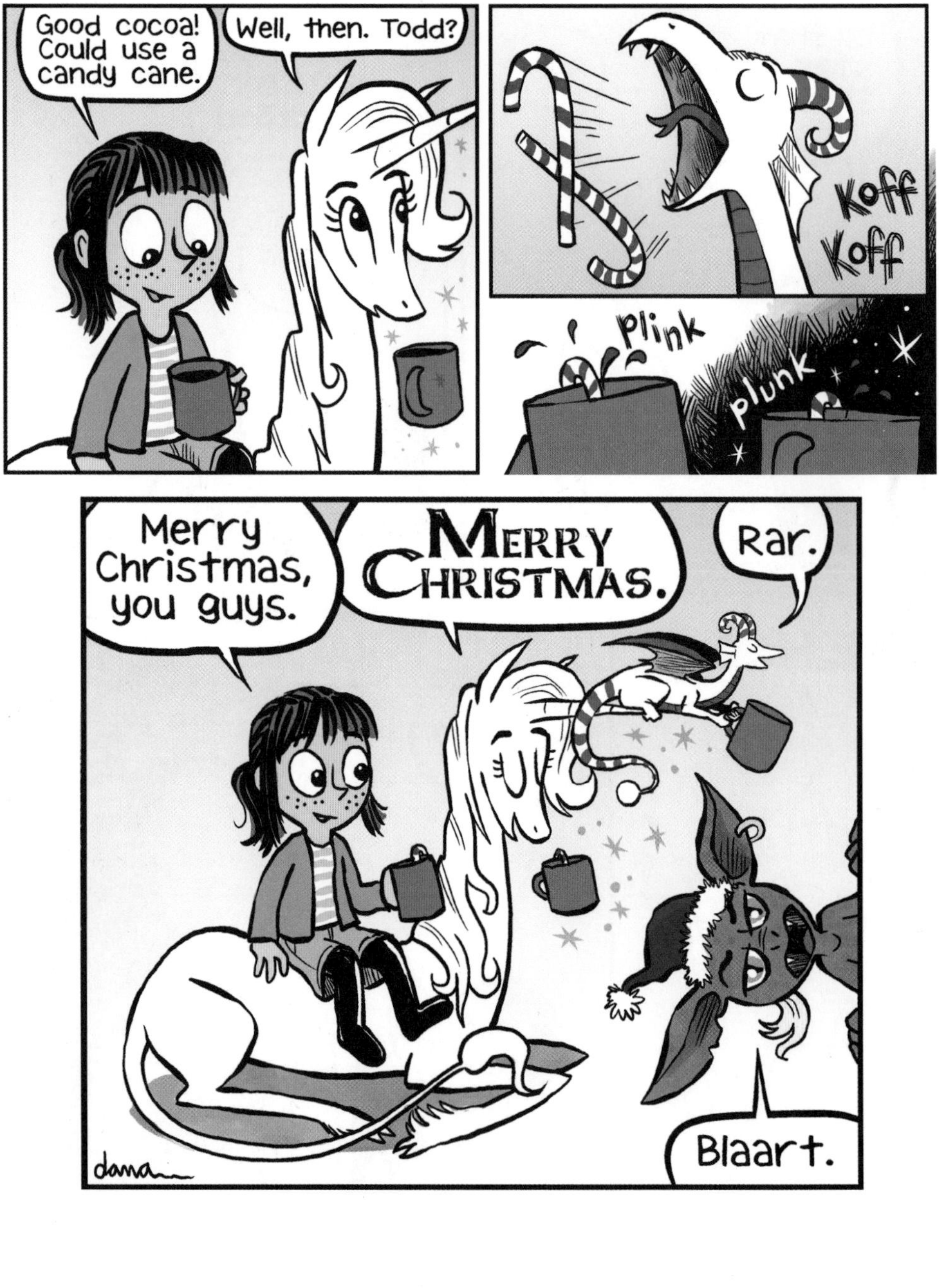
Good cocoa! Could use a candy cane.
Well, then. Todd?
Koff Koff
plink
plunk
Merry Christmas, you guys.
MERRY CHRISTMAS.
Rar.
Blaart.
dana

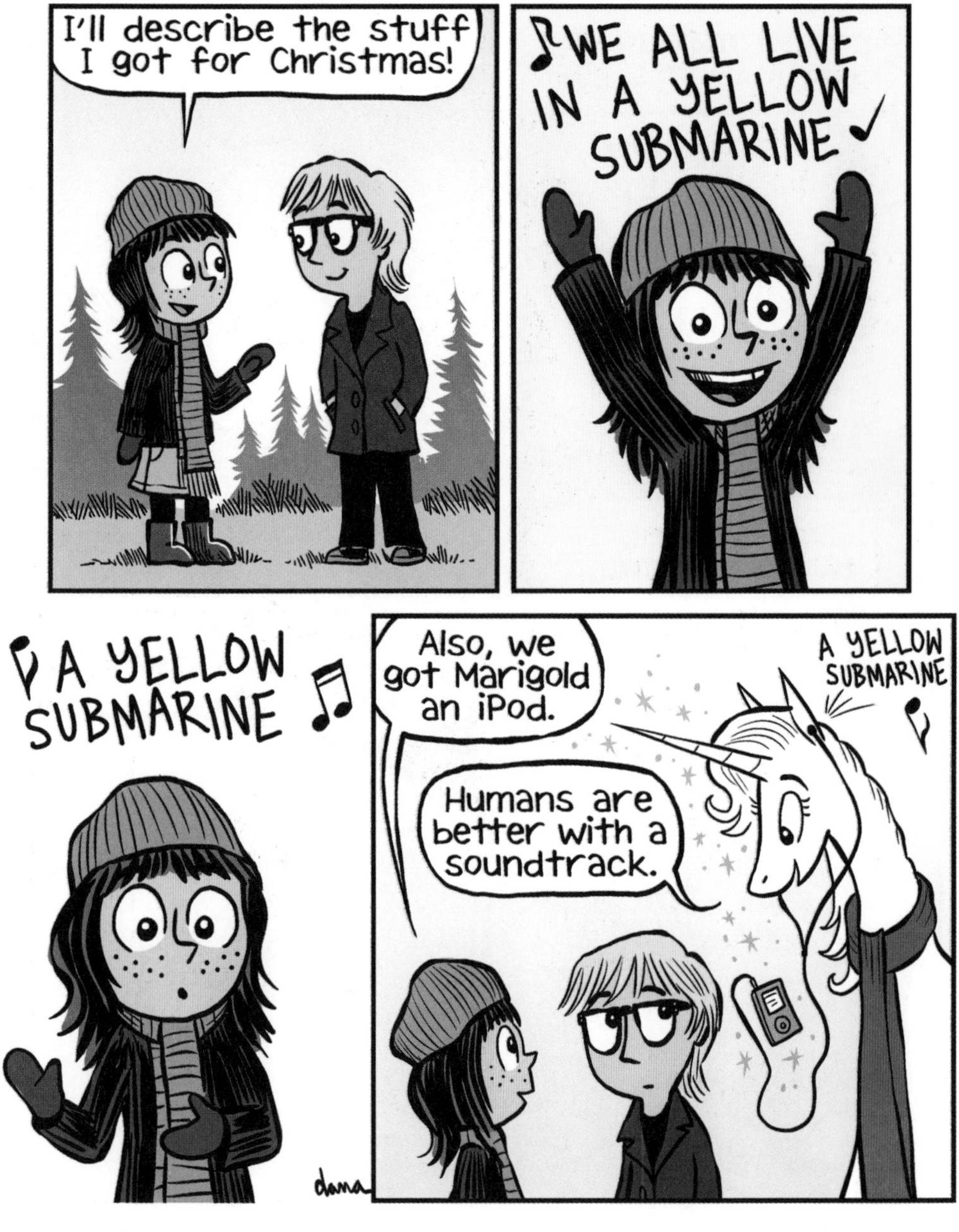
I'll describe the stuff I got for Christmas!
WE ALL LIVE IN A YELLOW SUBMARINE
A YELLOW SUBMARINE
Also, we got Marigold an iPod.
A YELLOW SUBMARINE
Humans are better with a soundtrack.
dana

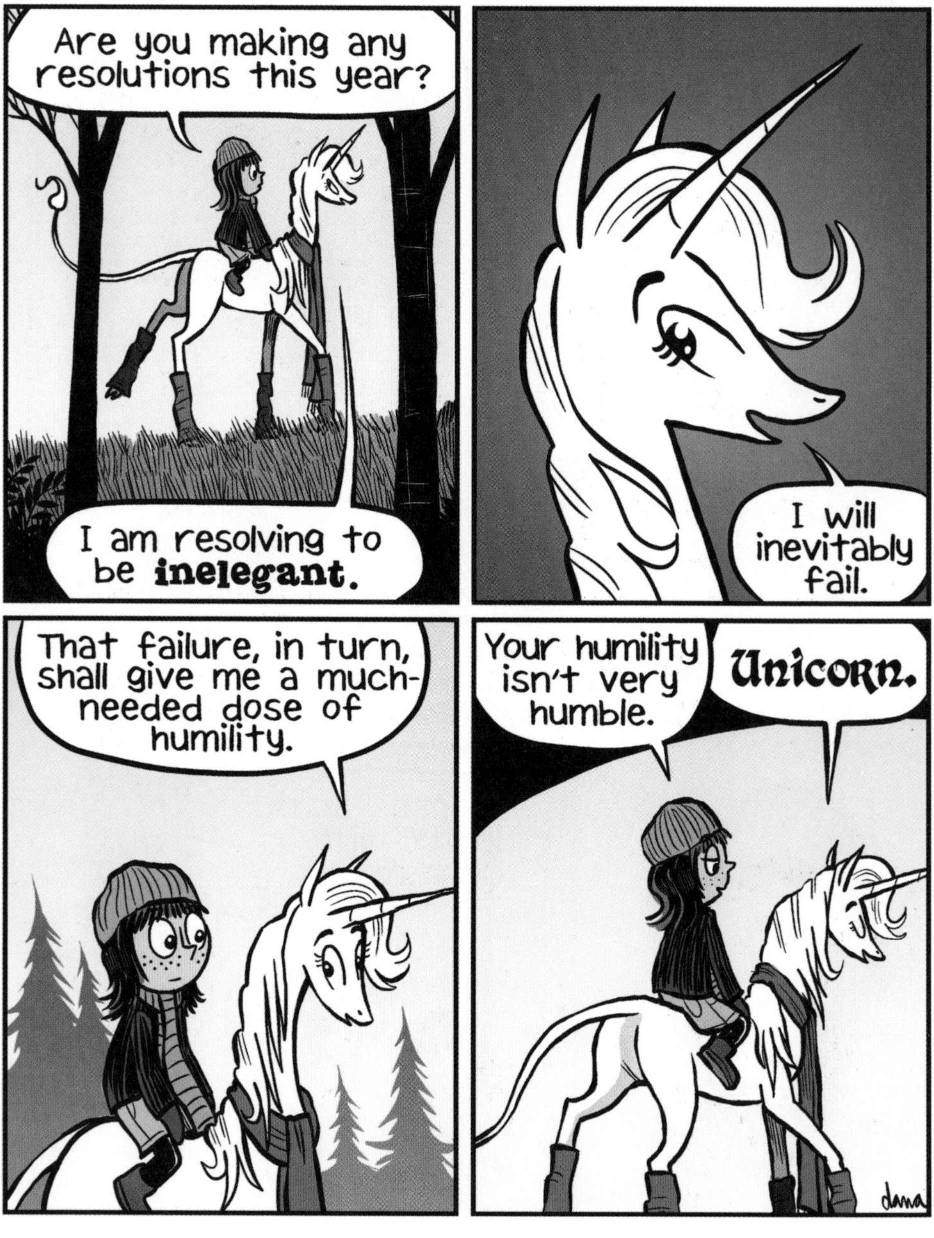
Are you making any resolutions this year?
I am resolving to be **inelegant**.
I will inevitably fail.
That failure, in turn, shall give me a much-needed dose of humility.
Your humility isn't very humble.
Unicorn.
dana

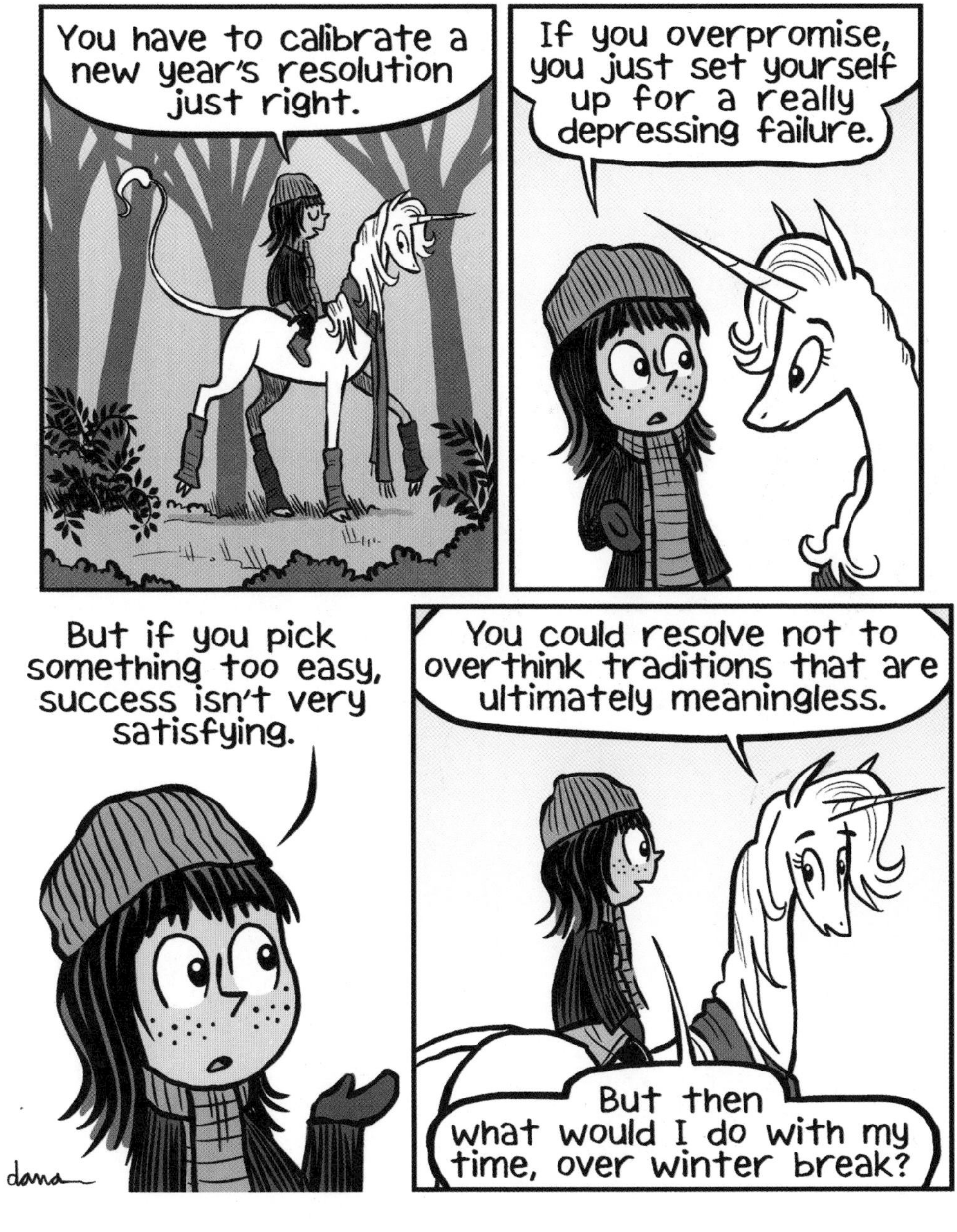
You have to calibrate a new year's resolution just right.
If you overpromise, you just set yourself up for a really depressing failure.
But if you pick something too easy, success isn't very satisfying.
dana
You could resolve not to overthink traditions that are ultimately meaningless.
But then what would I do with my time, over winter break?

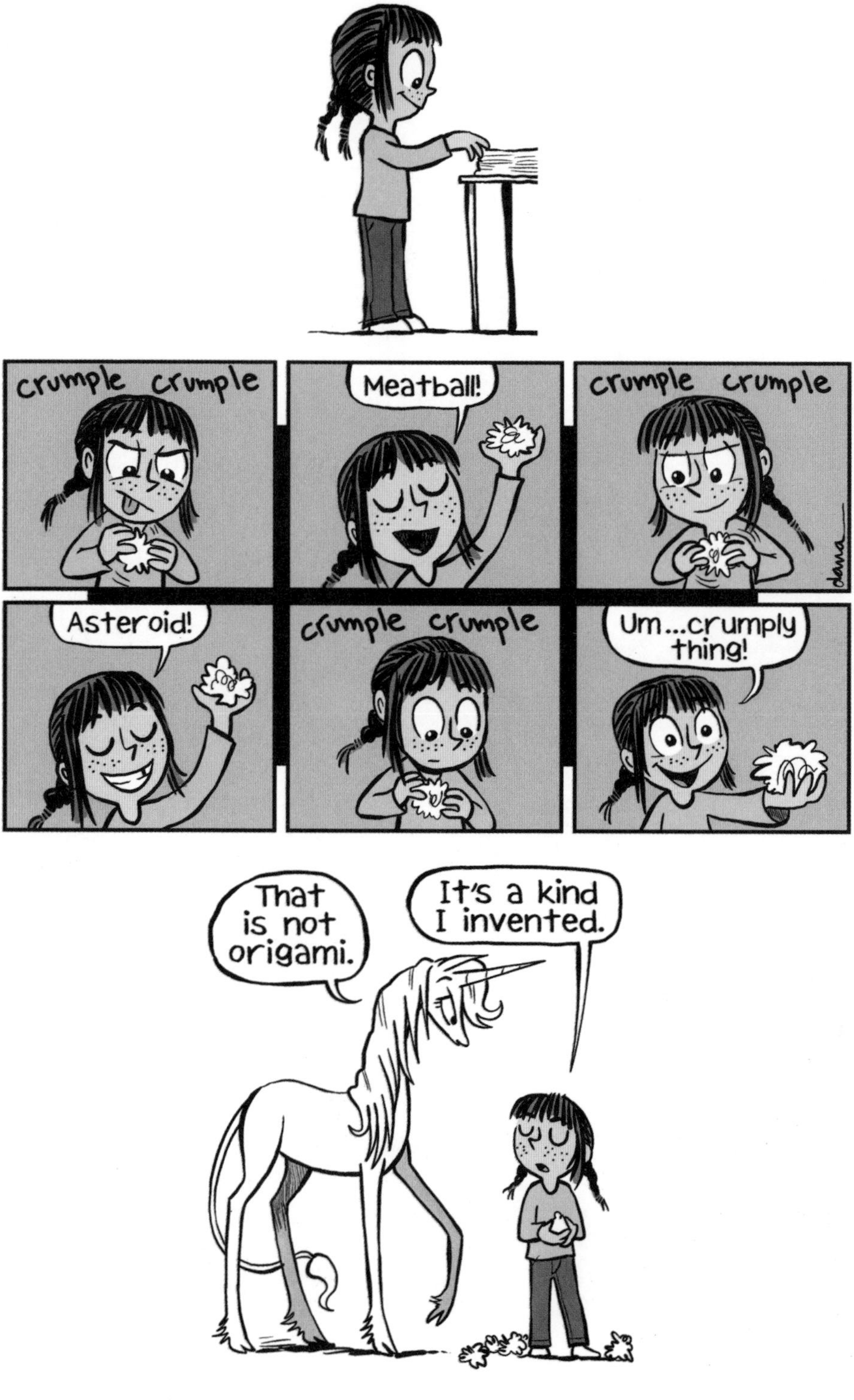
crumple crumple
Meatball!
crumple crumple
dana
Asteroid!
crumple crumple
Um...crumply thing!
That is not origami.
It's a kind I invented.

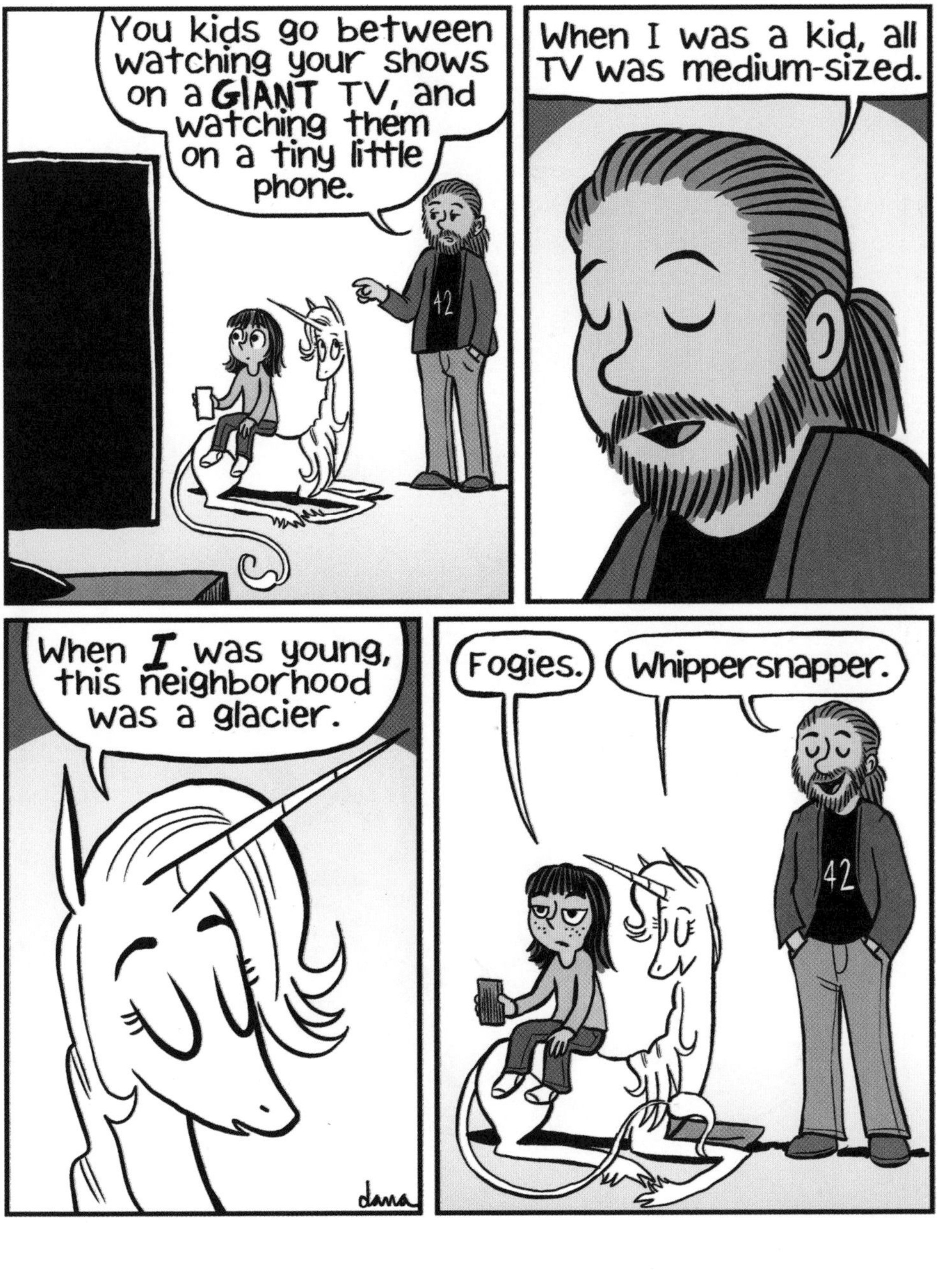
You kids go between watching your shows on a GIANT TV, and watching them on a tiny little phone.
When I was a kid, all TV was medium-sized.
When I was young, this neighborhood was a glacier.
Fogies.
Whippersnapper.
dana

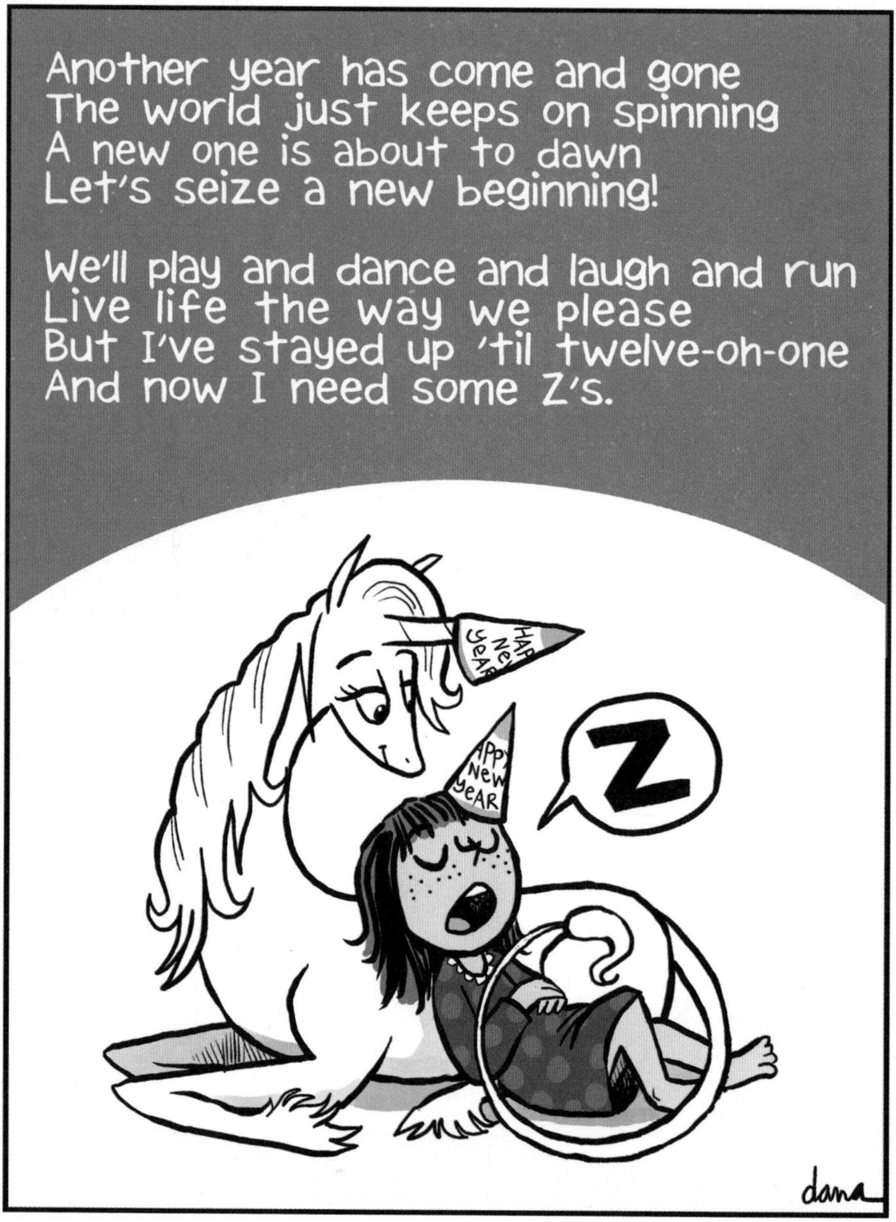
Another year has come and gone
The world just keeps on spinning
A new one is about to dawn
Let's seize a new beginning!

We'll play and dance and laugh and run
Live life the way we please
But I've stayed up 'til twelve-oh-one
And now I need some Z's.
Z
dana

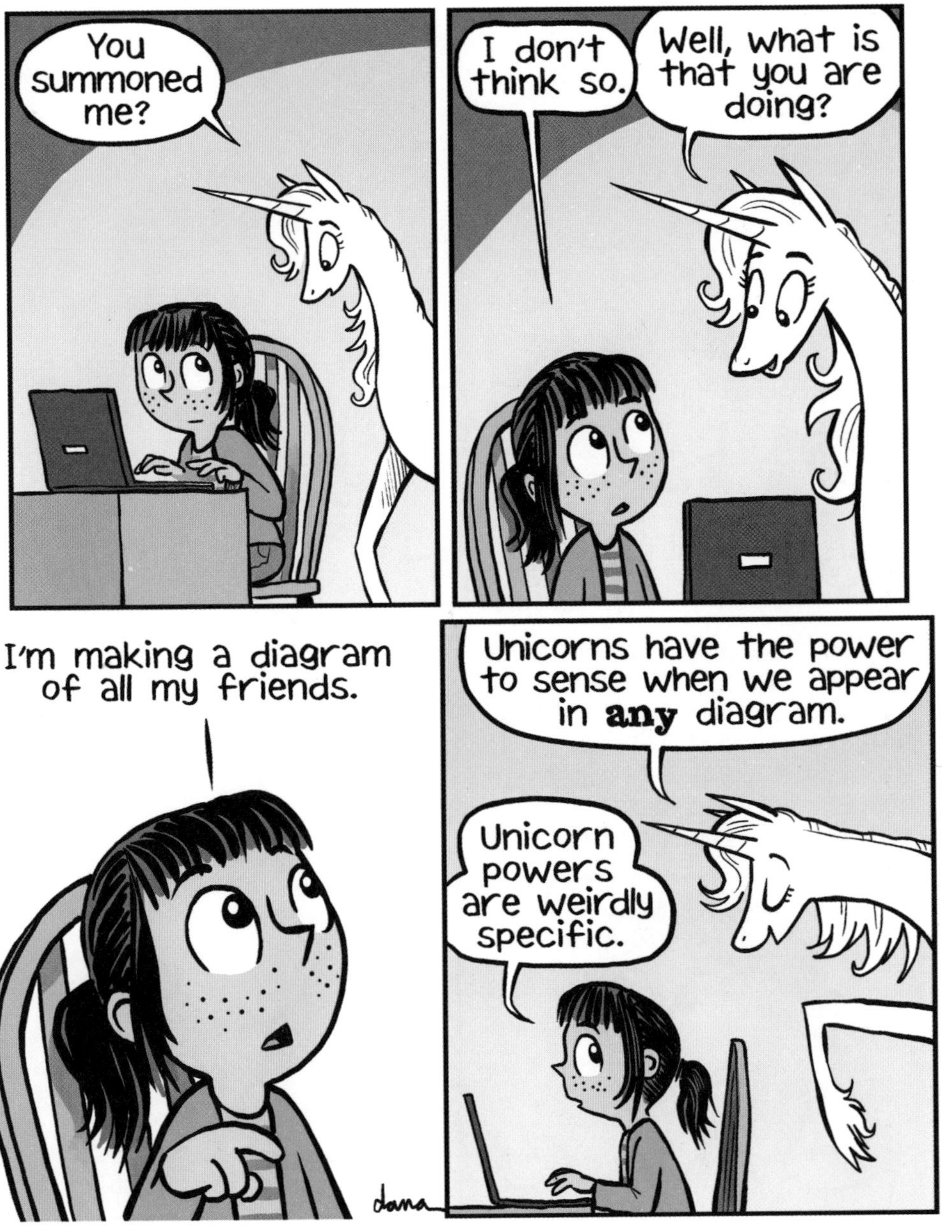
You summoned me?
I don't think so.
Well, what is that you are doing?
I'm making a diagram of all my friends.
Unicorns have the power to sense when we appear in **any** diagram.
Unicorn powers are weirdly specific.
dana

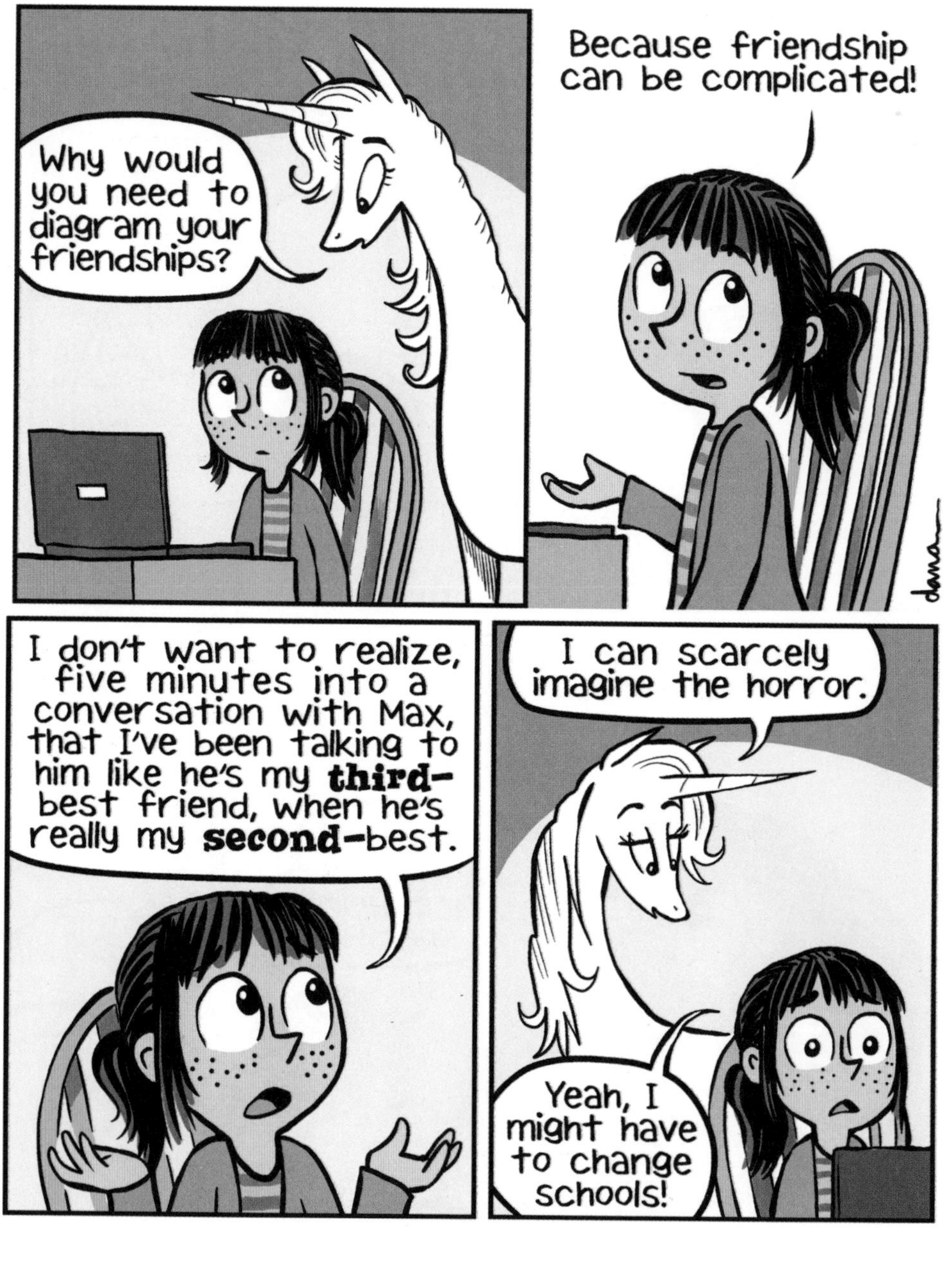
Why would you need to diagram your friendships?
Because friendship can be complicated!
dana
I don't want to realize, five minutes into a conversation with Max, that I've been talking to him like he's my **third**-best friend, when he's really my **second**-best.
I can scarcely imagine the horror.
Yeah, I might have to change schools!

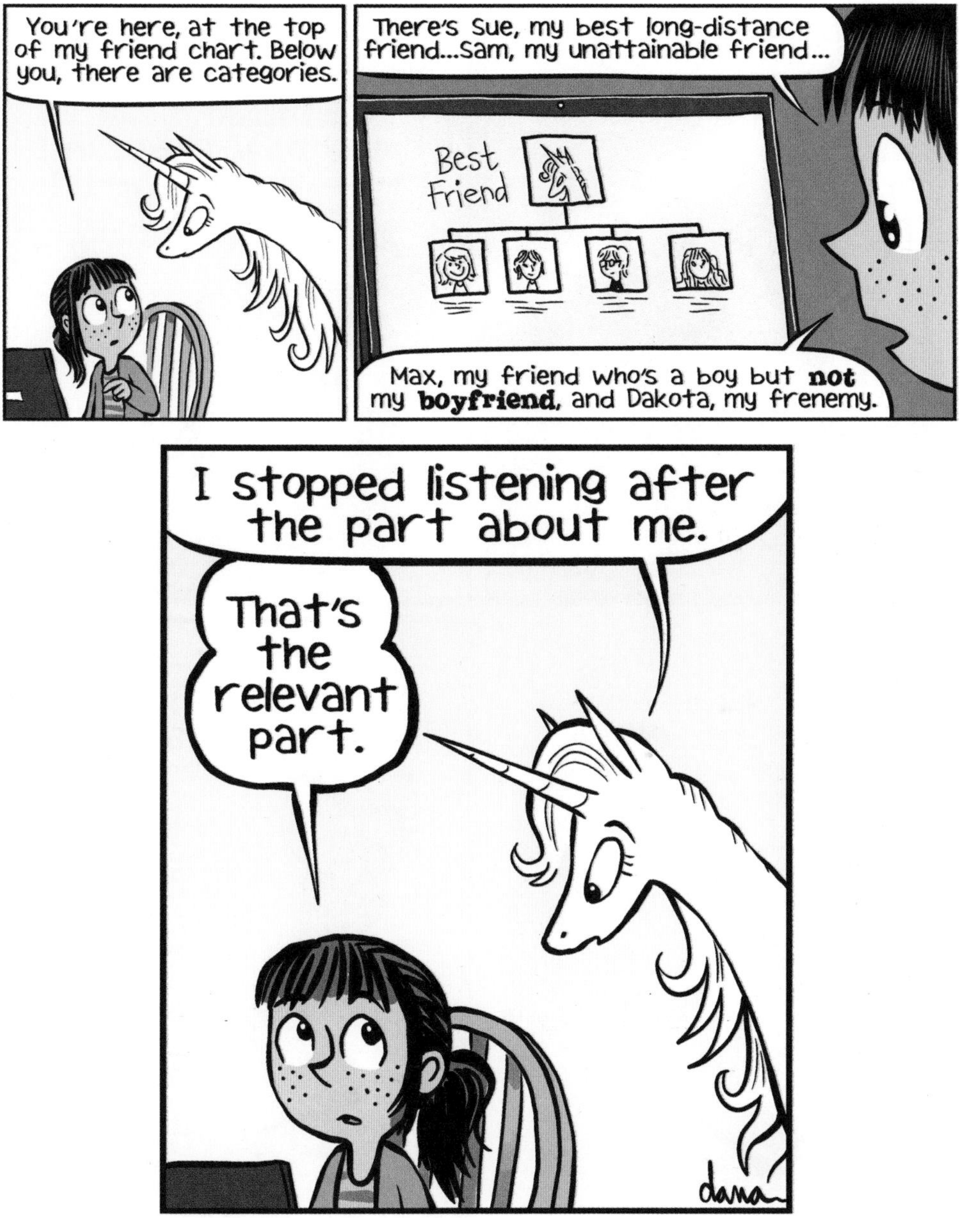
You're here, at the top of my friend chart. Below you, there are categories.
There's Sue, my best long-distance friend...Sam, my unattainable friend...
Best Friend
Max, my friend who's a boy but **not** my **boyfriend**, and Dakota, my frenemy.
I stopped listening after the part about me.
That's the relevant part.

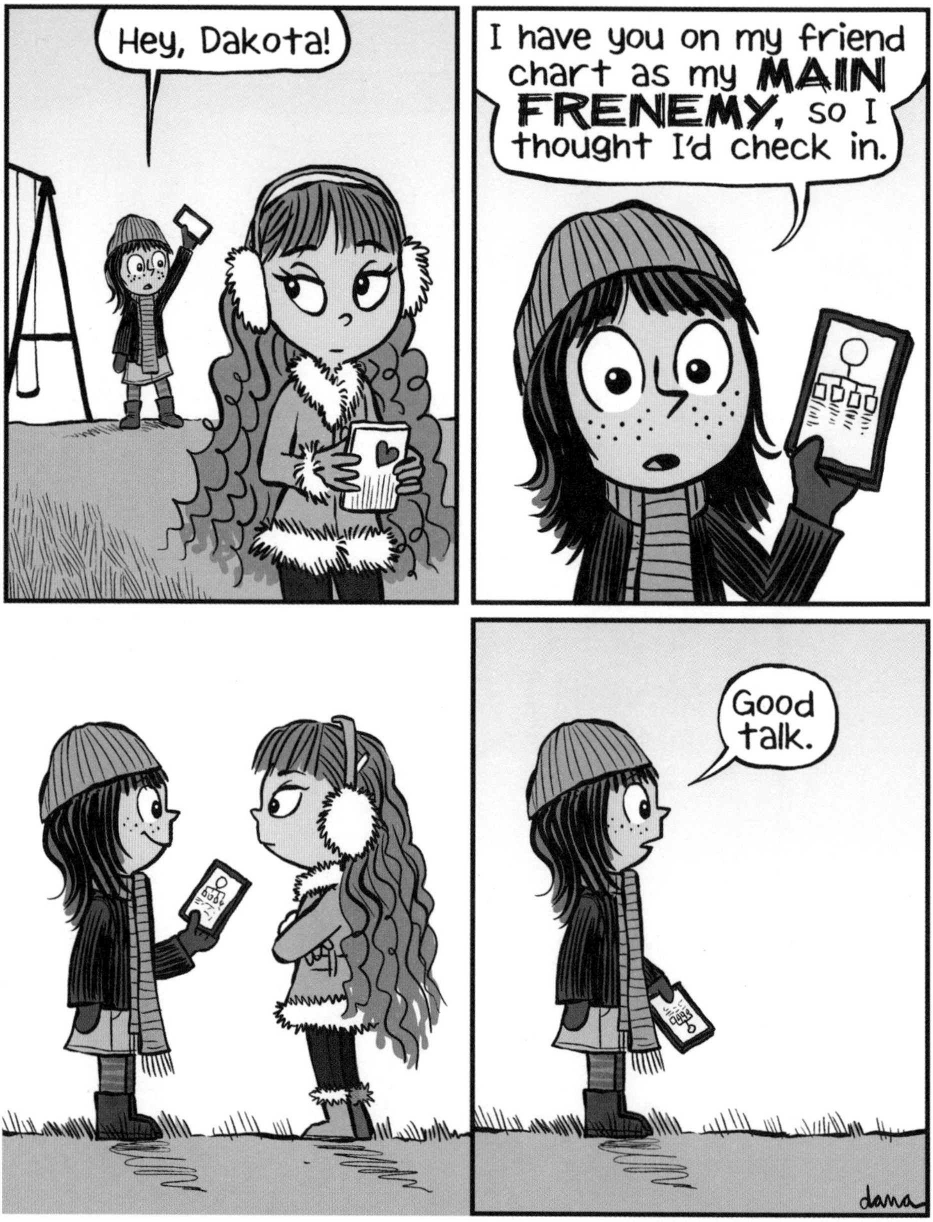
Hey, Dakota!
I have you on my friend chart as my MAIN FRENEMY, so I thought I'd check in.
Good talk.
dana

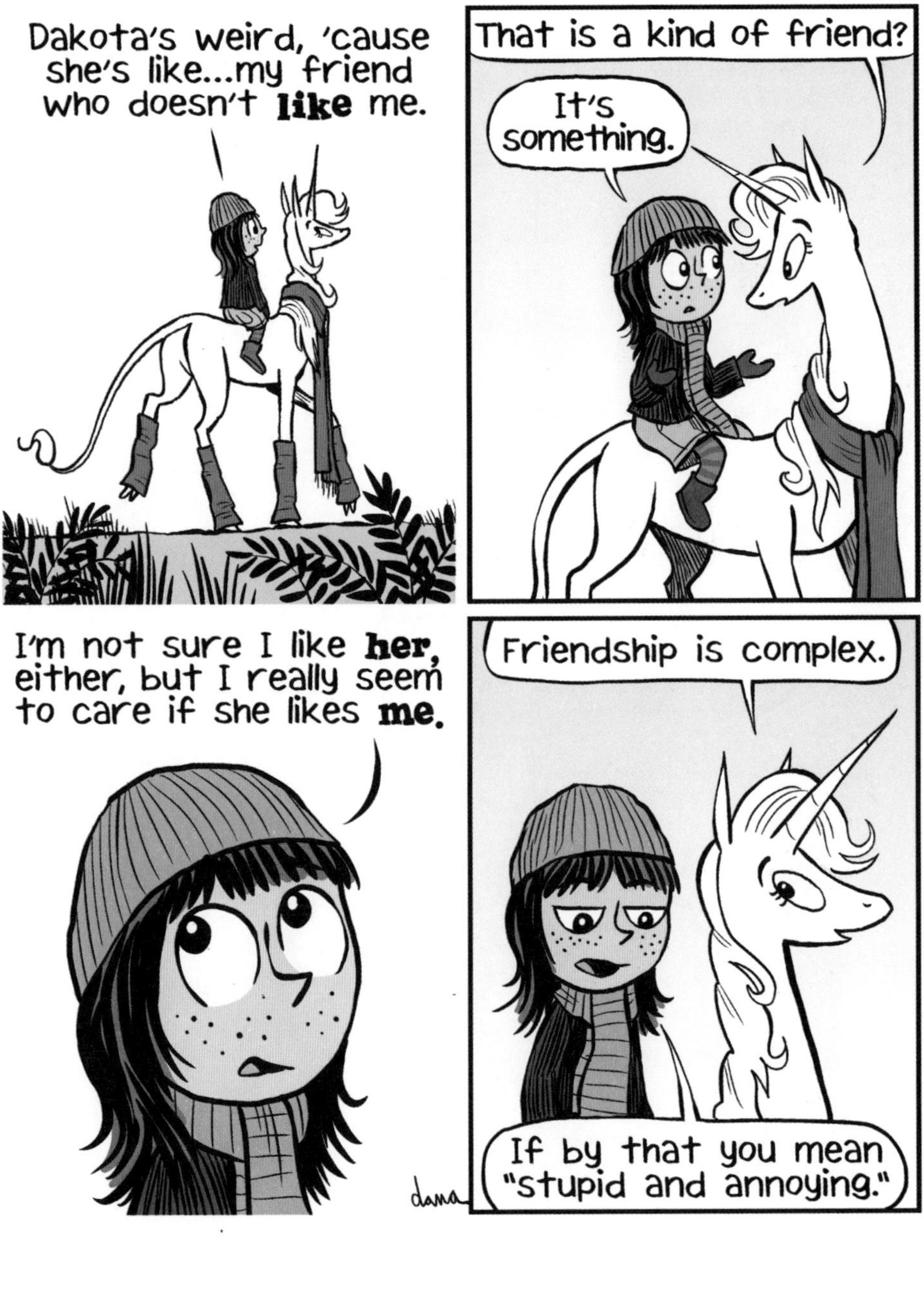
Dakota's weird, 'cause she's like...my friend who doesn't **like** me.
That is a kind of friend?
It's something.
I'm not sure I like **her**, either, but I really seem to care if she likes **me**.
Friendship is complex.
If by that you mean "stupid and annoying."
dana

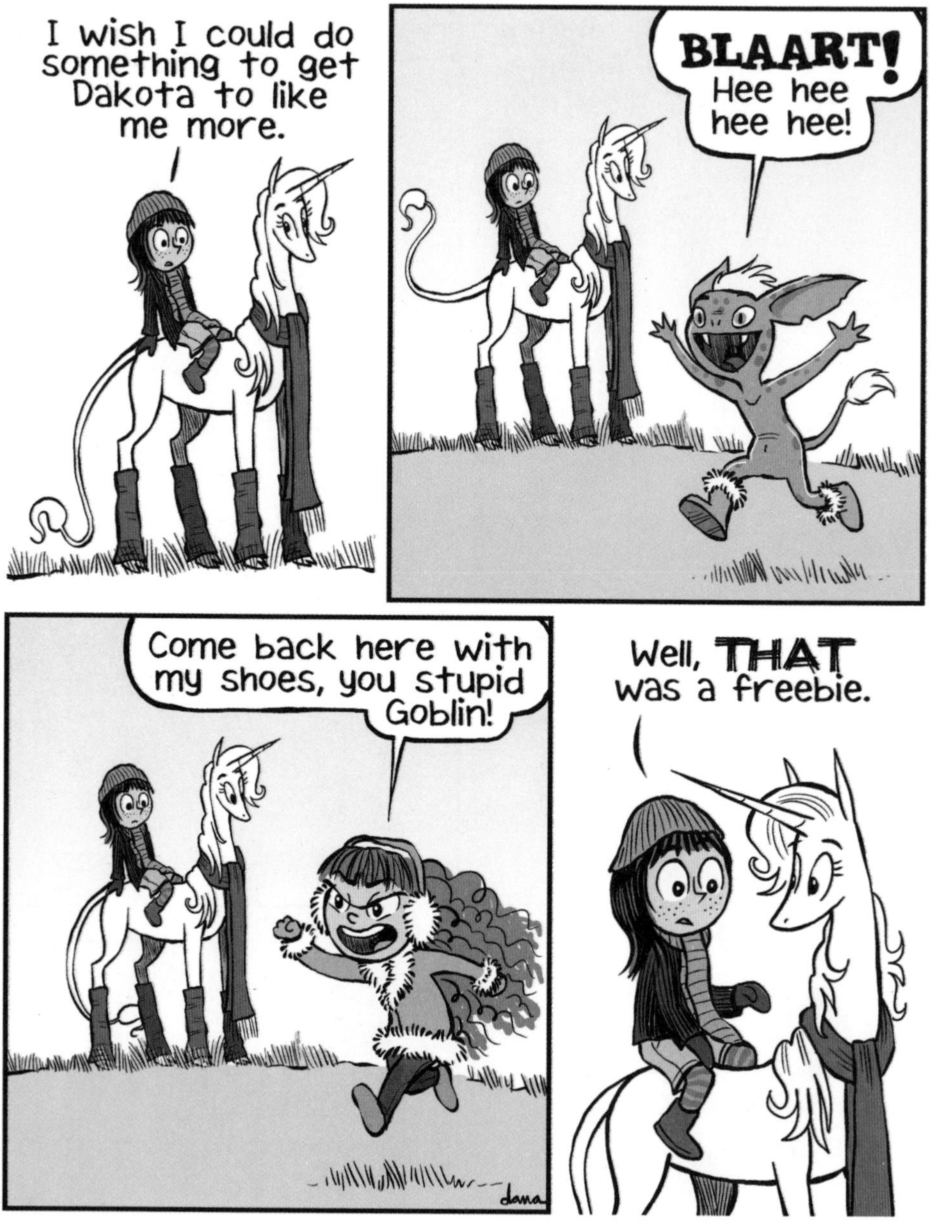
I wish I could do something to get Dakota to like me more.
BLAART! Hee hee hee hee!
Come back here with my shoes, you stupid Goblin!
Well, THAT was a freebie.
dana

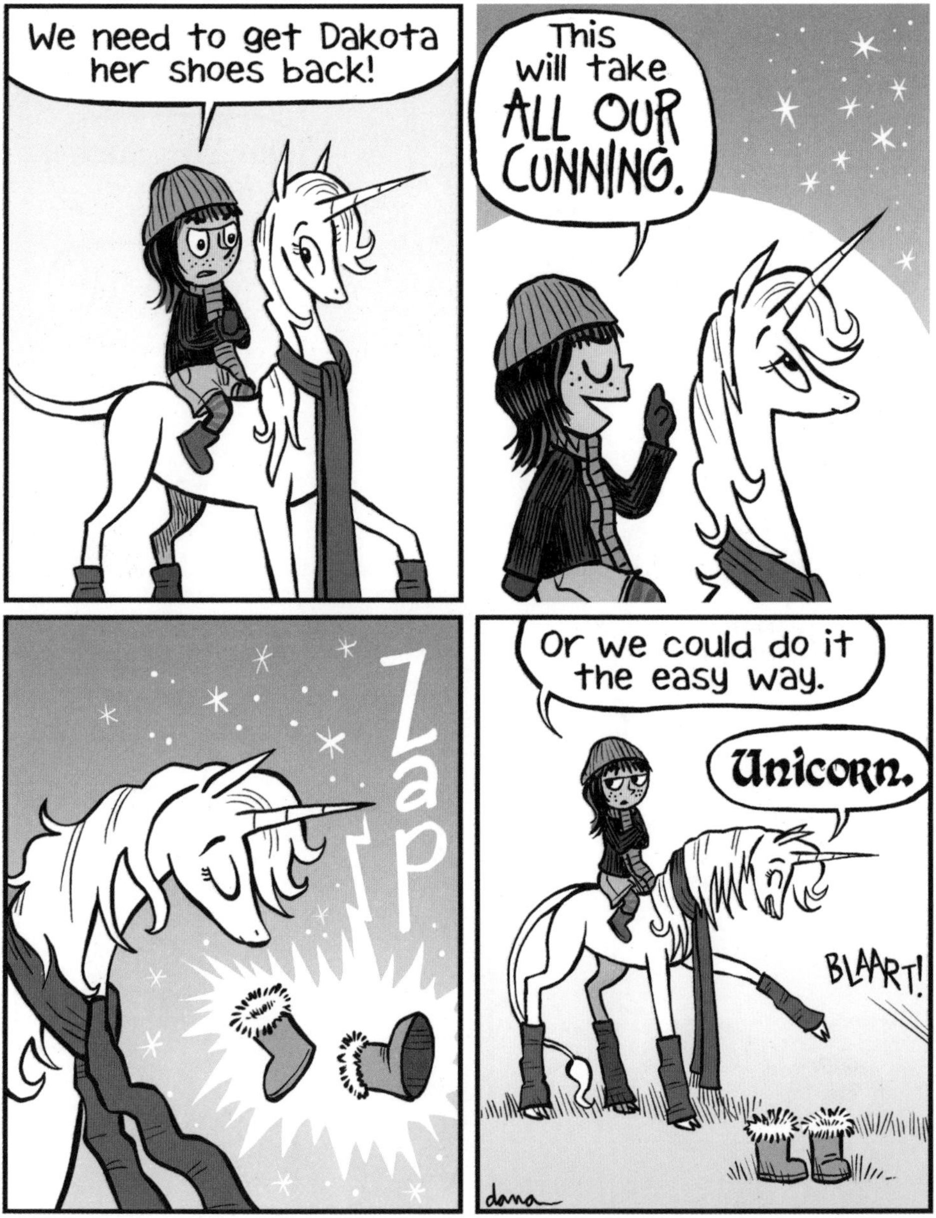

We need to get Dakota her shoes back!
This will take ALL OUR CUNNING.
Zap
Or we could do it the easy way.
Unicorn.
BLAART!
dana

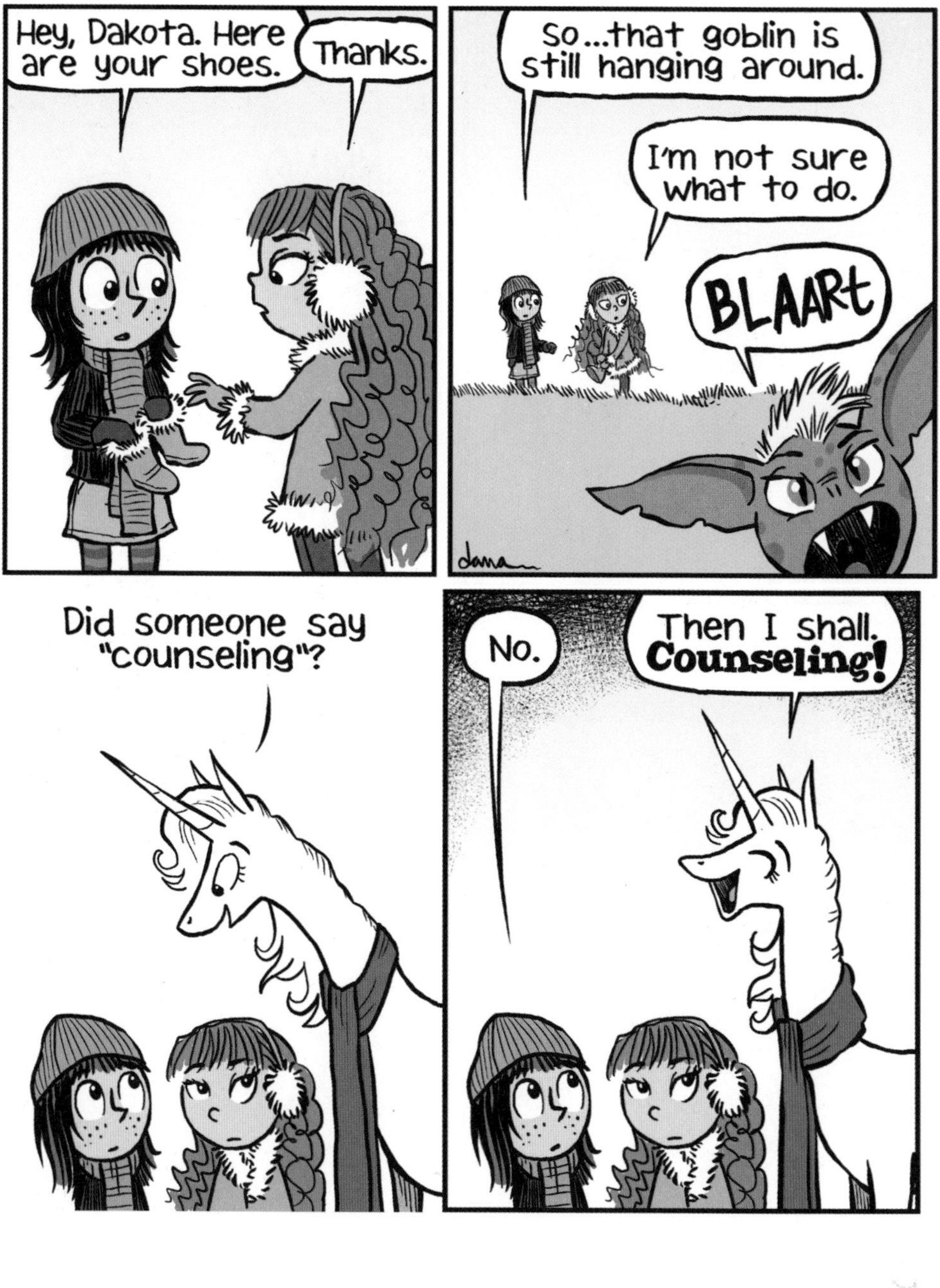
Hey, Dakota. Here are your shoes.
Thanks.
So...that goblin is still hanging around.
I'm not sure what to do.
BLAART
dana
Did someone say "counseling"?
No.
Then I shall. **Counseling!**

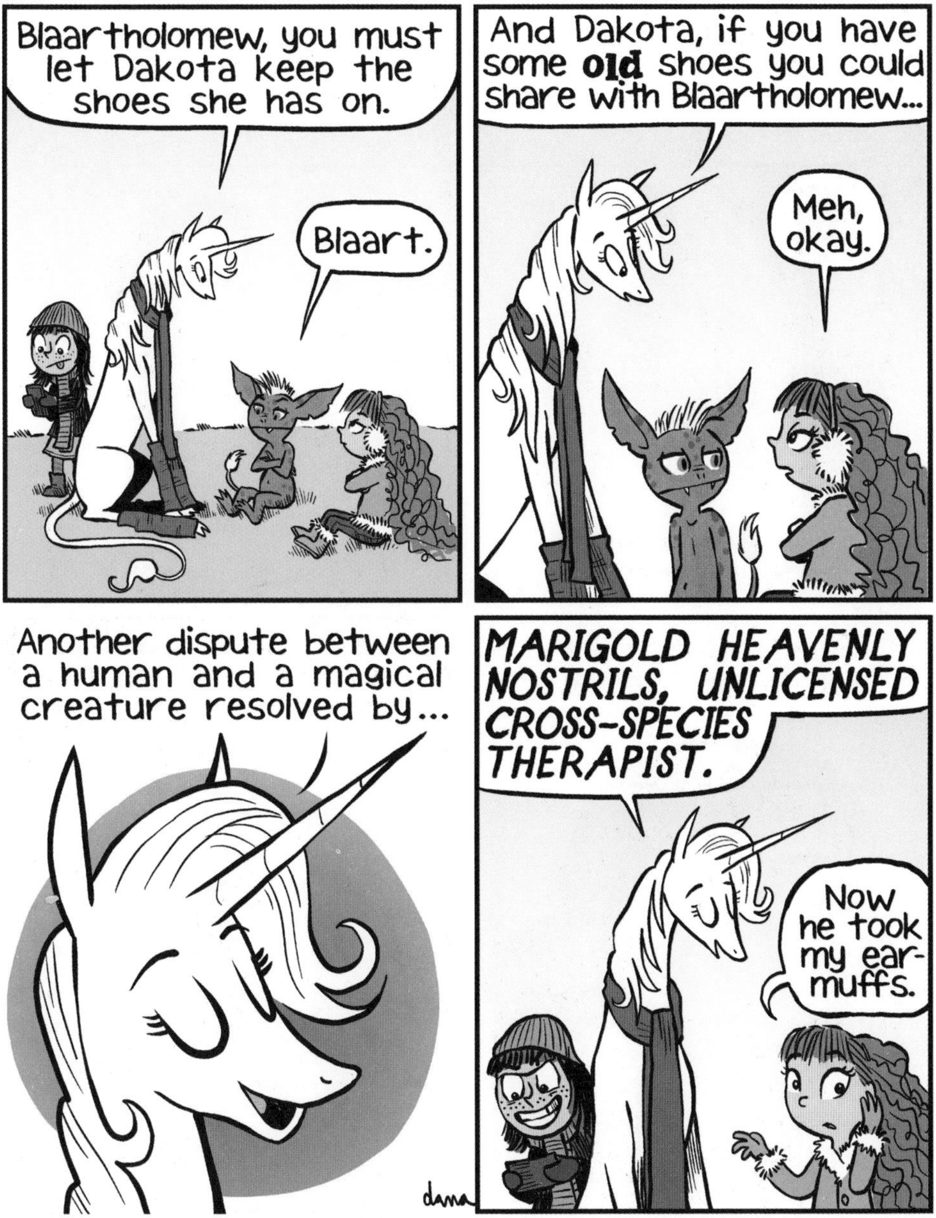
Blaartholomew, you must let Dakota keep the shoes she has on.
Blaart.
And Dakota, if you have some **old** shoes you could share with Blaartholomew...
Meh, okay.
Another dispute between a human and a magical creature resolved by...
MARIGOLD HEAVENLY NOSTRILS, UNLICENSED CROSS-SPECIES THERAPIST.
Now he took my ear-muffs.
dana

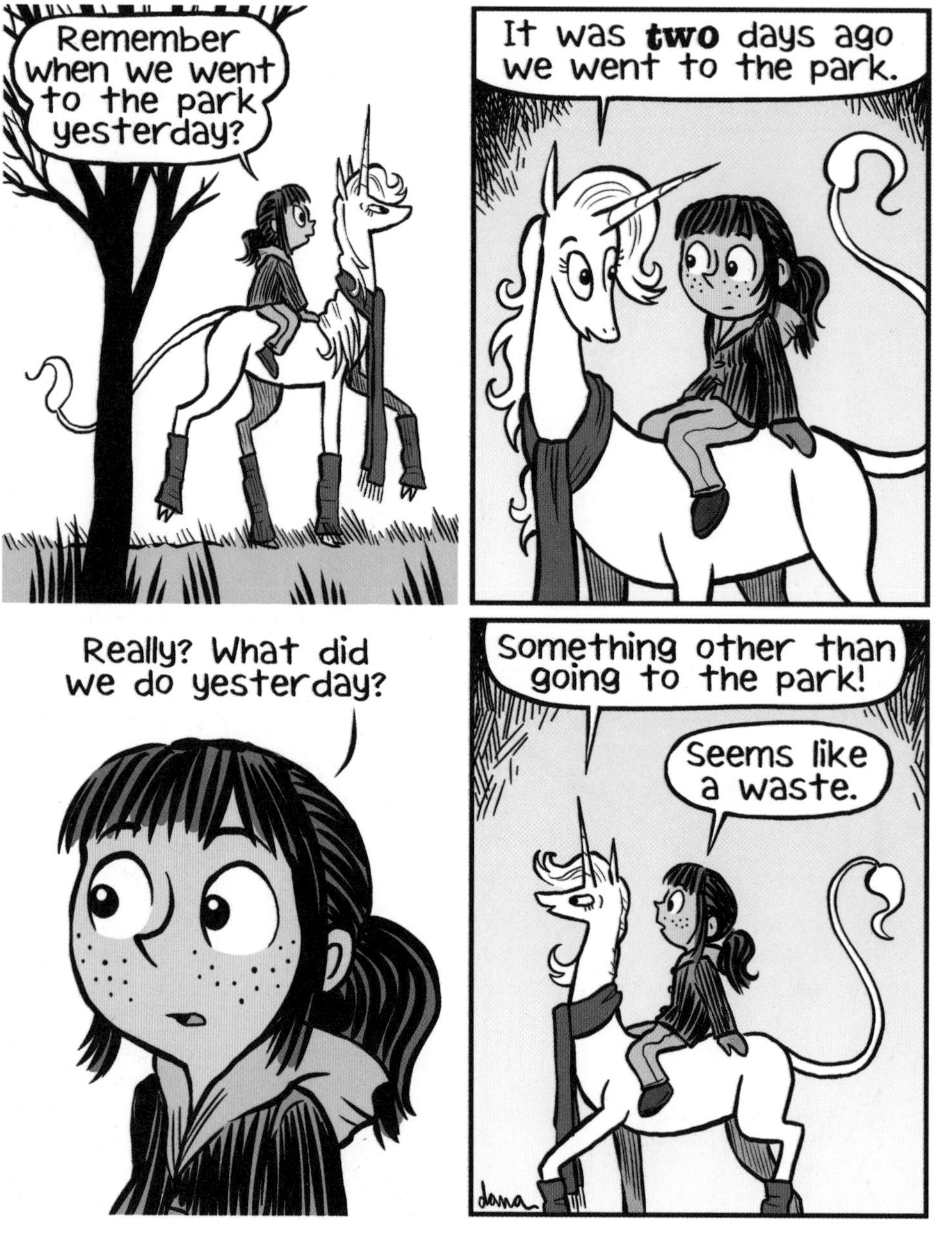
Remember when we went to the park yesterday?
It was **two** days ago we went to the park.
Really? What did we do yesterday?
Something other than going to the park!
Seems like a waste.
dana

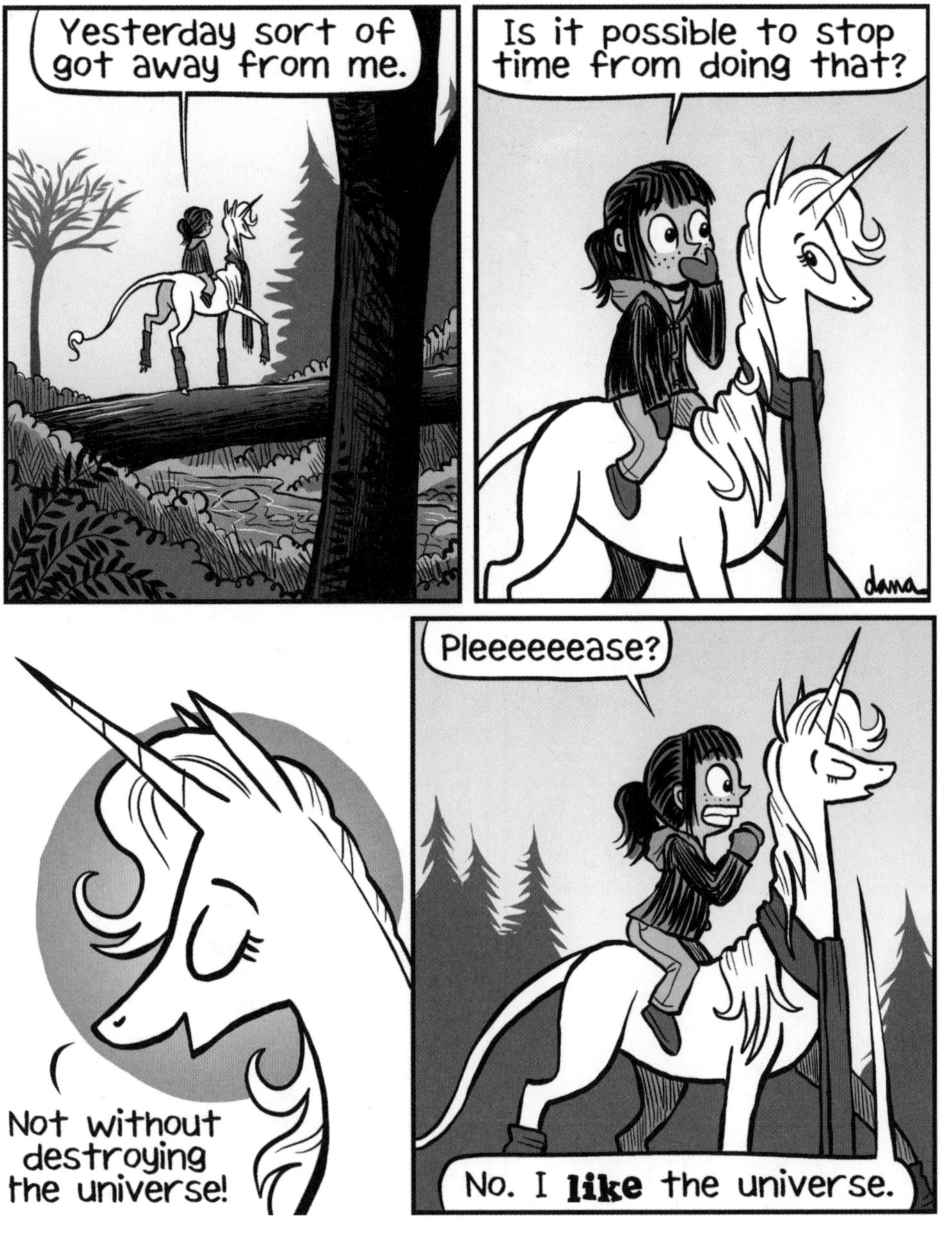
Yesterday sort of got away from me.
Is it possible to stop time from doing that?
dana
Not without destroying the universe!
Pleeeeeease?
No. I **like** the universe.

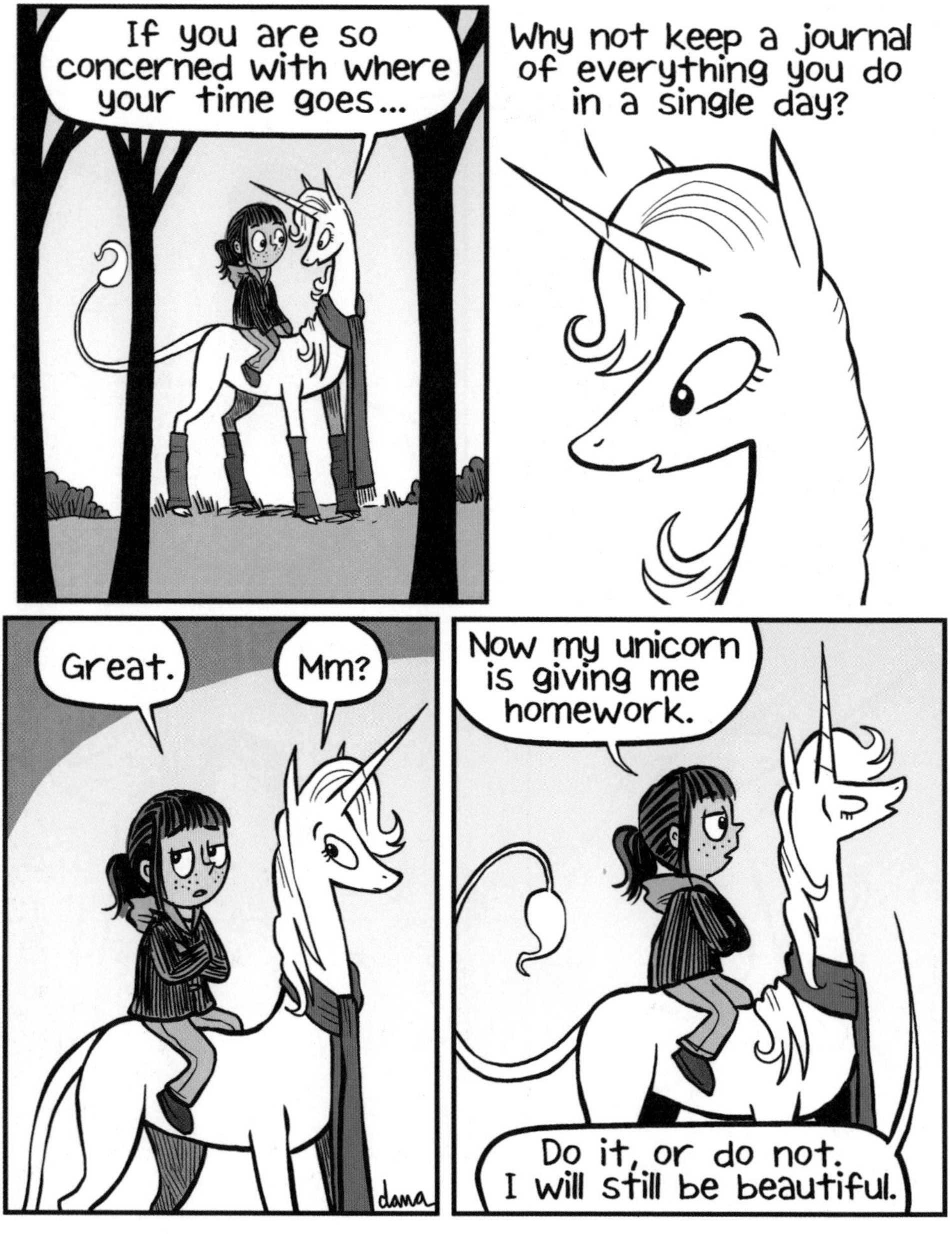

If you are so concerned with where your time goes...
Why not keep a journal of everything you do in a single day?
Great.
Mm?
dana
Now my unicorn is giving me homework.
Do it, or do not. I will still be beautiful.

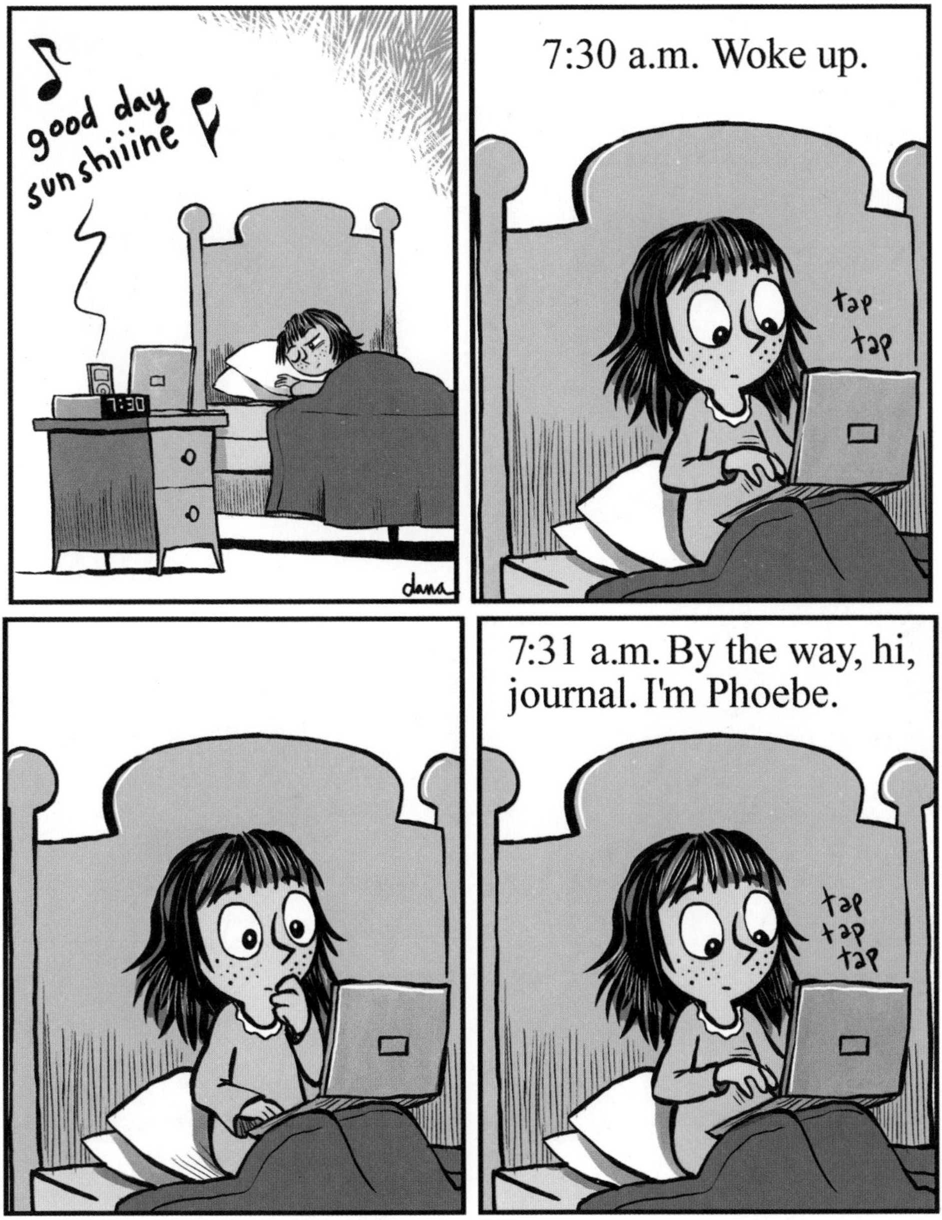
good day sunshiiine
dana
7:30 a.m. Woke up.
tap tap
7:31 a.m. By the way, hi, journal. I'm Phoebe.
tap tap tap

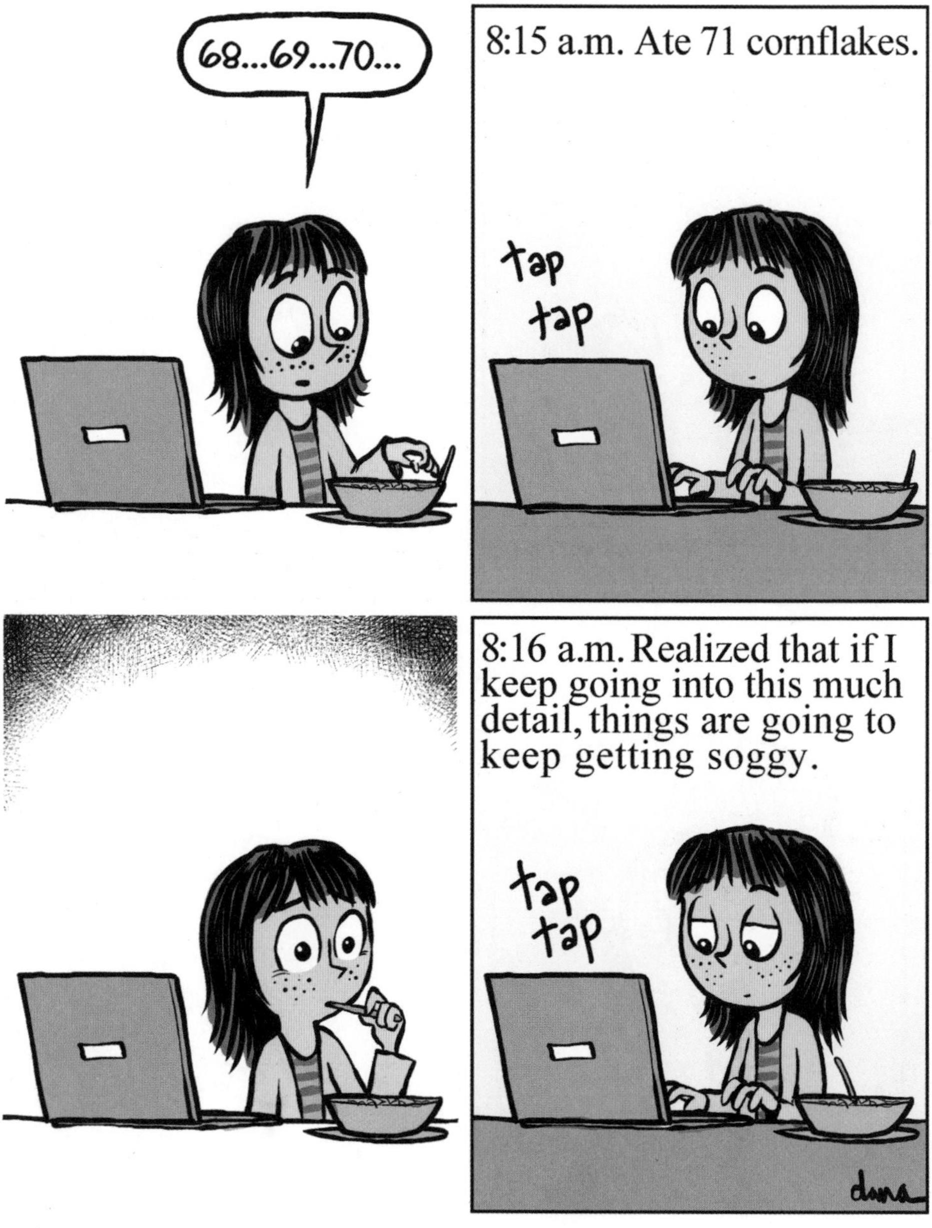
68...69...70...
8:15 a.m. Ate 71 cornflakes.
tap tap
8:16 a.m. Realized that if I keep going into this much detail, things are going to keep getting soggy.
tap tap
dana

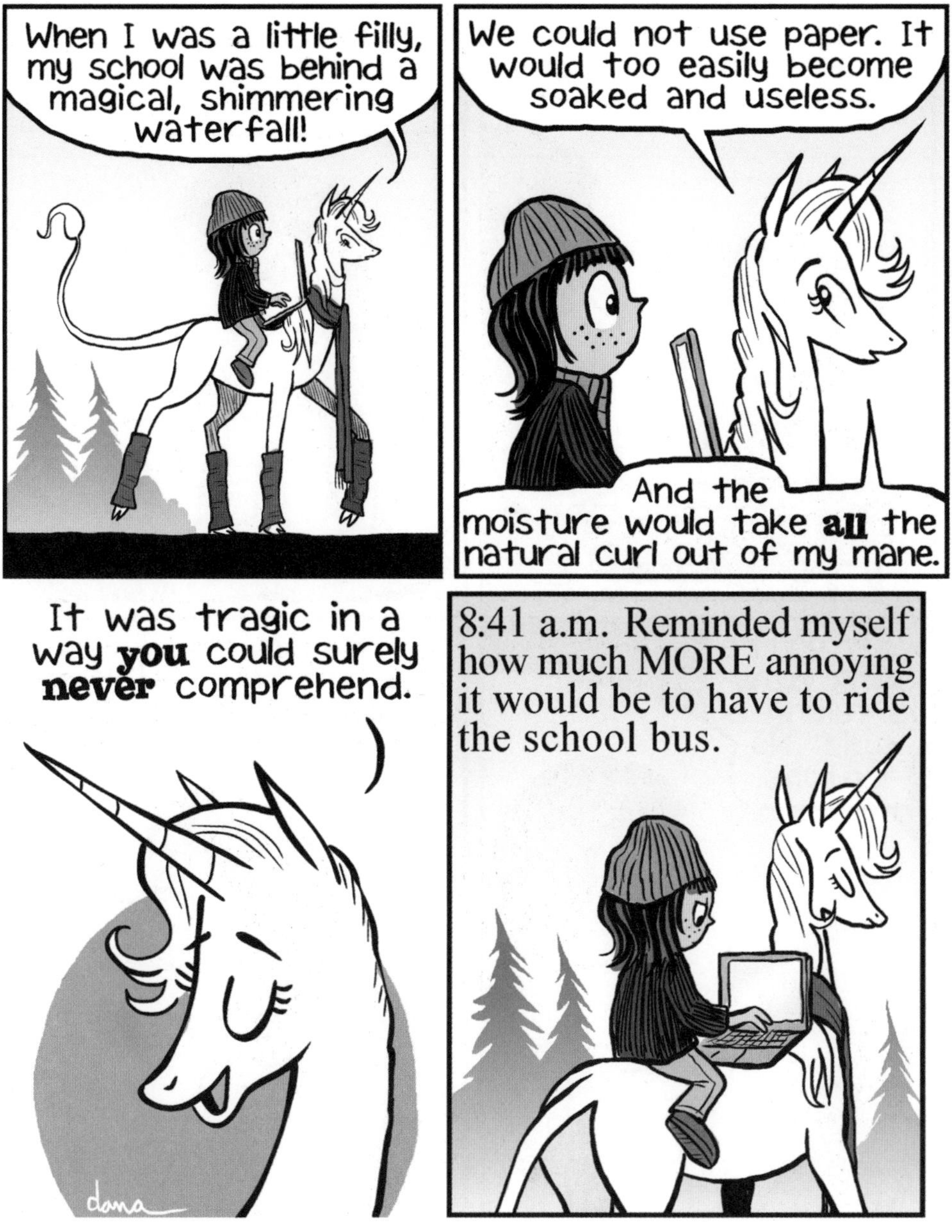
When I was a little filly, my school was behind a magical, shimmering waterfall!
We could not use paper. It would too easily become soaked and useless.
And the moisture would take **all** the natural curl out of my mane.
It was tragic in a way **you** could surely **never** comprehend.
8:41 a.m. Reminded myself how much MORE annoying it would be to have to ride the school bus.
dana

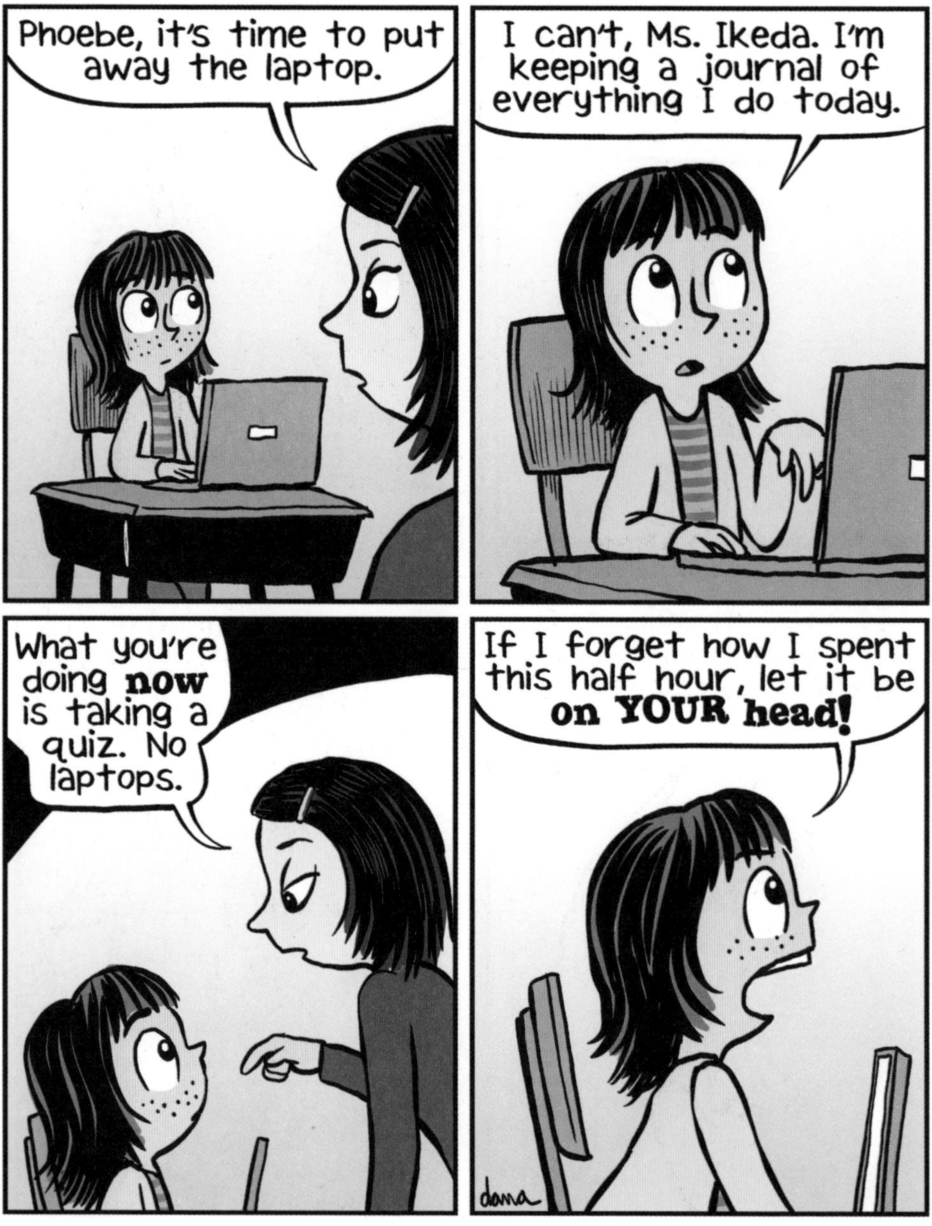
Phoebe, it's time to put away the laptop.
I can't, Ms. Ikeda. I'm keeping a journal of everything I do today.
What you're doing **now** is taking a quiz. No laptops.
If I forget how I spent this half hour, let it be **on YOUR head!**
dana

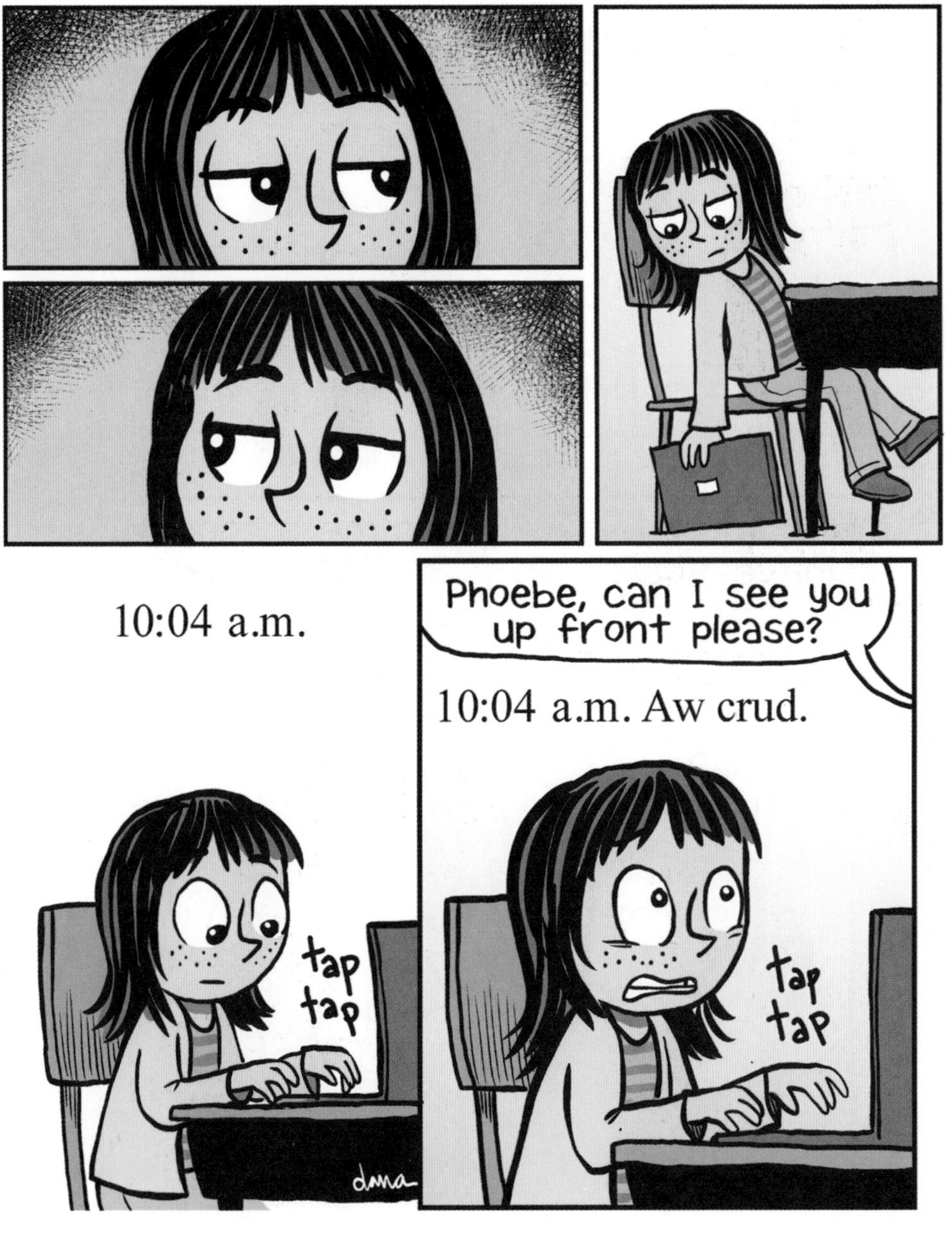
10:04 a.m.
tap tap
Phoebe, can I see you up front please?
10:04 a.m. Aw crud.
tap tap
dana

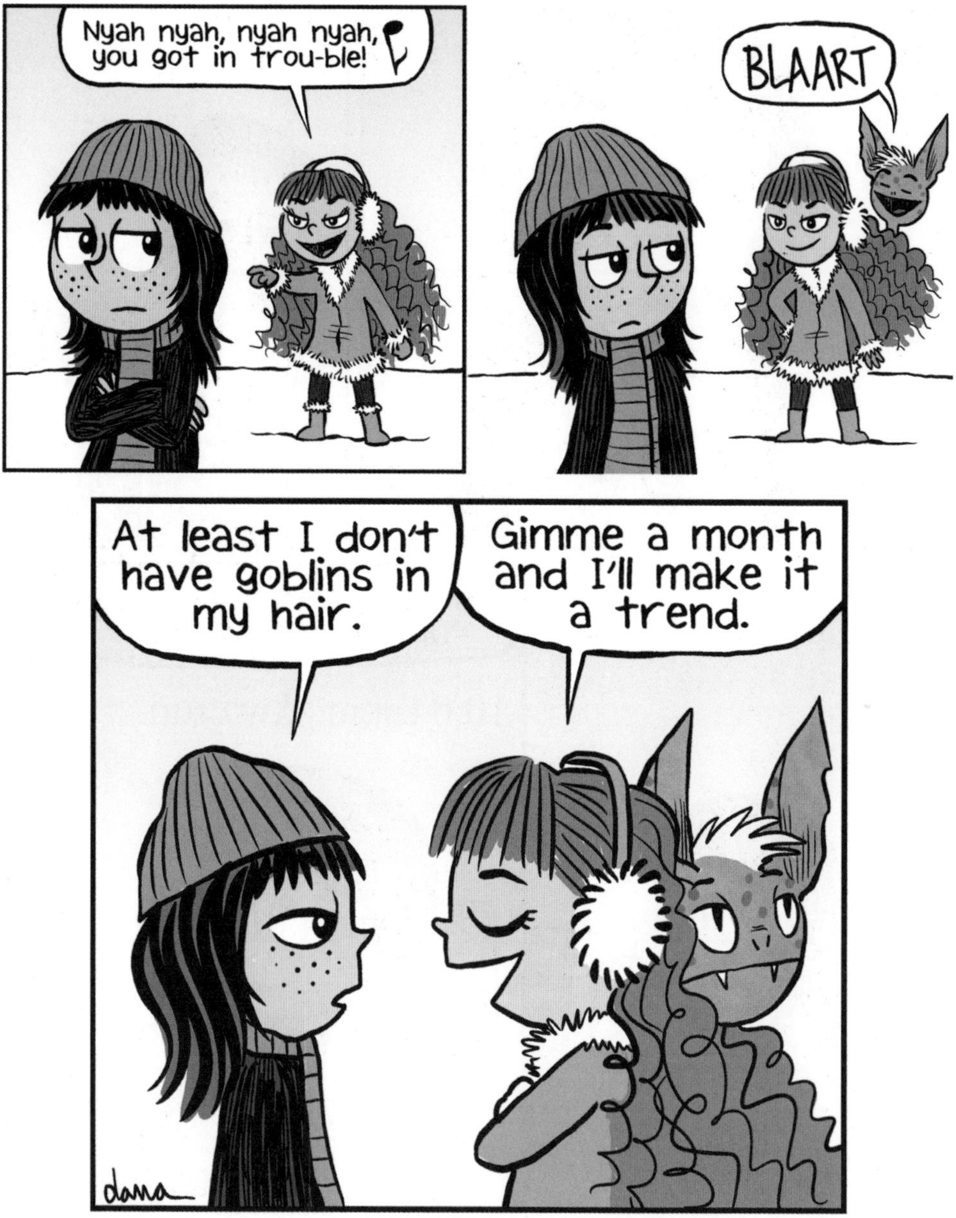
Nyah nyah, nyah nyah, you got in trou-ble!
BLAART
At least I don't have goblins in my hair.
Gimme a month and I'll make it a trend.
dana

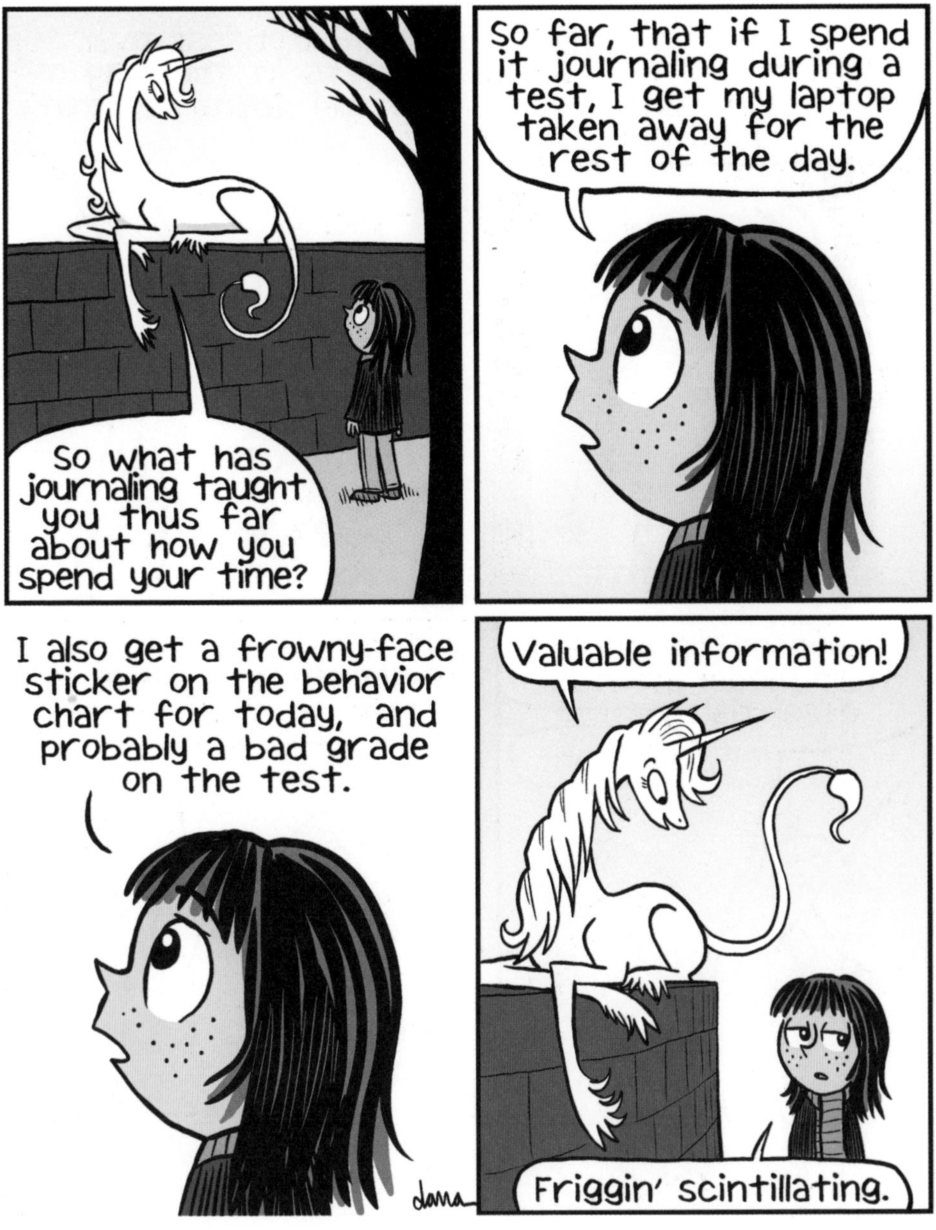
So what has journaling taught you thus far about how you spend your time?
So far, that if I spend it journaling during a test, I get my laptop taken away for the rest of the day.
I also get a frowny-face sticker on the behavior chart for today, and probably a bad grade on the test.
Valuable information!
Friggin' scintillating.
dana

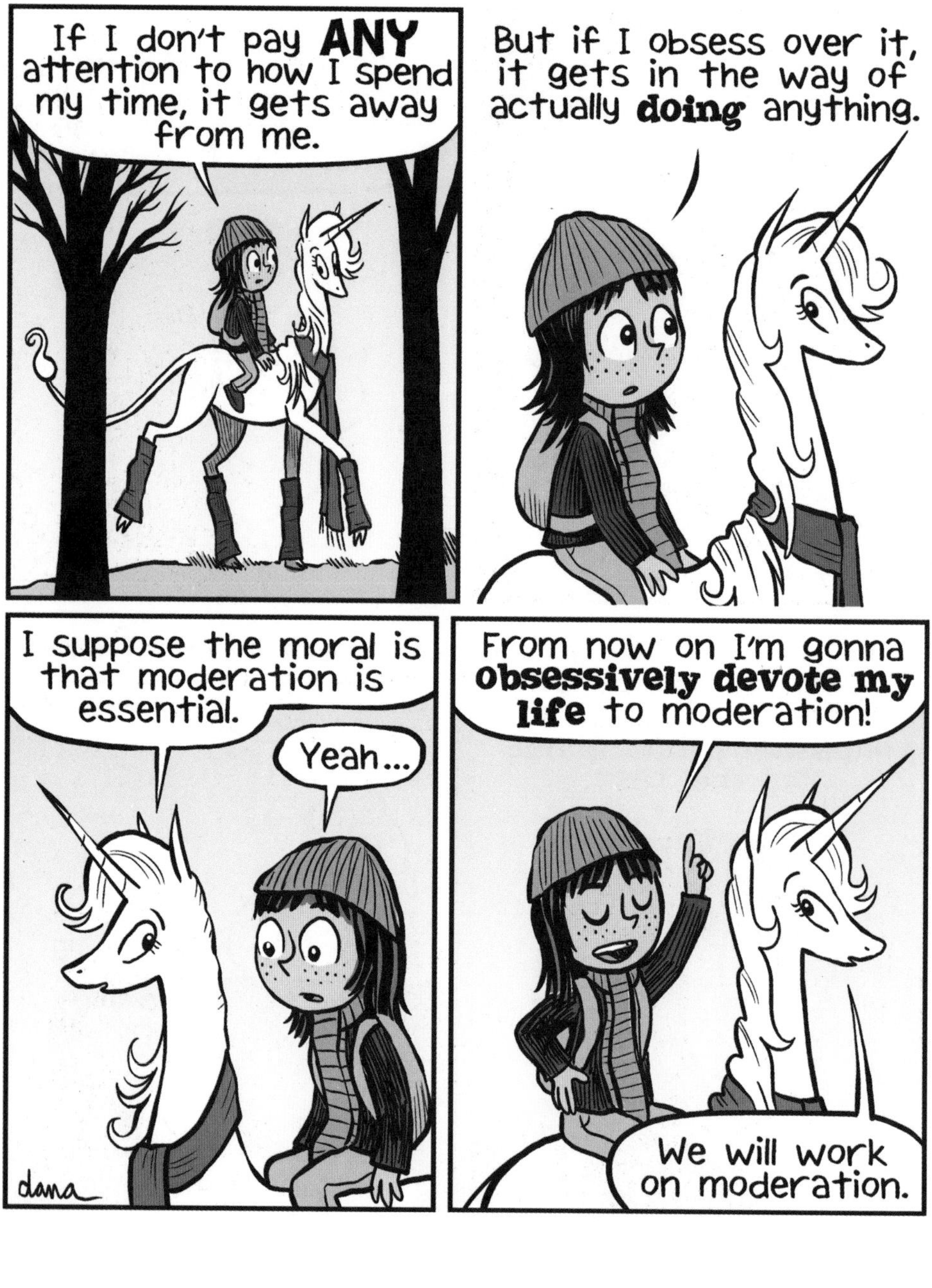
If I don't pay **ANY** attention to how I spend my time, it gets away from me.
But if I obsess over it, it gets in the way of actually **doing** anything.
I suppose the moral is that moderation is essential.
Yeah...
dana
From now on I'm gonna **obsessively devote my life** to moderation!
We will work on moderation.

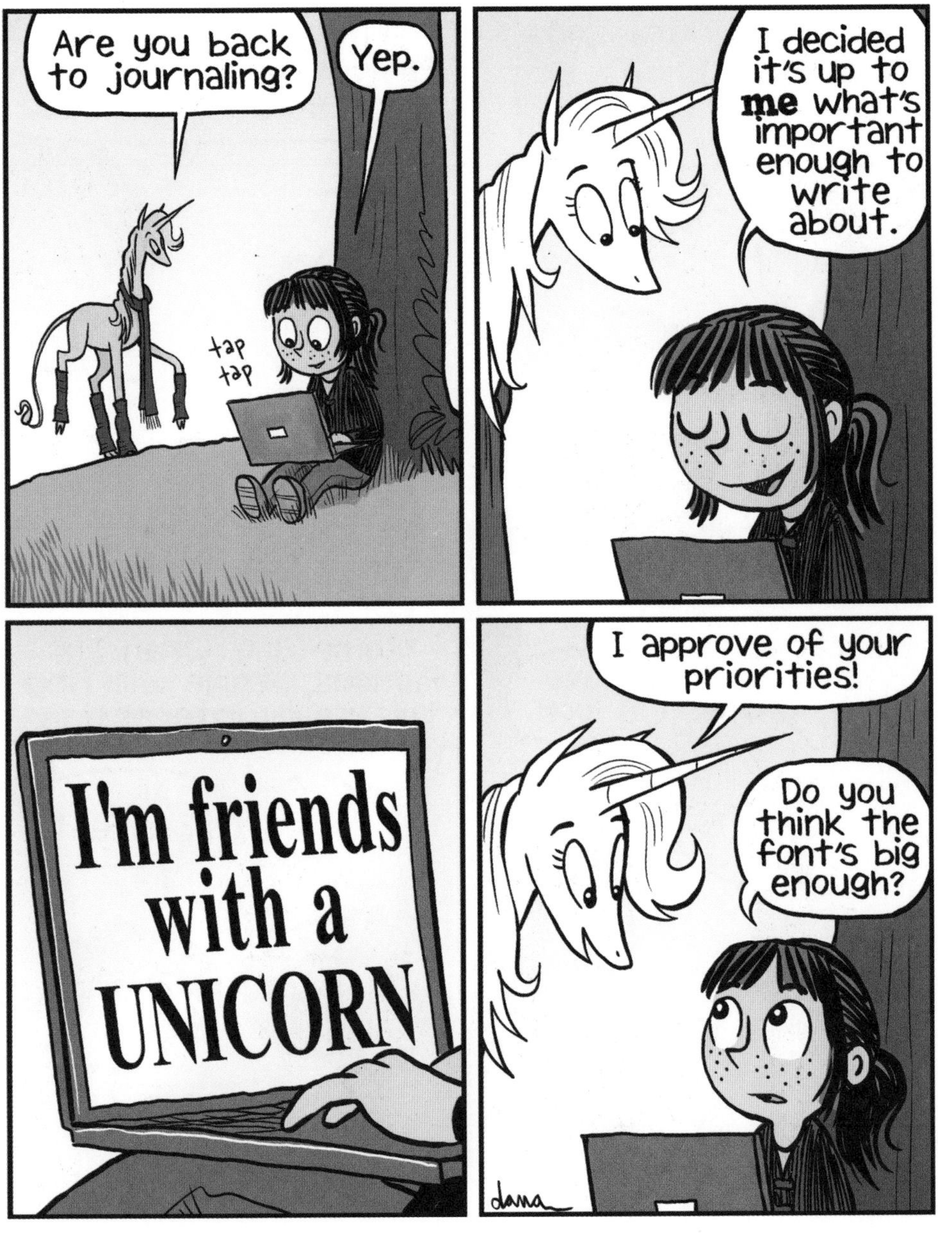

Are you back to journaling?
Yep.
tap tap
I decided it's up to **me** what's important enough to write about.
I'm friends with a UNICORN
I approve of your priorities!
Do you think the font's big enough?
dana

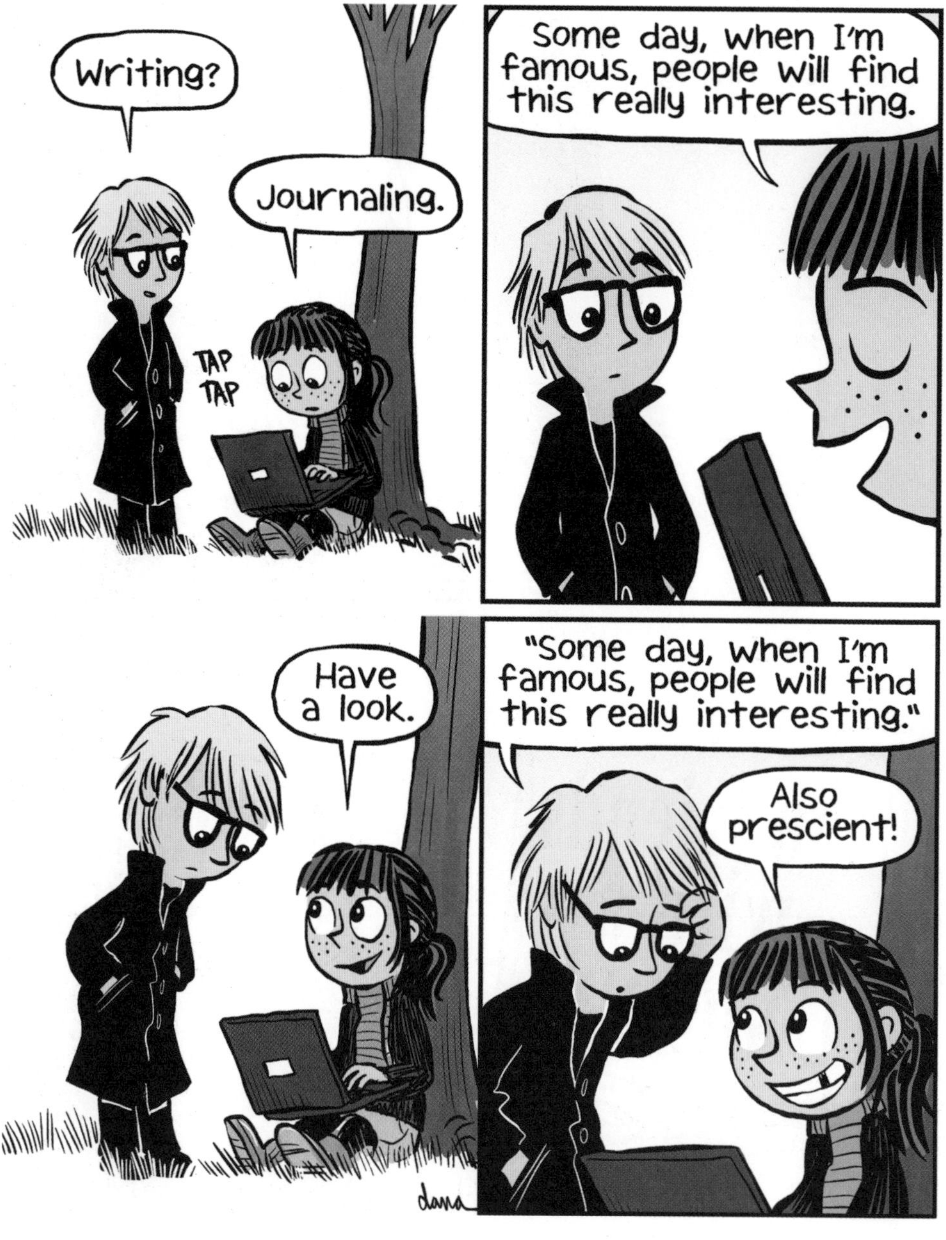
Writing?
Journaling.
TAP TAP
Some day, when I'm famous, people will find this really interesting.
Have a look.
"Some day, when I'm famous, people will find this really interesting."
Also prescient!
dana

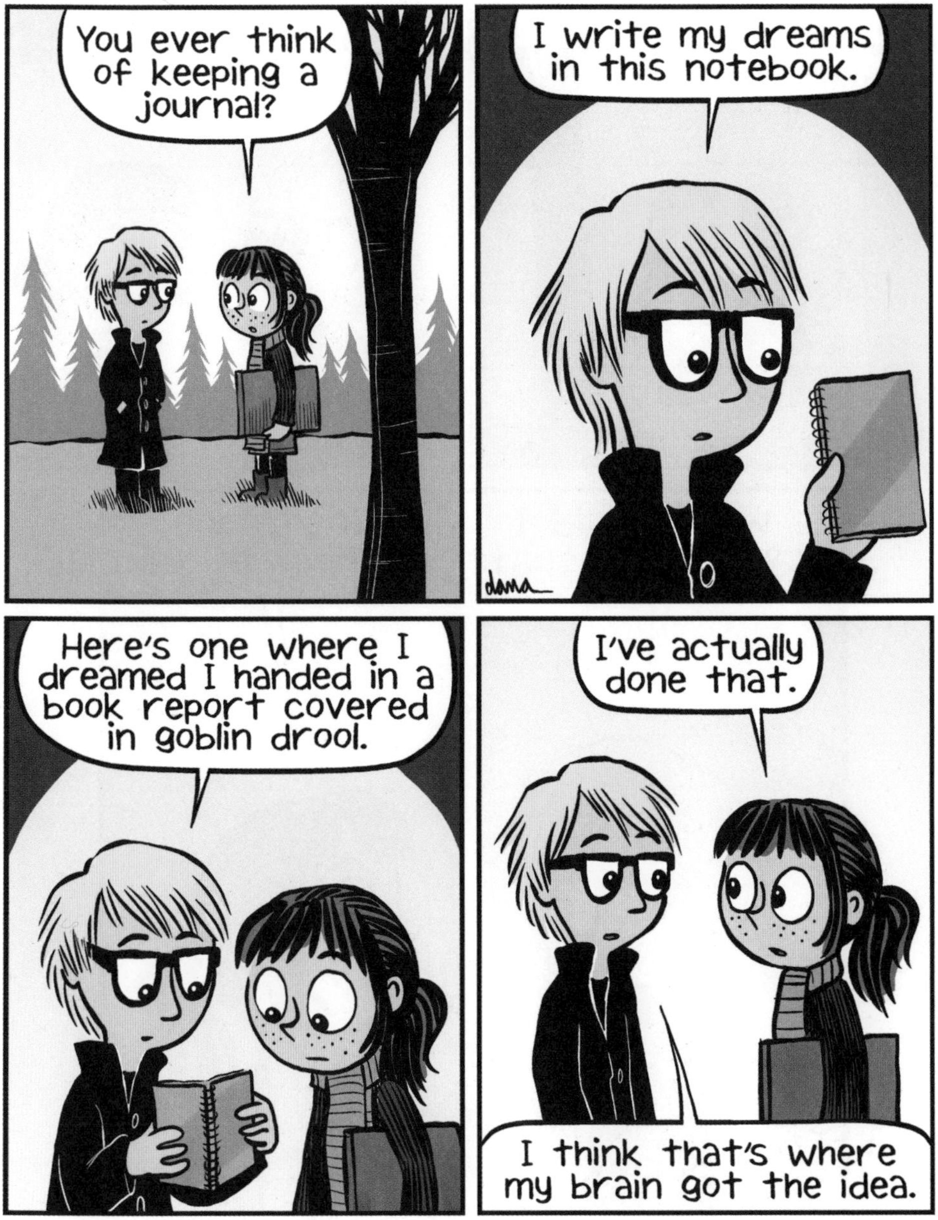
You ever think of keeping a journal?
I write my dreams in this notebook.
dana
Here's one where I dreamed I handed in a book report covered in goblin drool.
I've actually done that.
I think that's where my brain got the idea.

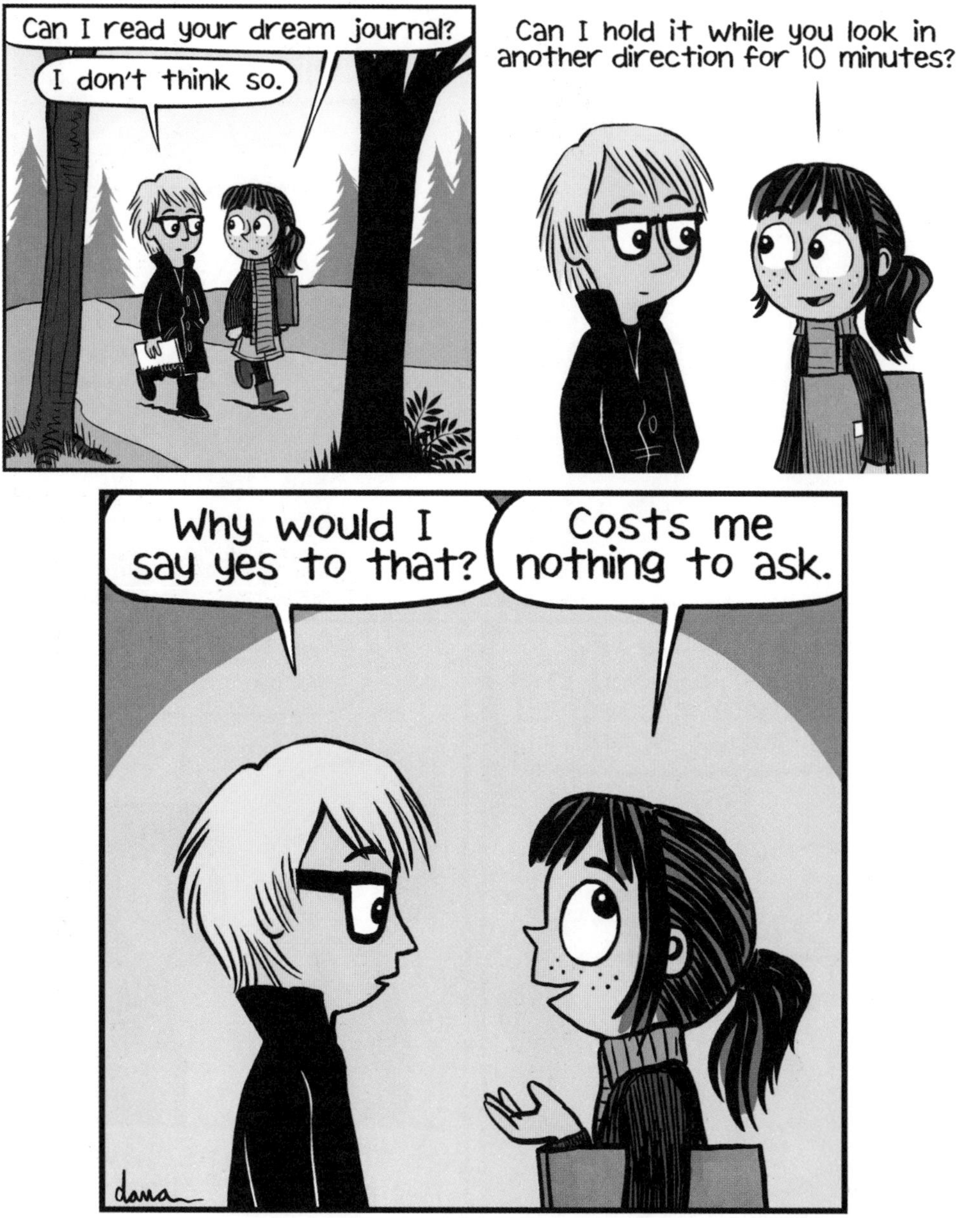
Can I read your dream journal?
I don't think so.
Can I hold it while you look in another direction for 10 minutes?
Why would I say yes to that?
Costs me nothing to ask.
dana

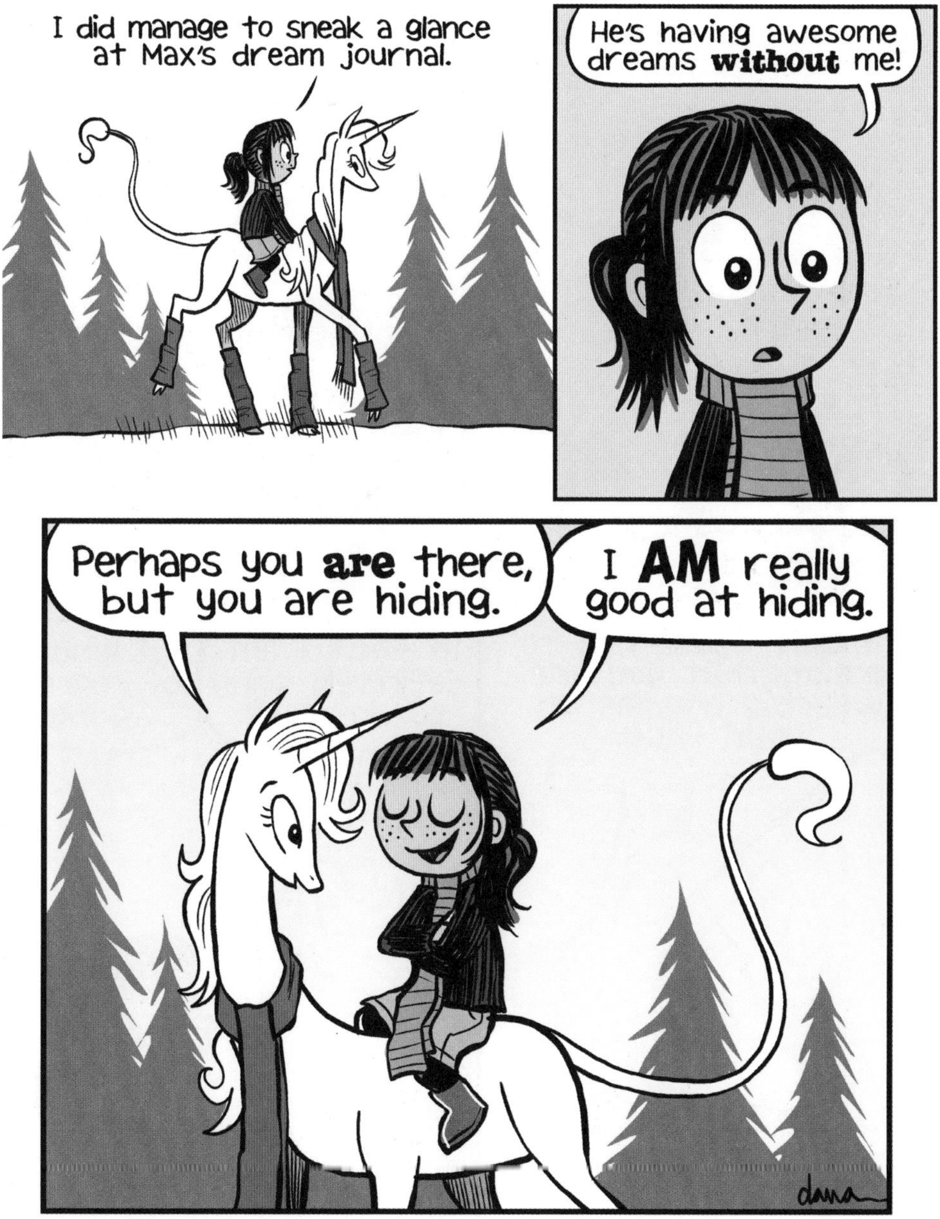
I did manage to sneak a glance at Max's dream journal.
He's having awesome dreams **without** me!
Perhaps you **are** there, but you are hiding.
I **AM** really good at hiding.
dana

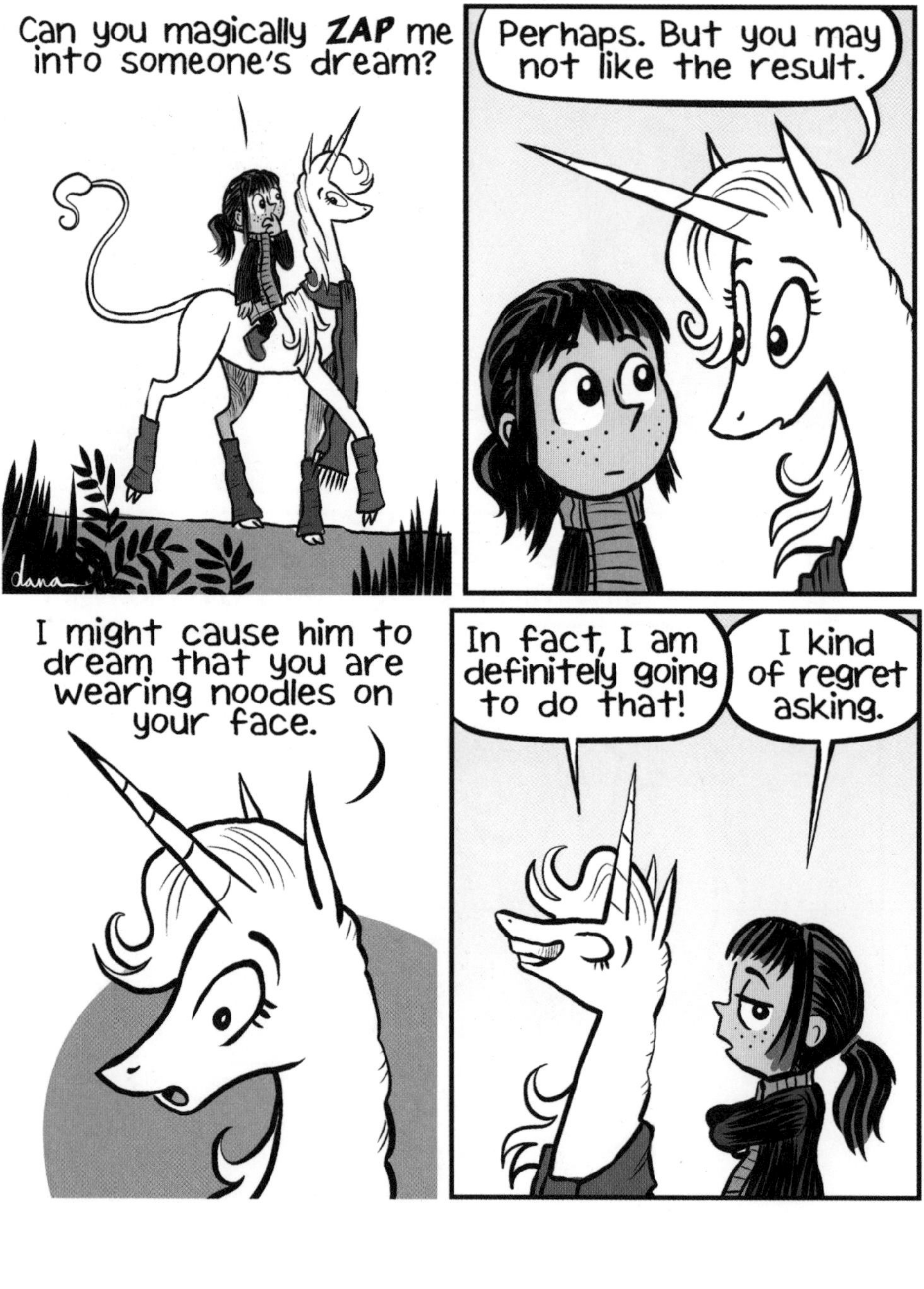
Can you magically **ZAP** me into someone's dream?
Perhaps. But you may not like the result.
I might cause him to dream that you are wearing noodles on your face.
In fact, I am definitely going to do that!
I kind of regret asking.
dana

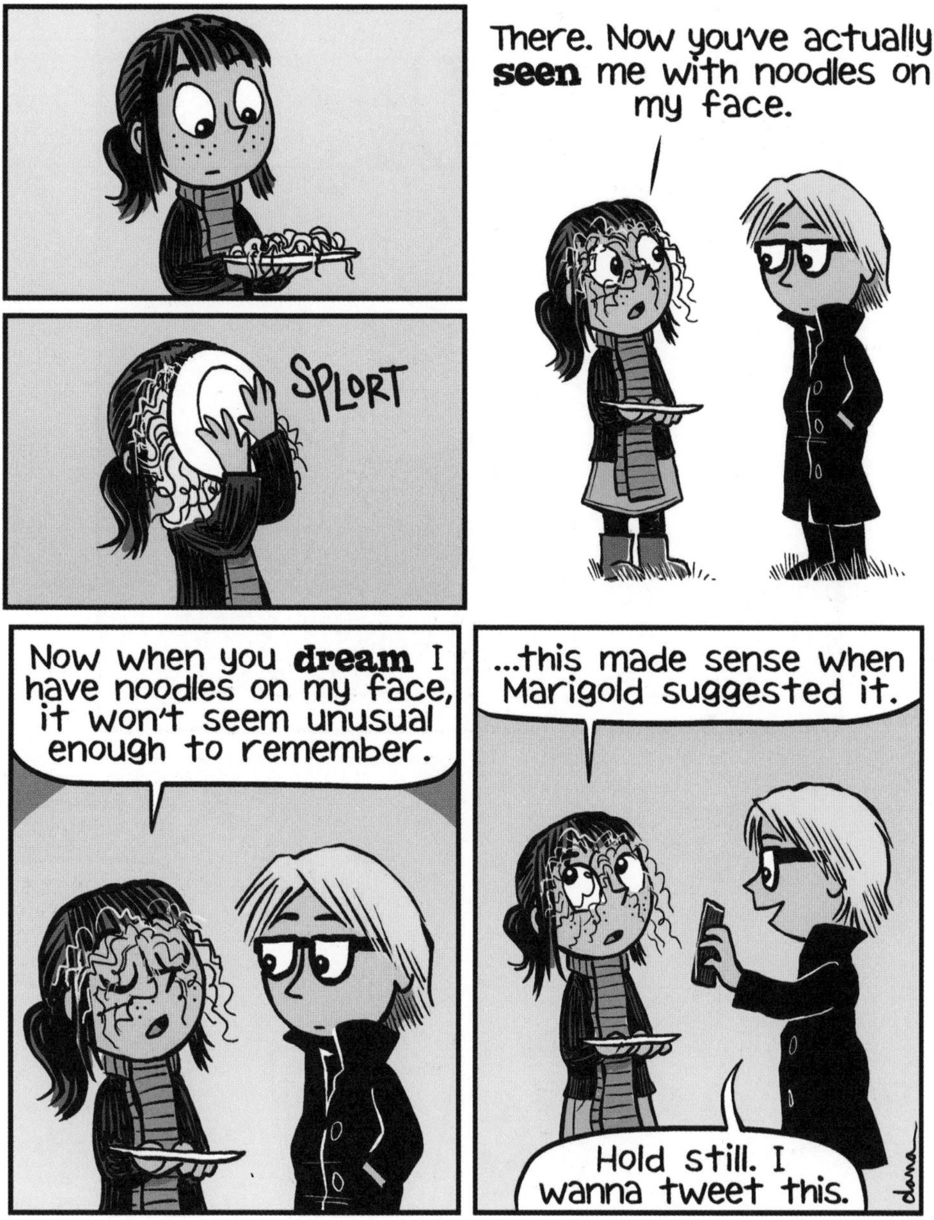
SPLORT
There. Now you've actually **seen** me with noodles on my face.
Now when you **dream** I have noodles on my face, it won't seem unusual enough to remember.
...this made sense when Marigold suggested it.
Hold still. I wanna tweet this.
dana

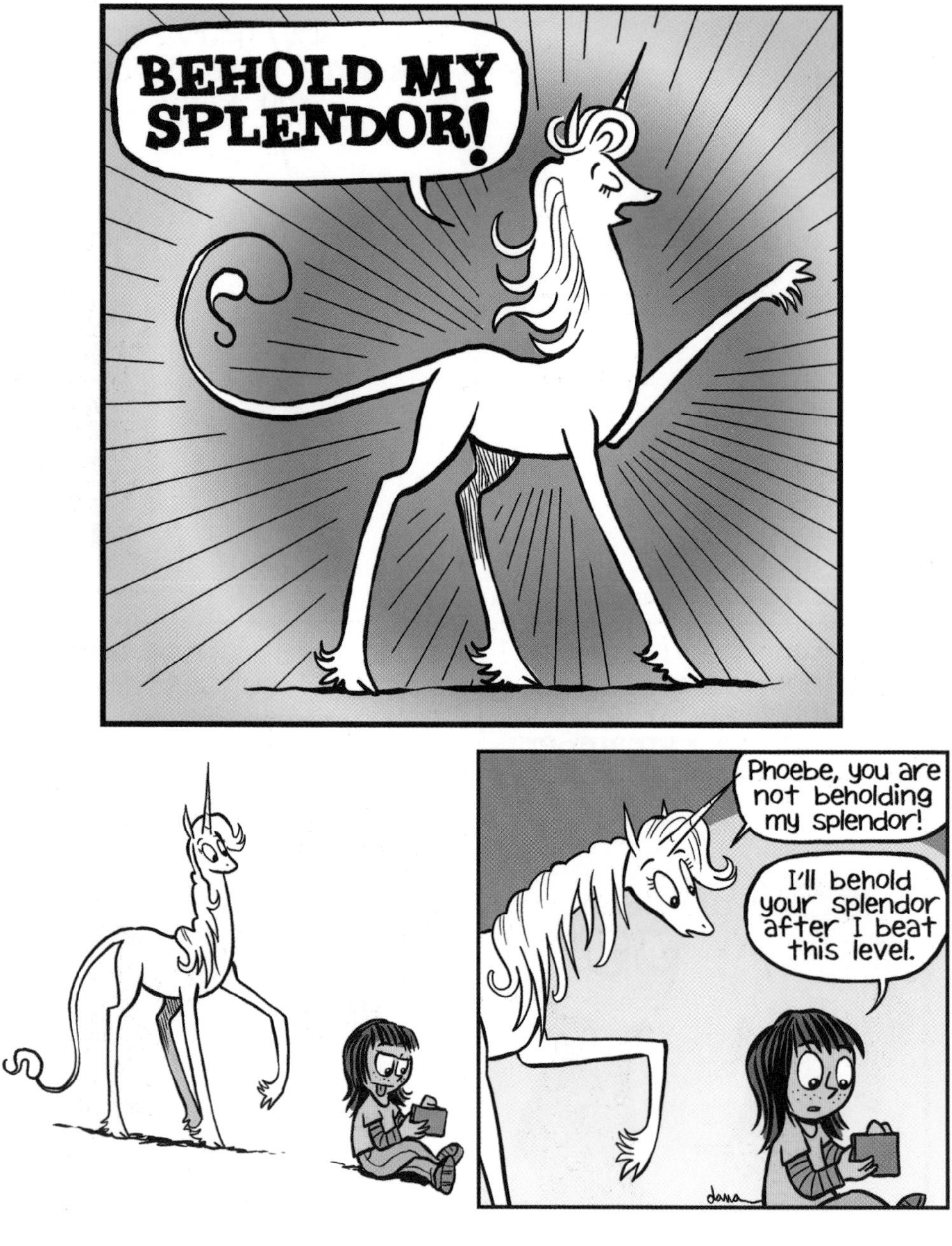
BEHOLD MY SPLENDOR!
Phoebe, you are not beholding my splendor!
I'll behold your splendor after I beat this level.

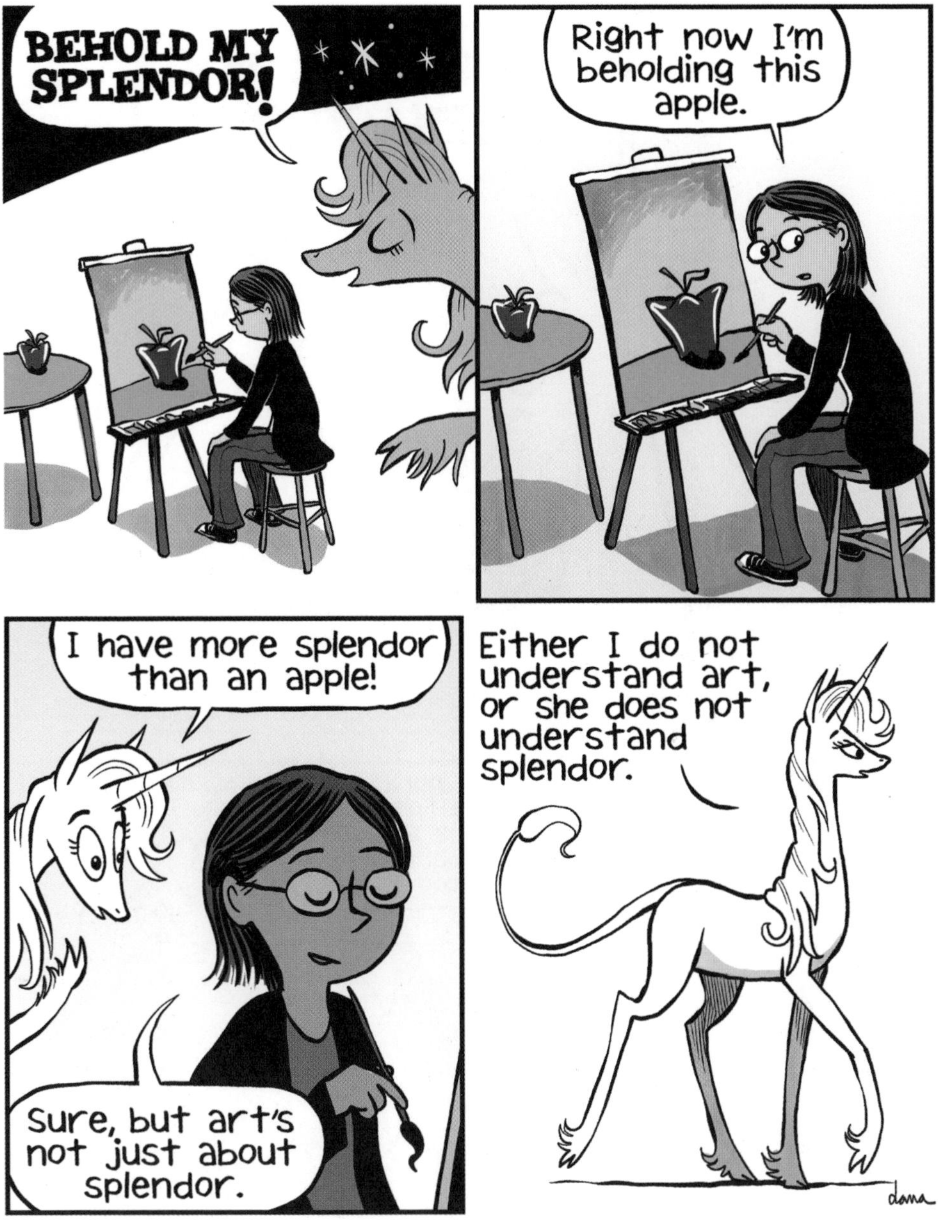
BEHOLD MY SPLENDOR!
Right now I'm beholding this apple.
I have more splendor than an apple!
Sure, but art's not just about splendor.
Either I do not understand art, or she does not understand splendor.
dana

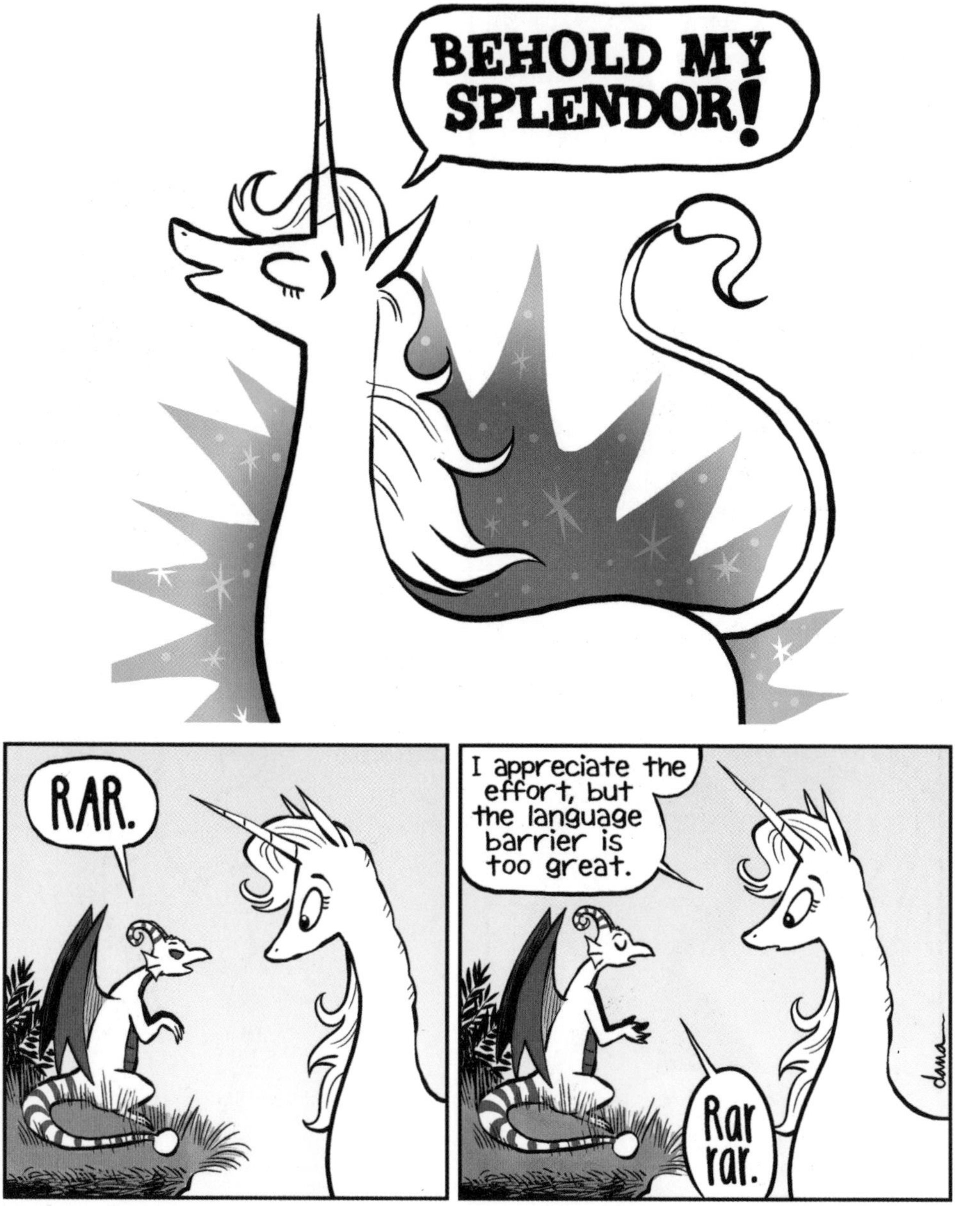
BEHOLD MY SPLENDOR!
RAR.
I appreciate the effort, but the language barrier is too great.
Rar rar.

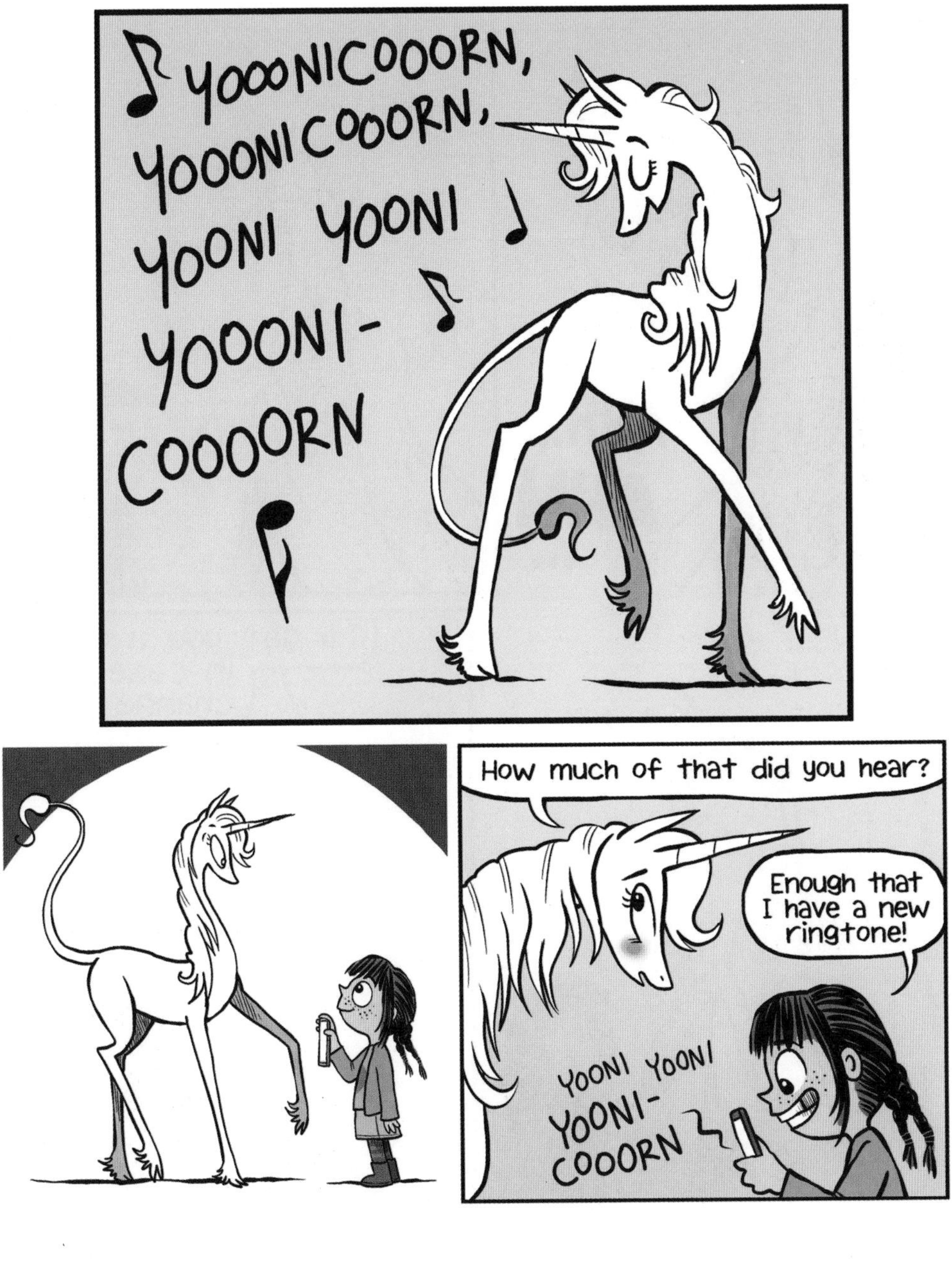
♪ YOOONICOOORN, YOOONICOOORN, YOONI YOONI ♩ YOOONI- ♪ COOOORN ♪
How much of that did you hear?
Enough that I have a new ringtone!
YOONI YOONI YOONI- COOORN

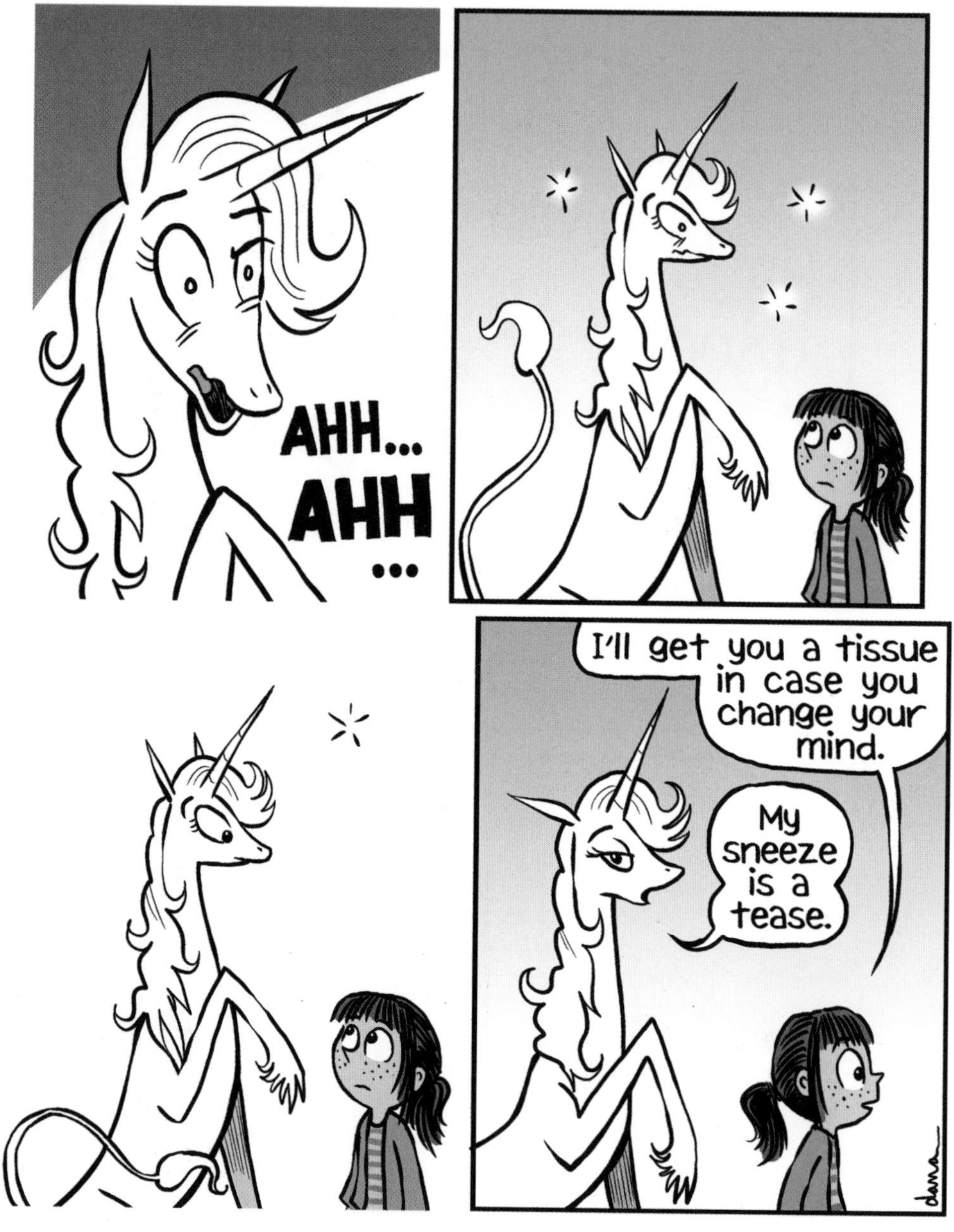
AHH... AHH ...
I'll get you a tissue in case you change your mind.
My sneeze is a tease.
dana

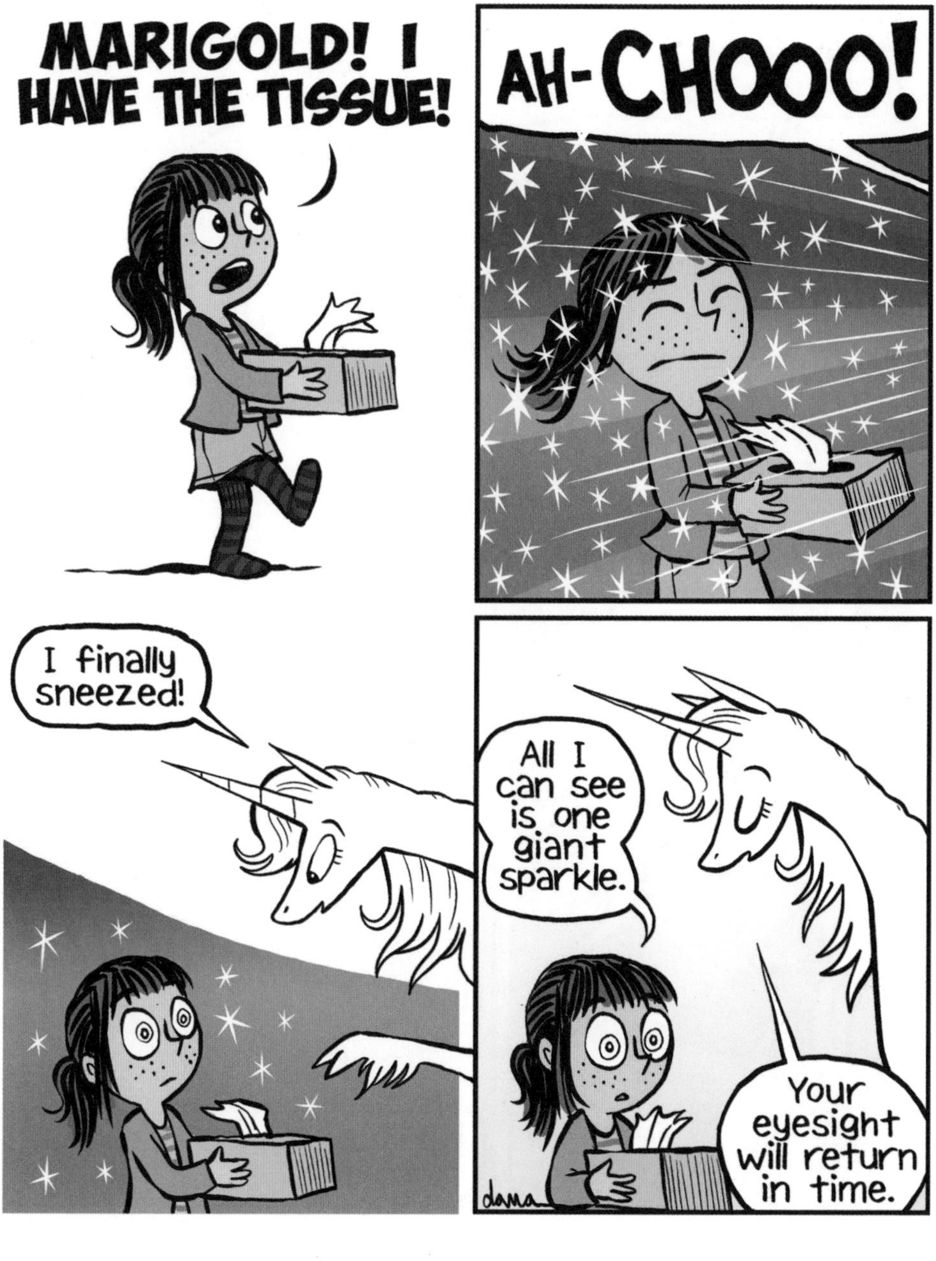
MARIGOLD! I HAVE THE TISSUE!
AH-CHOOO!
I finally sneezed!
All I can see is one giant sparkle.
Your eyesight will return in time.
dana

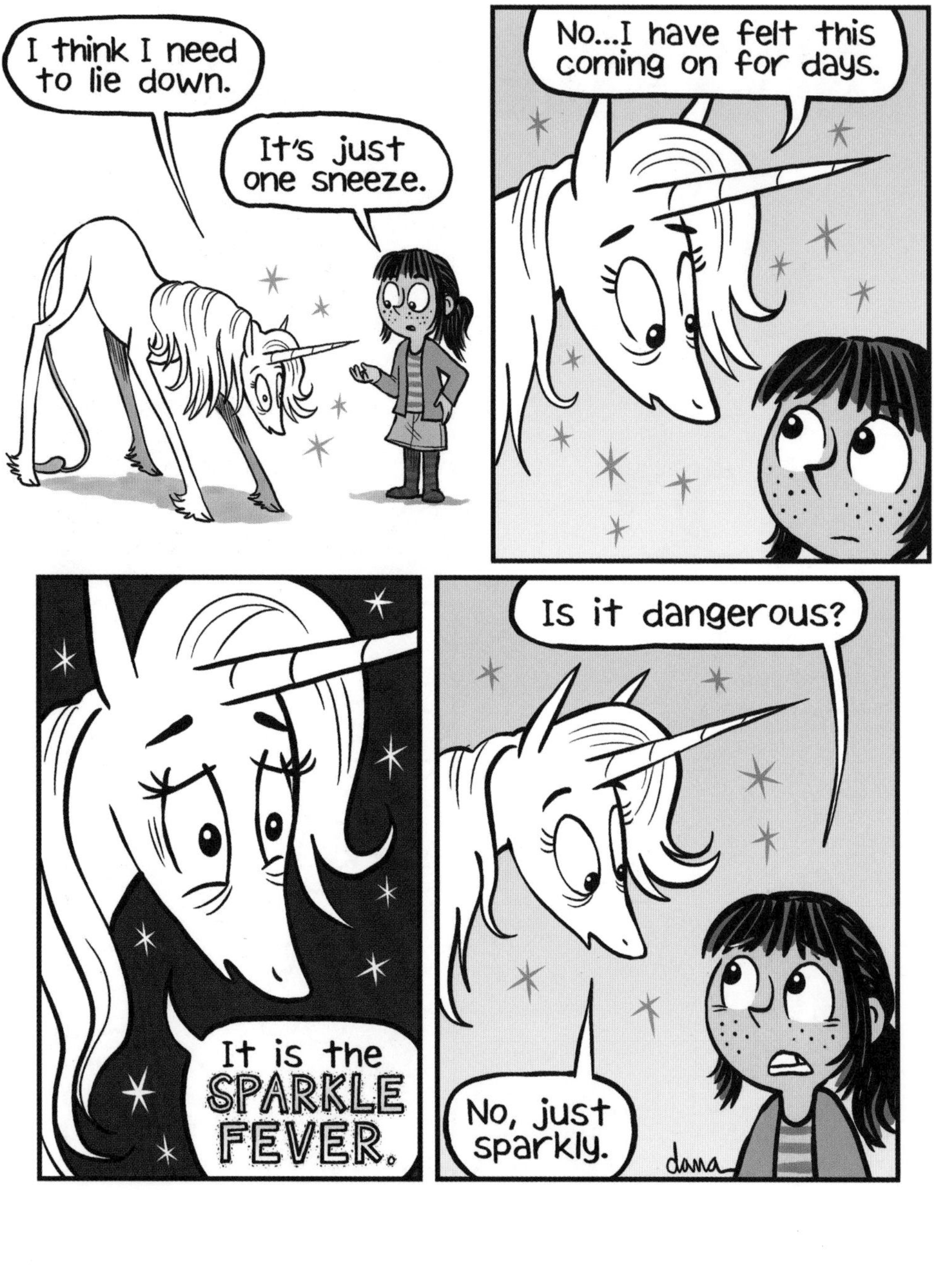
I think I need to lie down.
It's just one sneeze.
No...I have felt this coming on for days.
It is the SPARKLE FEVER.
Is it dangerous?
No, just sparkly.
dana

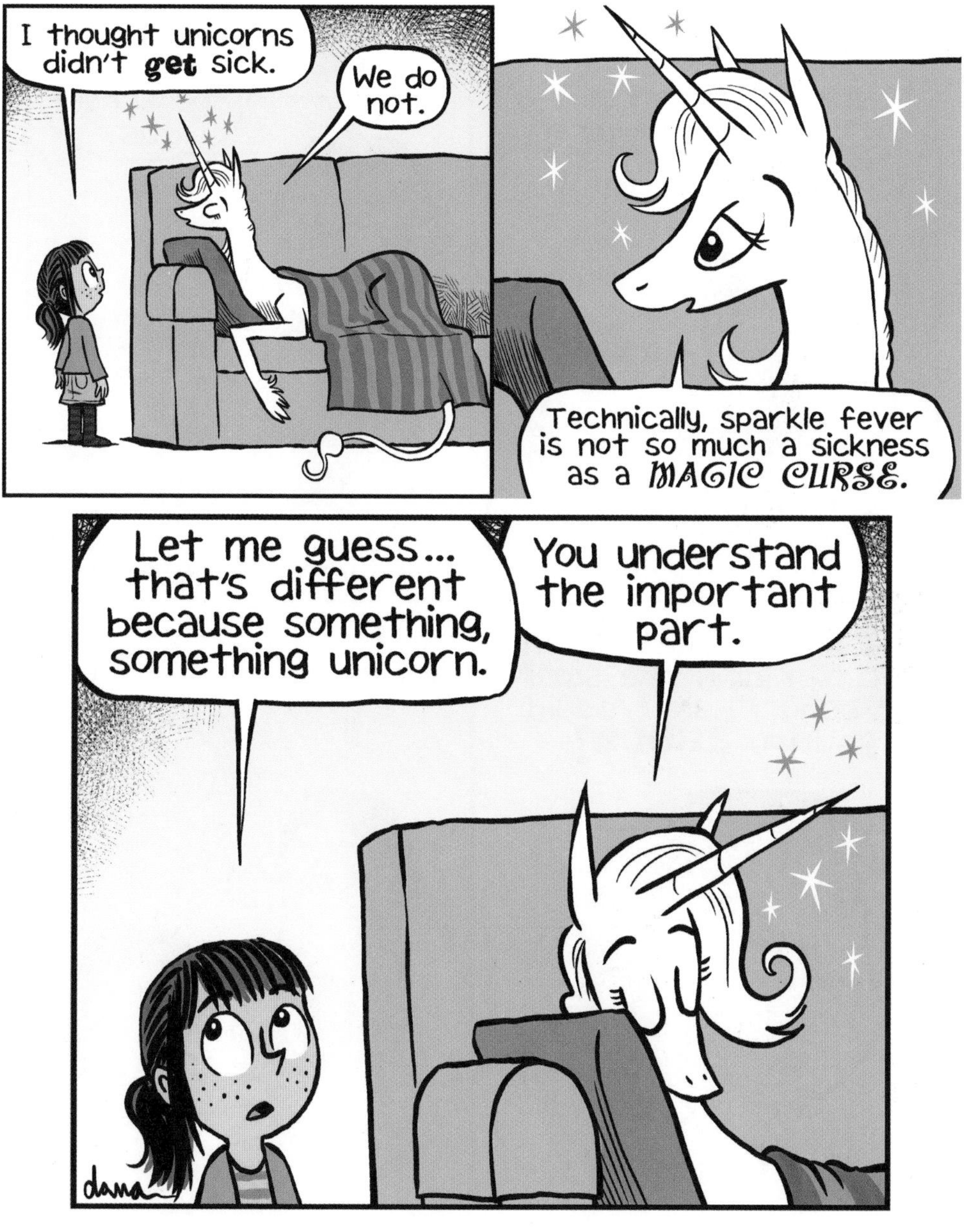
I thought unicorns didn't **get** sick.
We do not.
Technically, sparkle fever is not so much a sickness as a MAGIC CURSE.
Let me guess... that's different because something, something unicorn.
You understand the important part.
dana

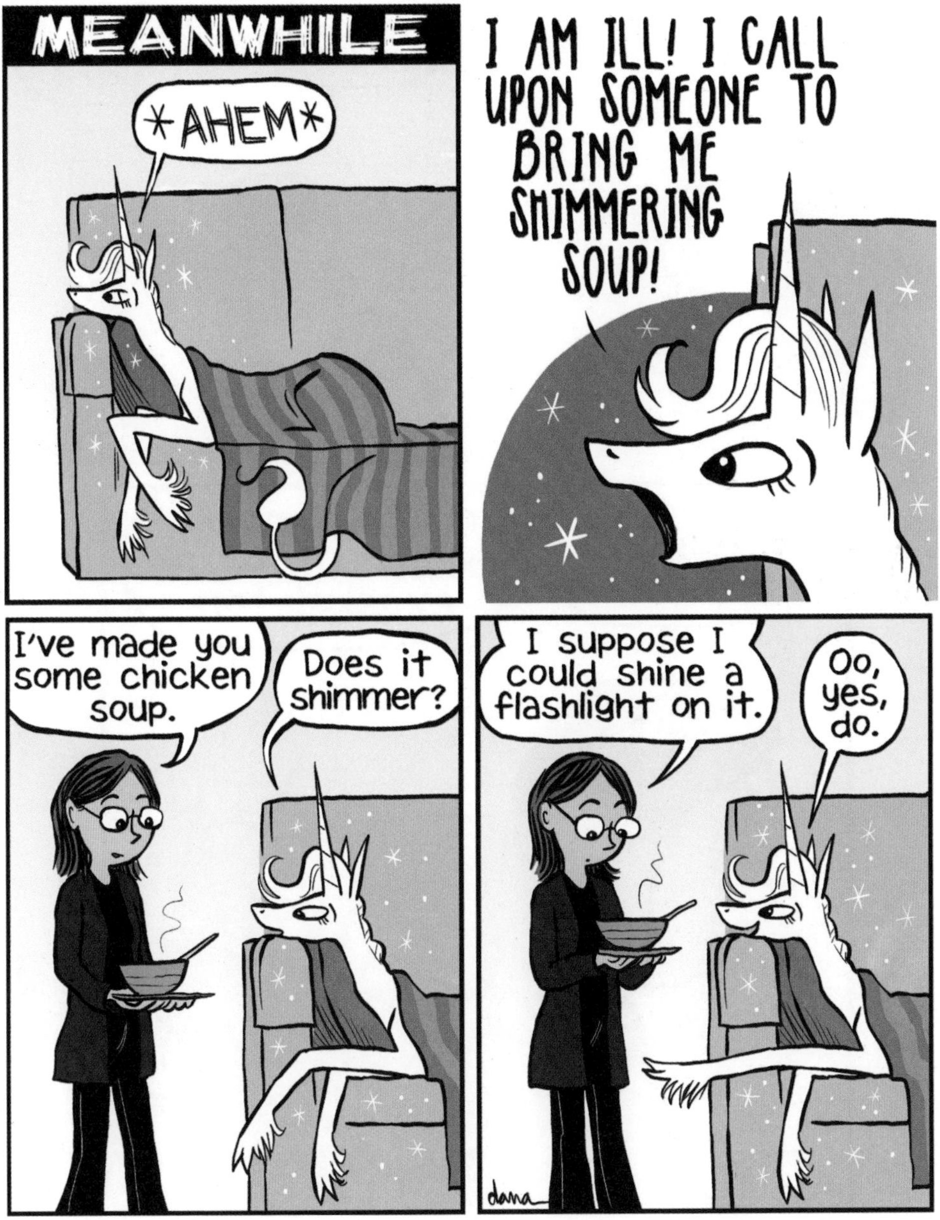
MEANWHILE
AHEM
I AM ILL! I CALL UPON SOMEONE TO BRING ME SHIMMERING SOUP!
I've made you some chicken soup.
Does it shimmer?
I suppose I could shine a flashlight on it.
Oo, yes, do.
dana

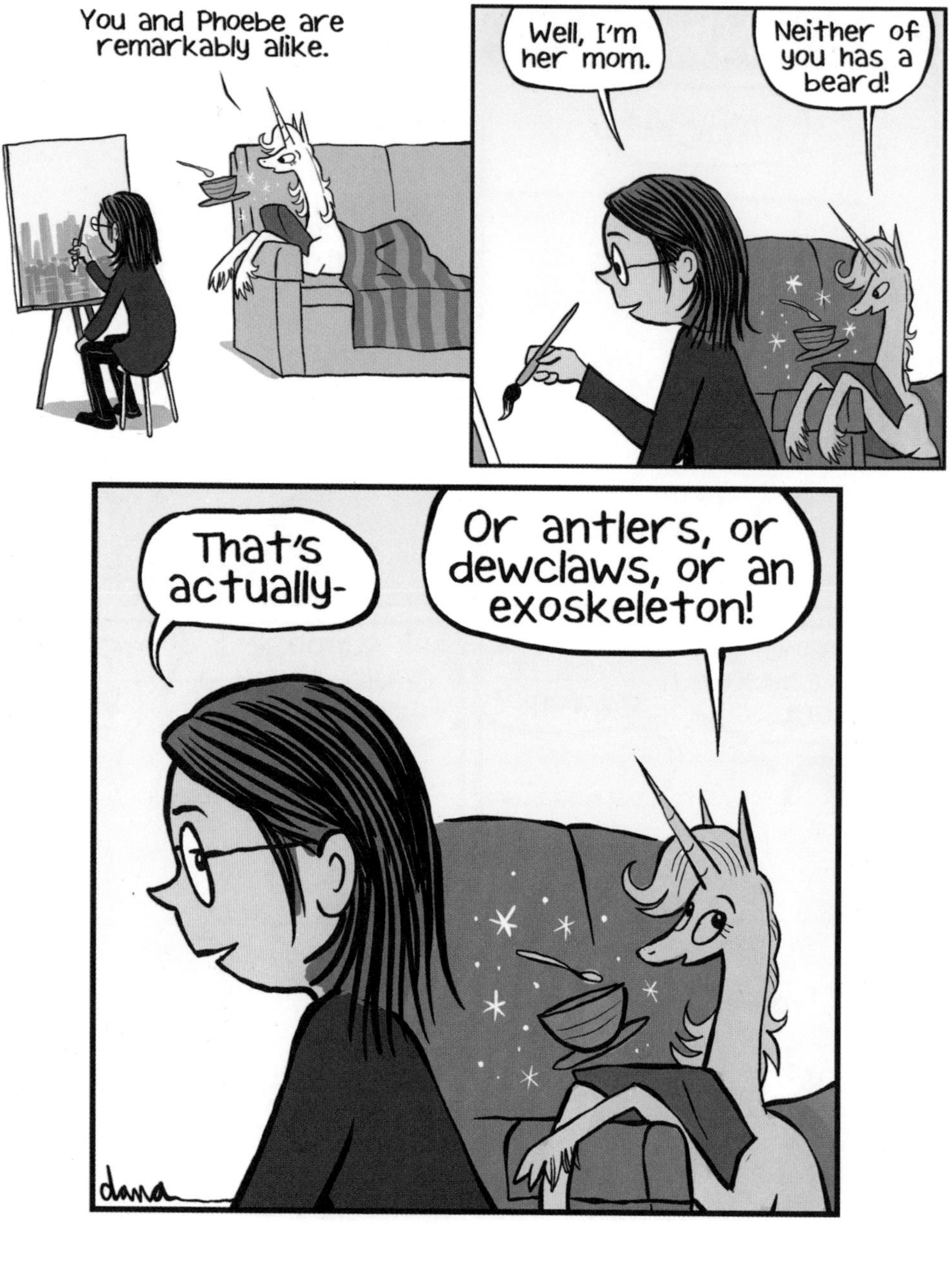
You and Phoebe are remarkably alike.
Well, I'm her mom.
Neither of you has a beard!
That's actually-
Or antlers, or dewclaws, or an exoskeleton!
dana

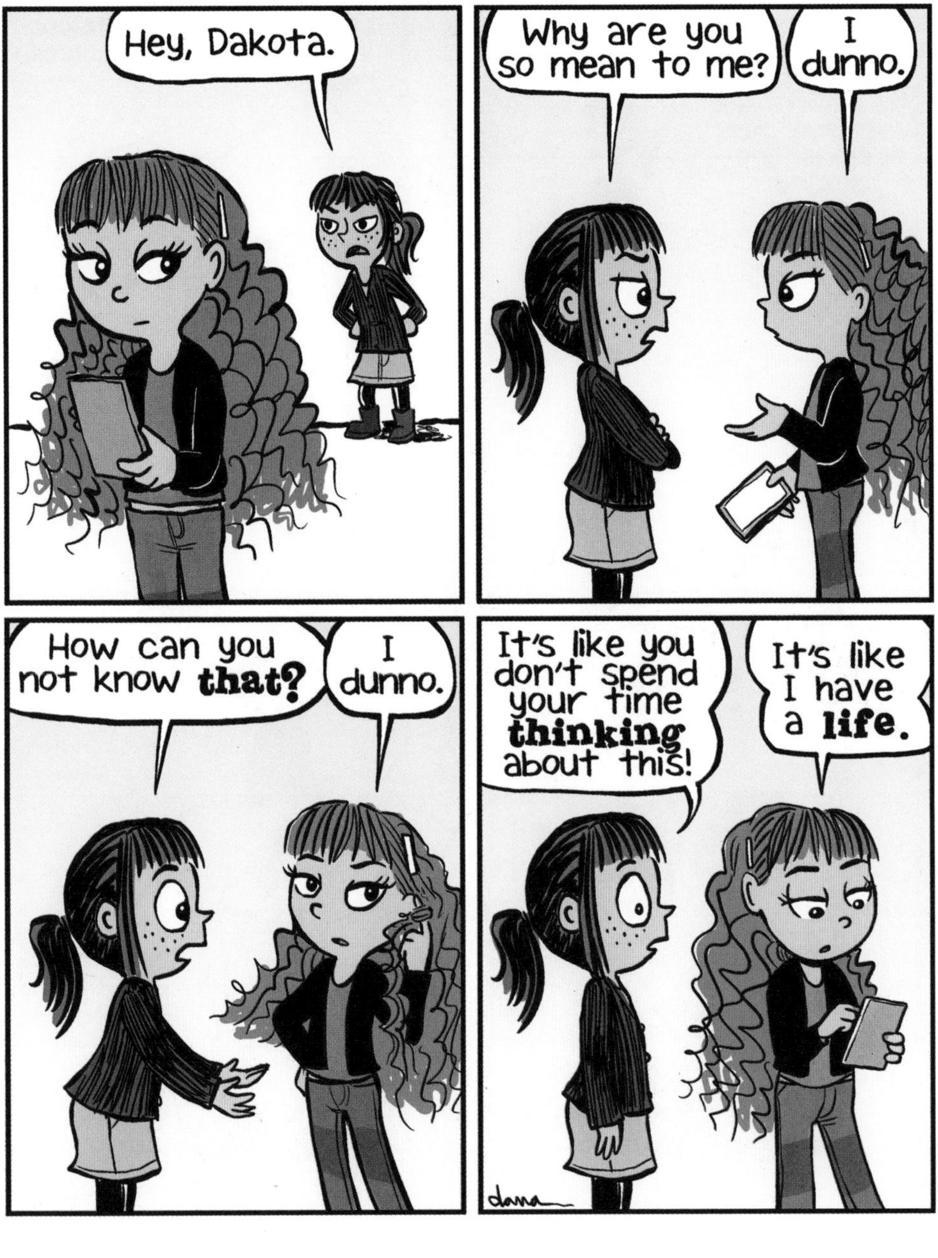
Hey, Dakota.
Why are you so mean to me?
I dunno.
How can you not know **that?**
I dunno.
It's like you don't spend your time **thinking** about this!
It's like I have a **life**.
dana

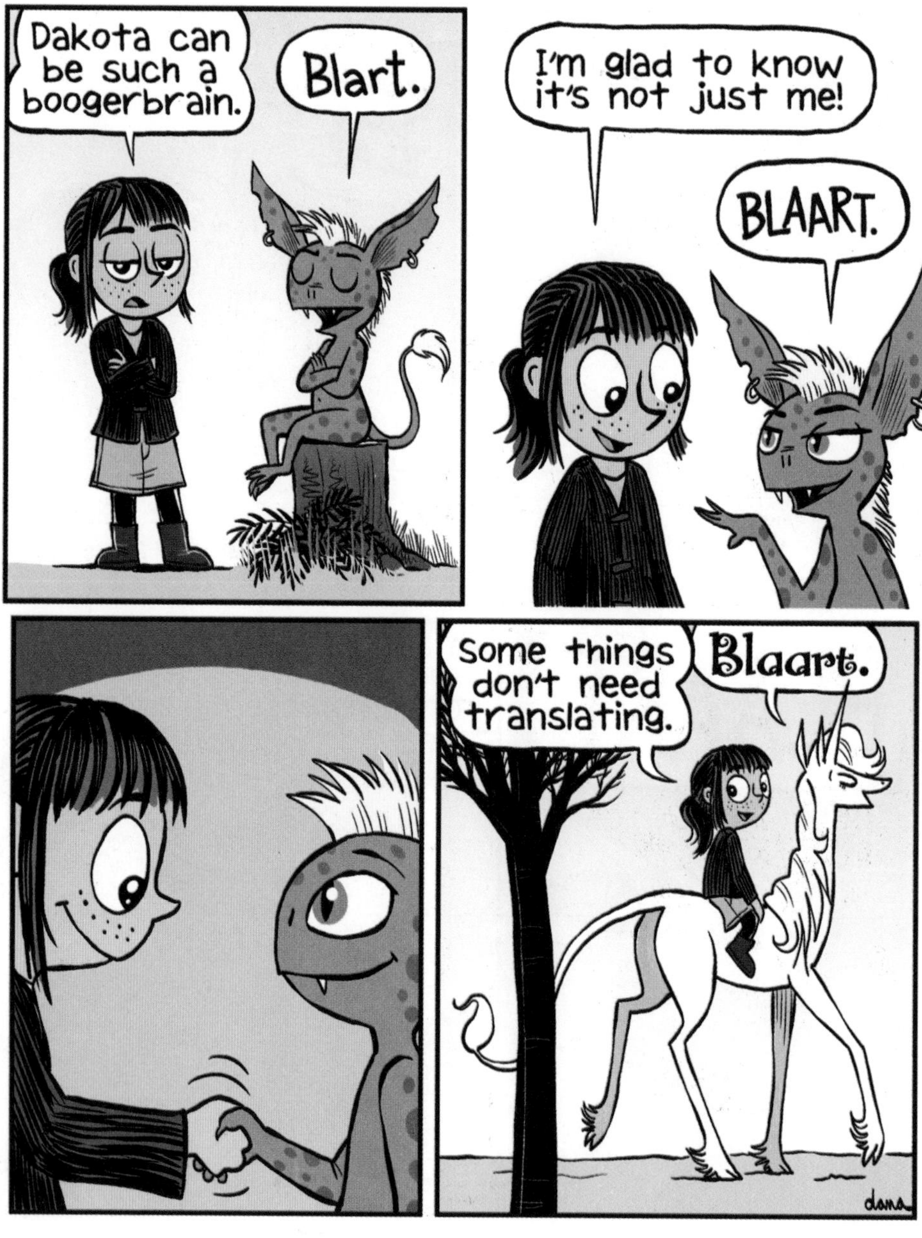
Dakota can be such a boogerbrain.
Blart.
I'm glad to know it's not just me!
BLAART.
Some things don't need translating.
Blaart.
dana

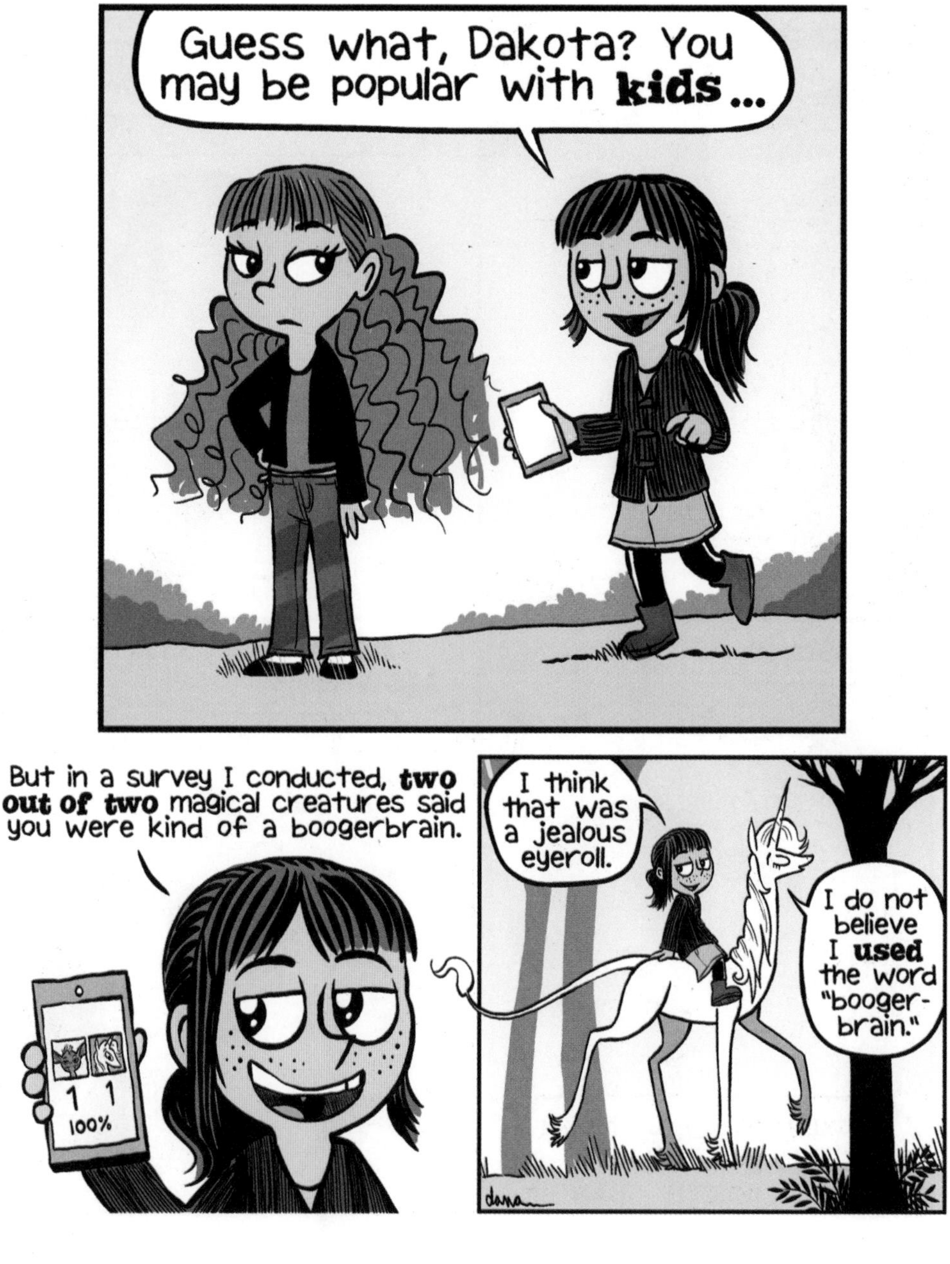
Guess what, Dakota? You may be popular with **kids**...
But in a survey I conducted, **two out of two** magical creatures said you were kind of a boogerbrain.
1 1
100%
I think that was a jealous eyeroll.
I do not believe I **used** the word "booger-brain."
dana

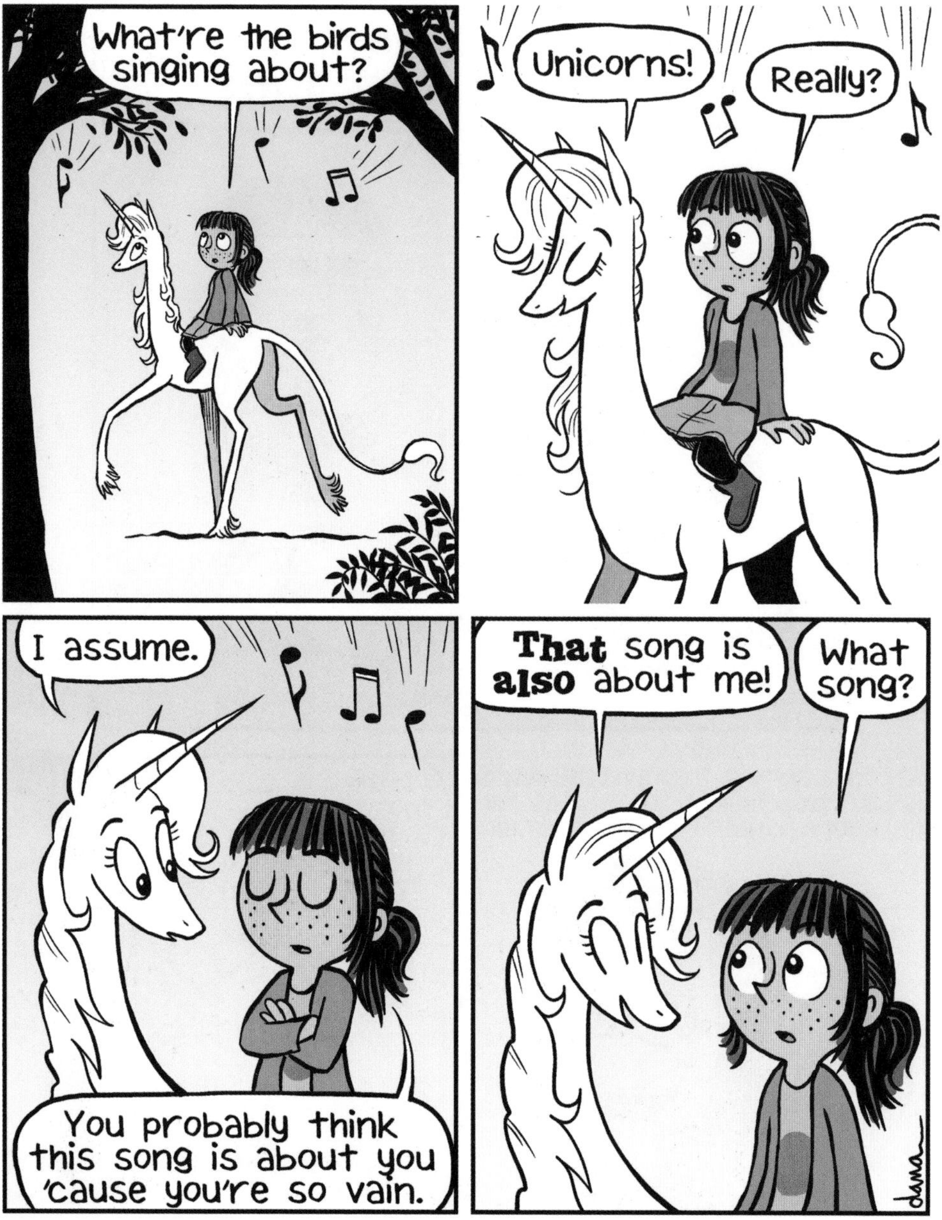
What're the birds singing about?
Unicorns!
Really?
I assume.
You probably think this song is about you 'cause you're so vain.
That song is **also** about me!
What song?
dana

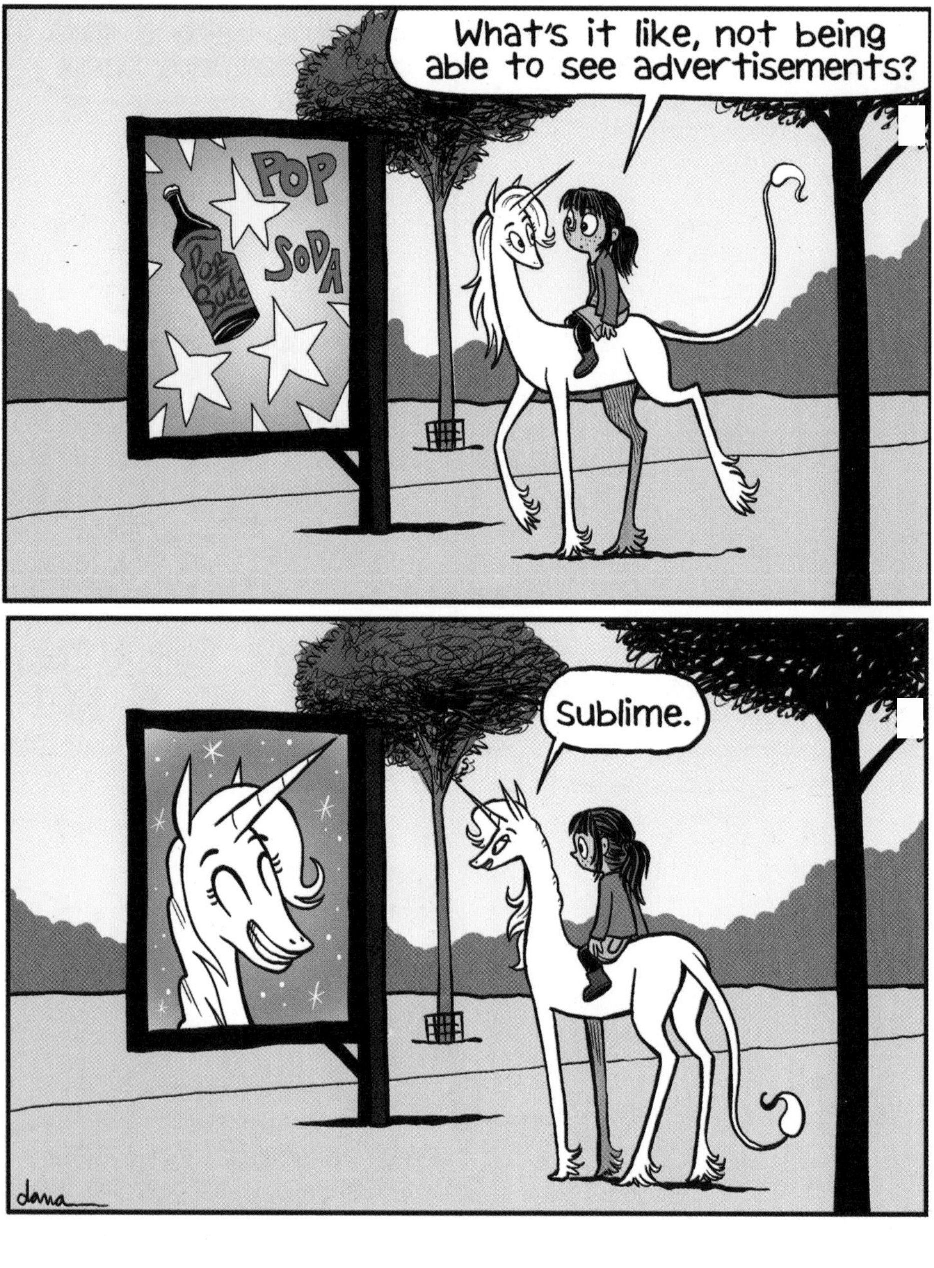
What's it like, not being able to see advertisements?
POP SODA
Pop Soda
sublime.
dana

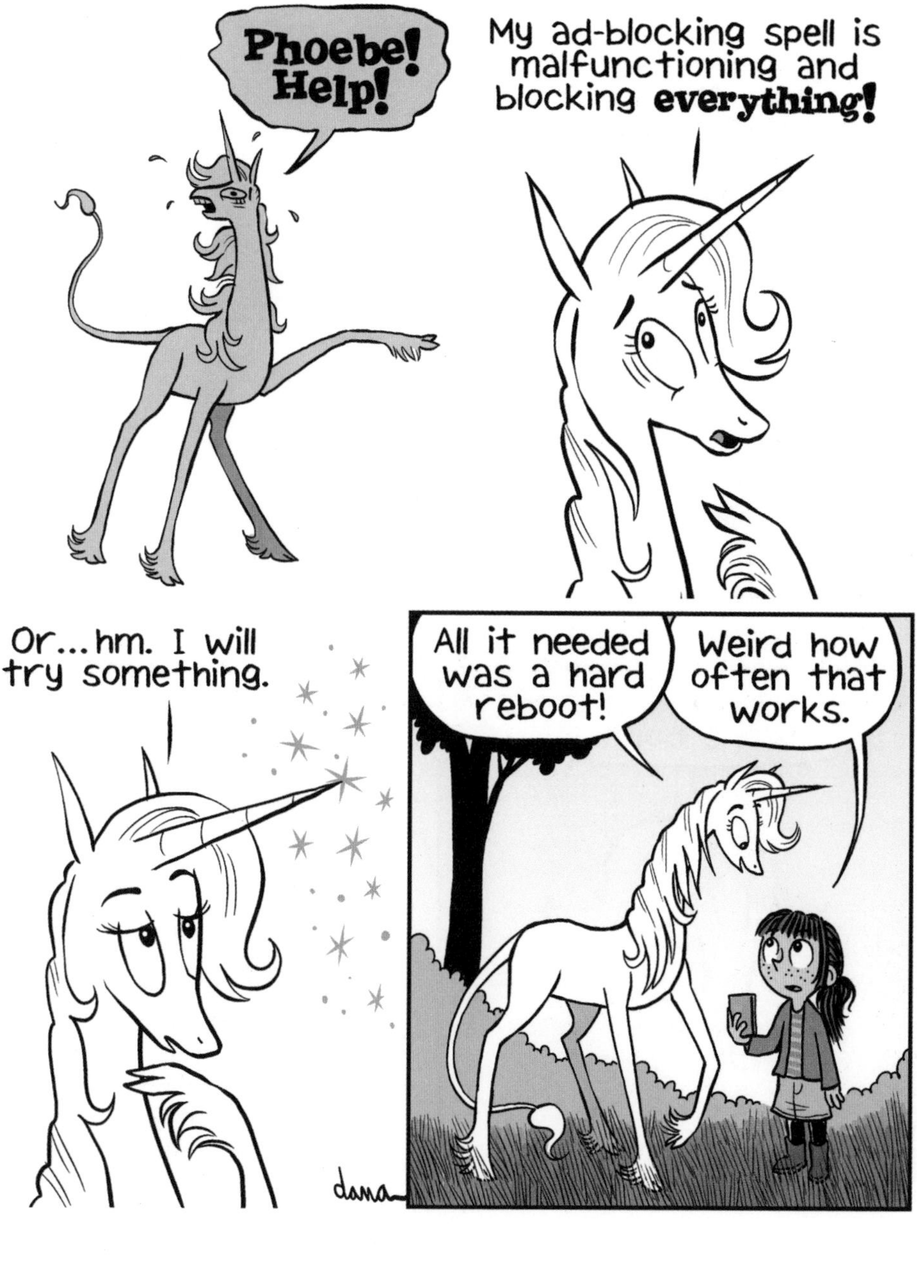
Phoebe! Help!
My ad-blocking spell is malfunctioning and blocking **everything!**
Or... hm. I will try something.
All it needed was a hard reboot!
Weird how often that works.
dana

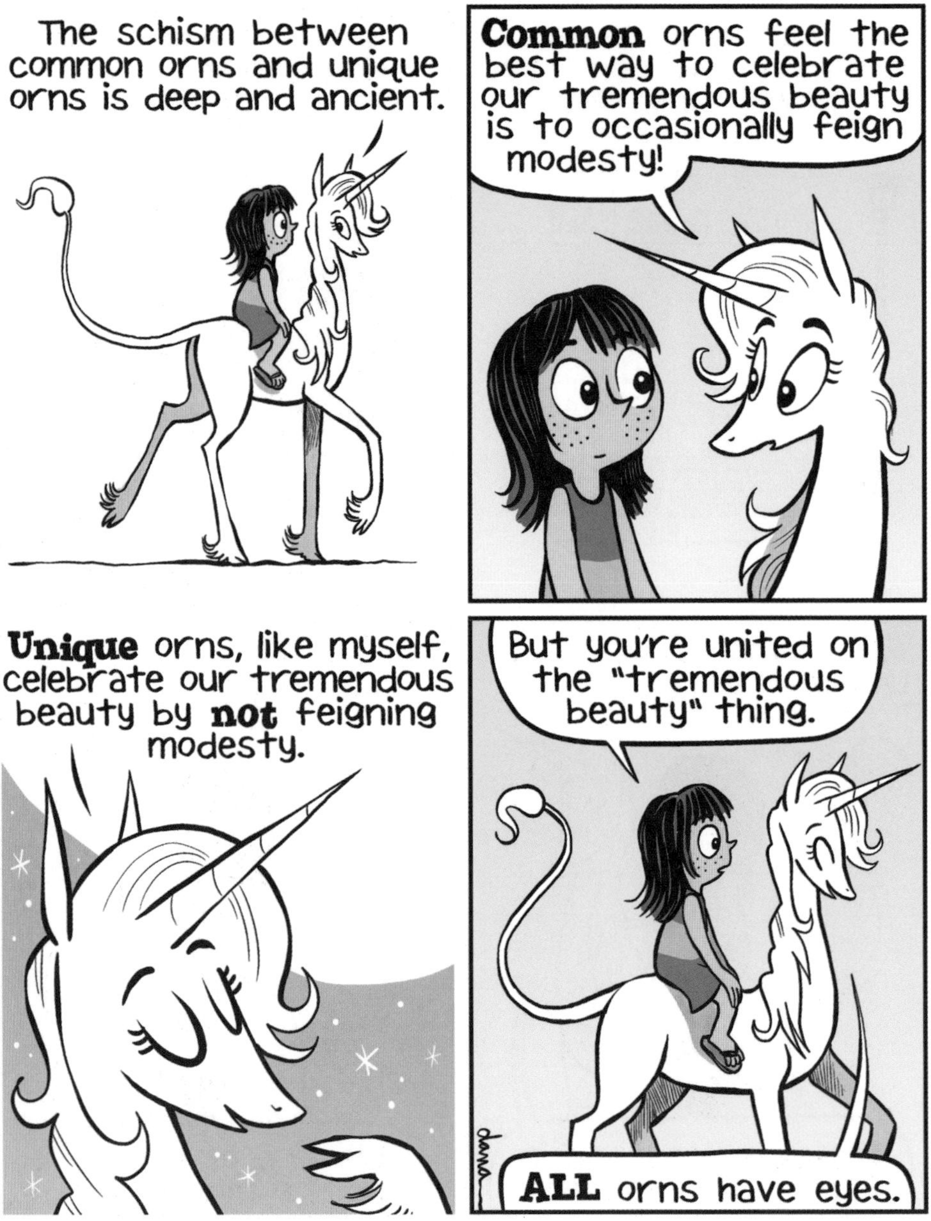
The schism between common orns and unique orns is deep and ancient.
Common orns feel the best way to celebrate our tremendous beauty is to occasionally feign modesty!
Unique orns, like myself, celebrate our tremendous beauty by not feigning modesty.
But you're united on the "tremendous beauty" thing.
ALL orns have eyes.

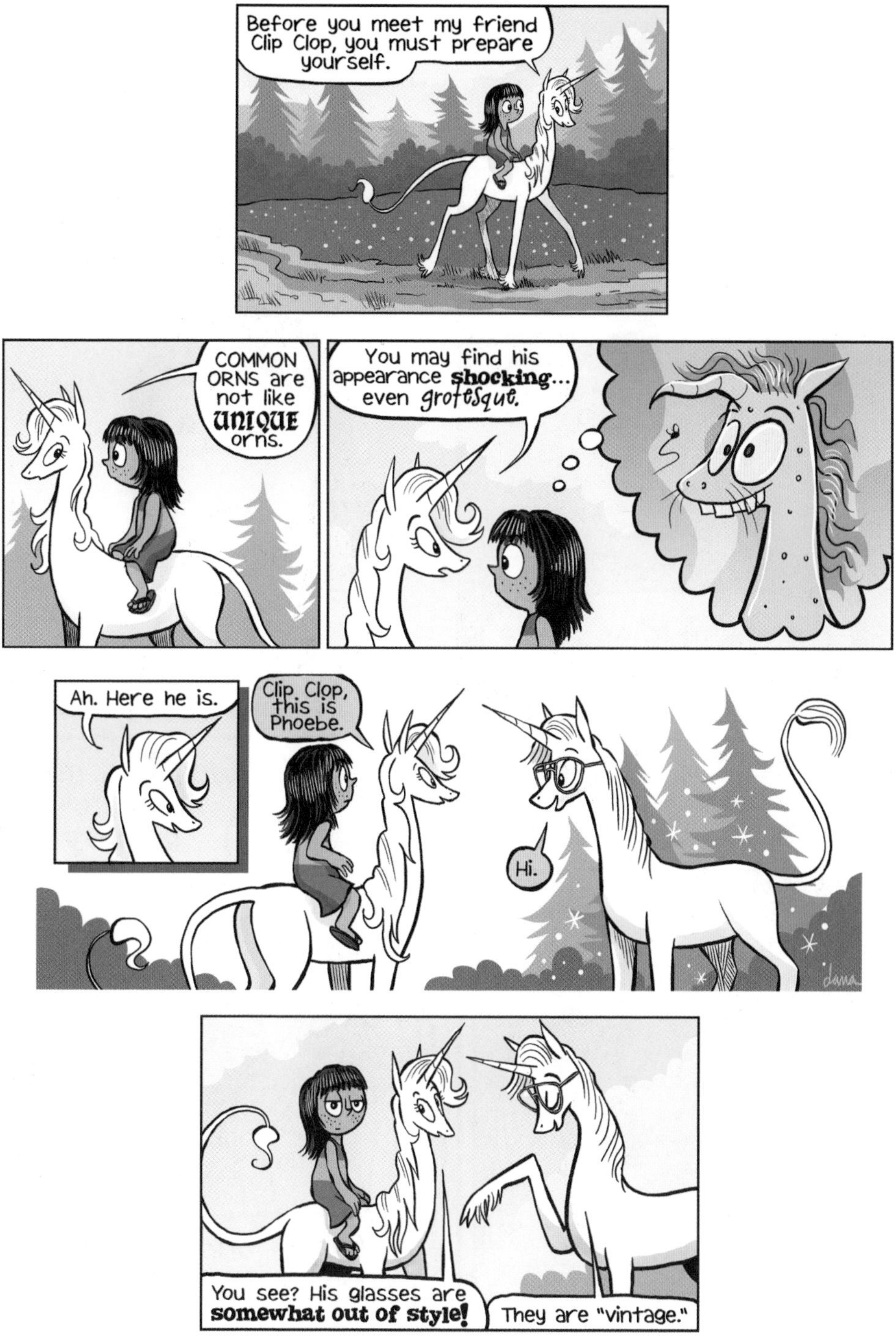
Before you meet my friend Clip Clop, you must prepare yourself.
COMMON ORNS are not like UNIQUE orns.
You may find his appearance shocking... even grotesque.
Ah. Here he is.
Clip Clop, this is Phoebe.
Hi.
You see? His glasses are somewhat out of style!
They are "vintage."

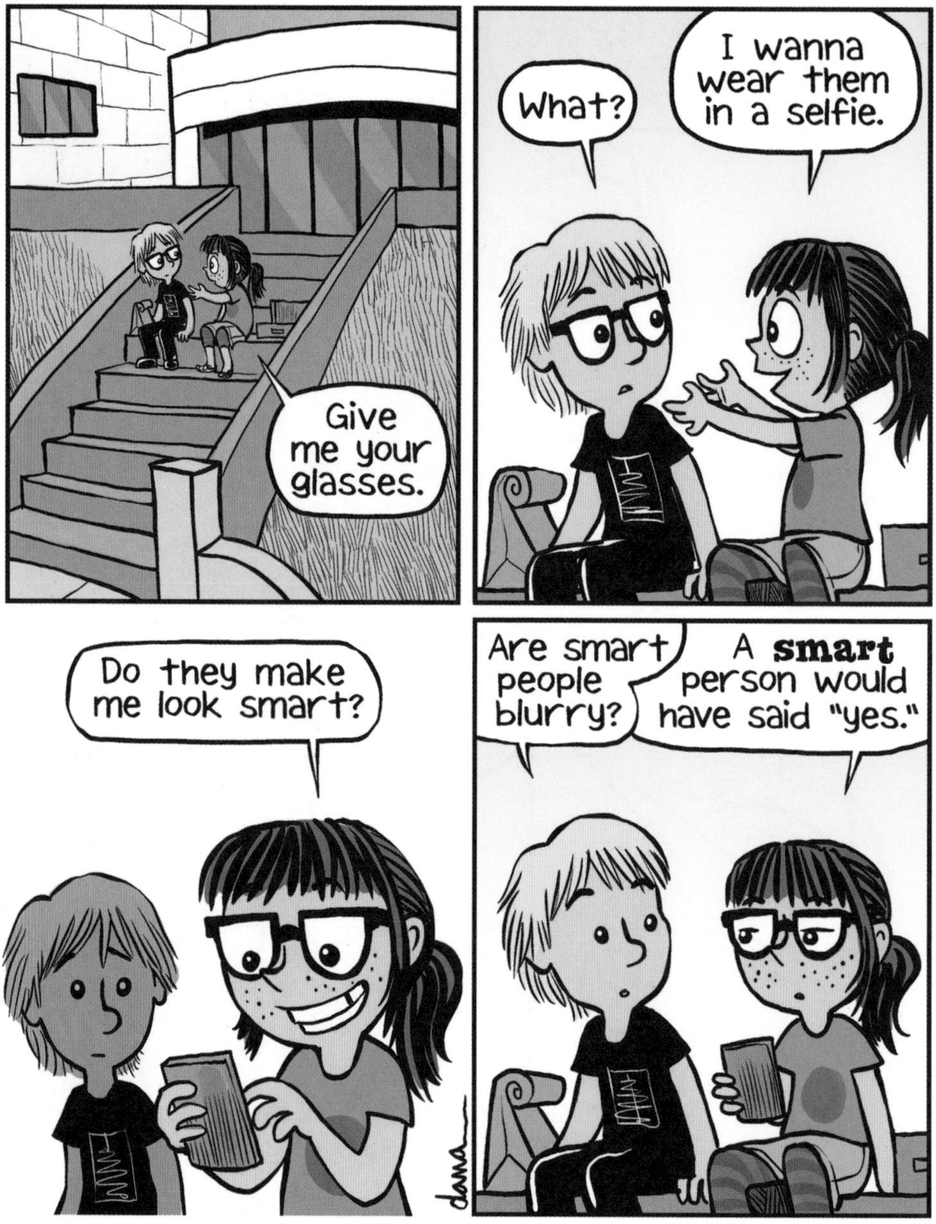
Give me your glasses.
What?
I wanna wear them in a selfie.
Do they make me look smart?
Are smart people blurry?
A **smart** person would have said "yes."
dana

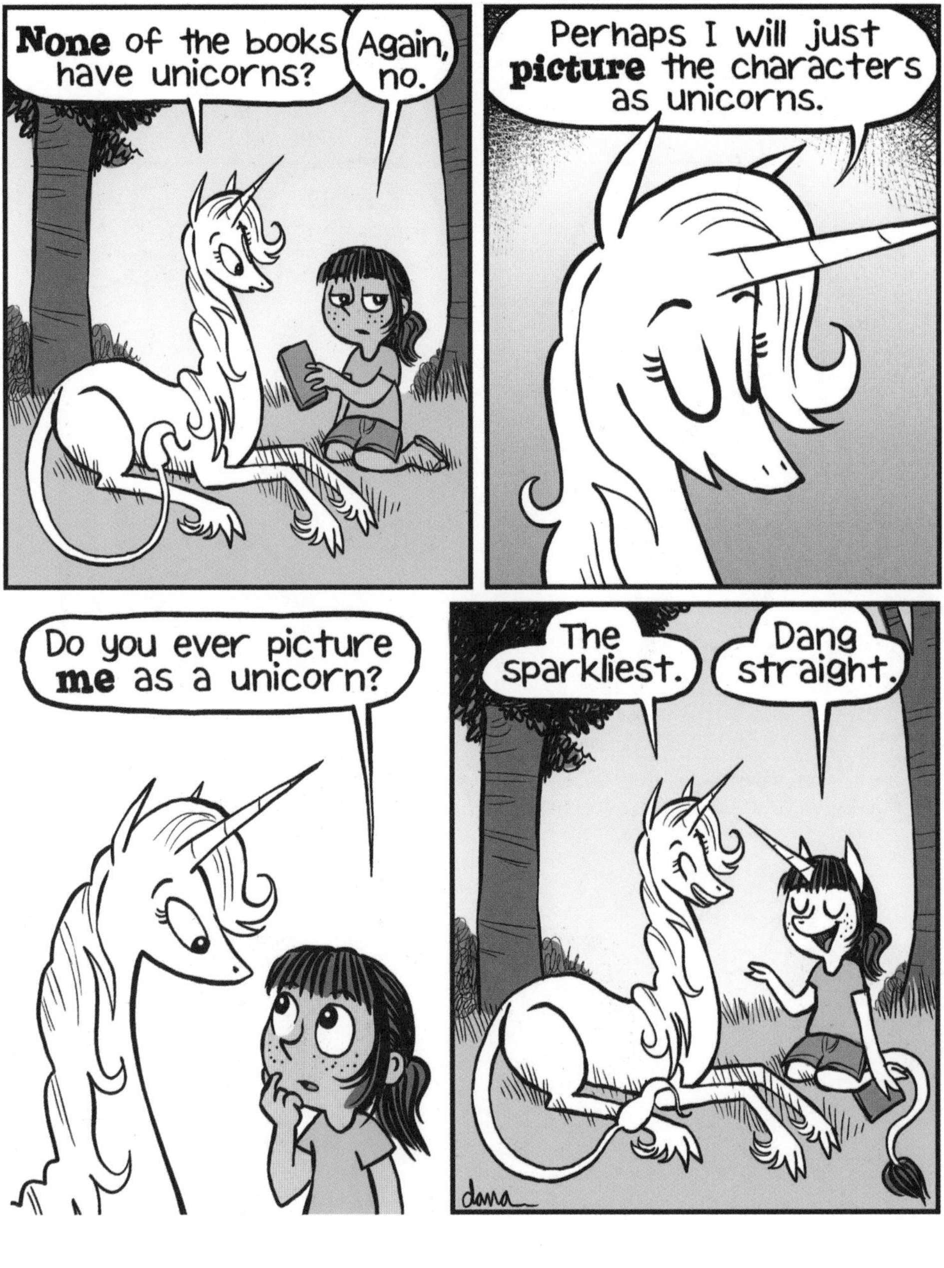
None of the books have unicorns?
Again, no.
Perhaps I will just **picture** the characters as unicorns.
Do you ever picture **me** as a unicorn?
The sparkliest.
Dang straight.
dana

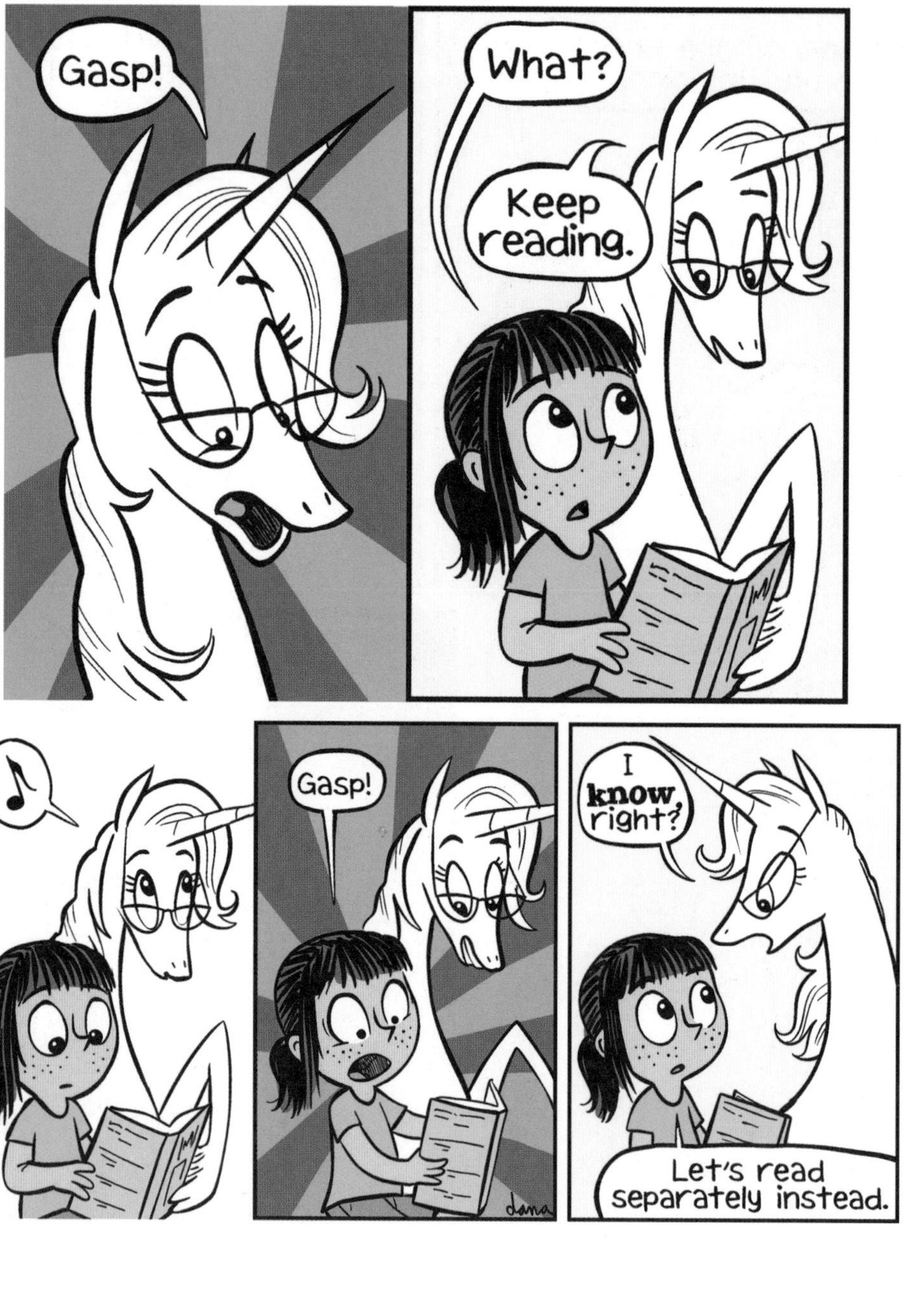
Gasp!
What?
Keep reading.
♪
Gasp!
I **know,** right?
Let's read separately instead.
dana

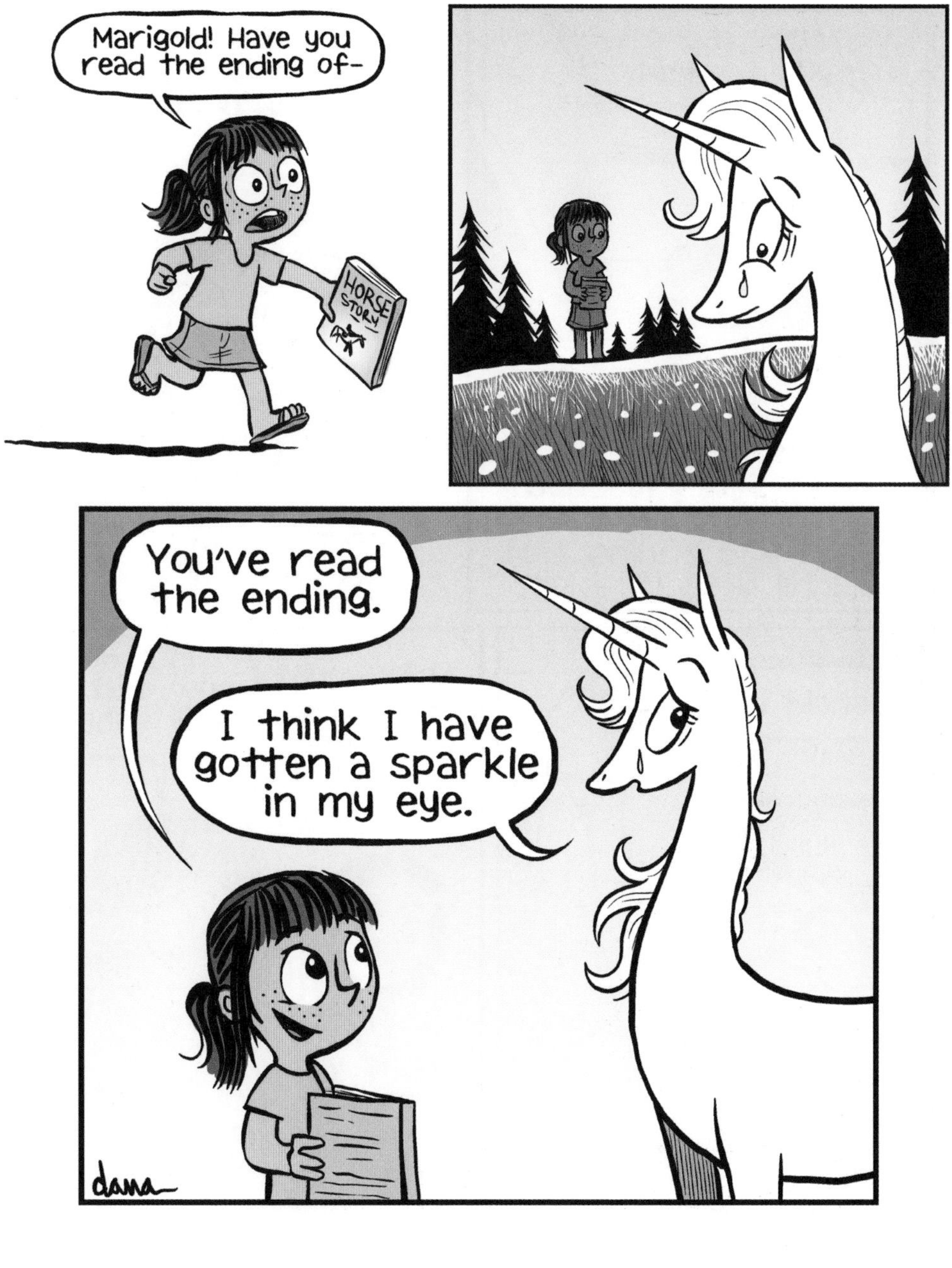
Marigold! Have you read the ending of-
HORSE STORY
You've read the ending.
I think I have gotten a sparkle in my eye.
dana

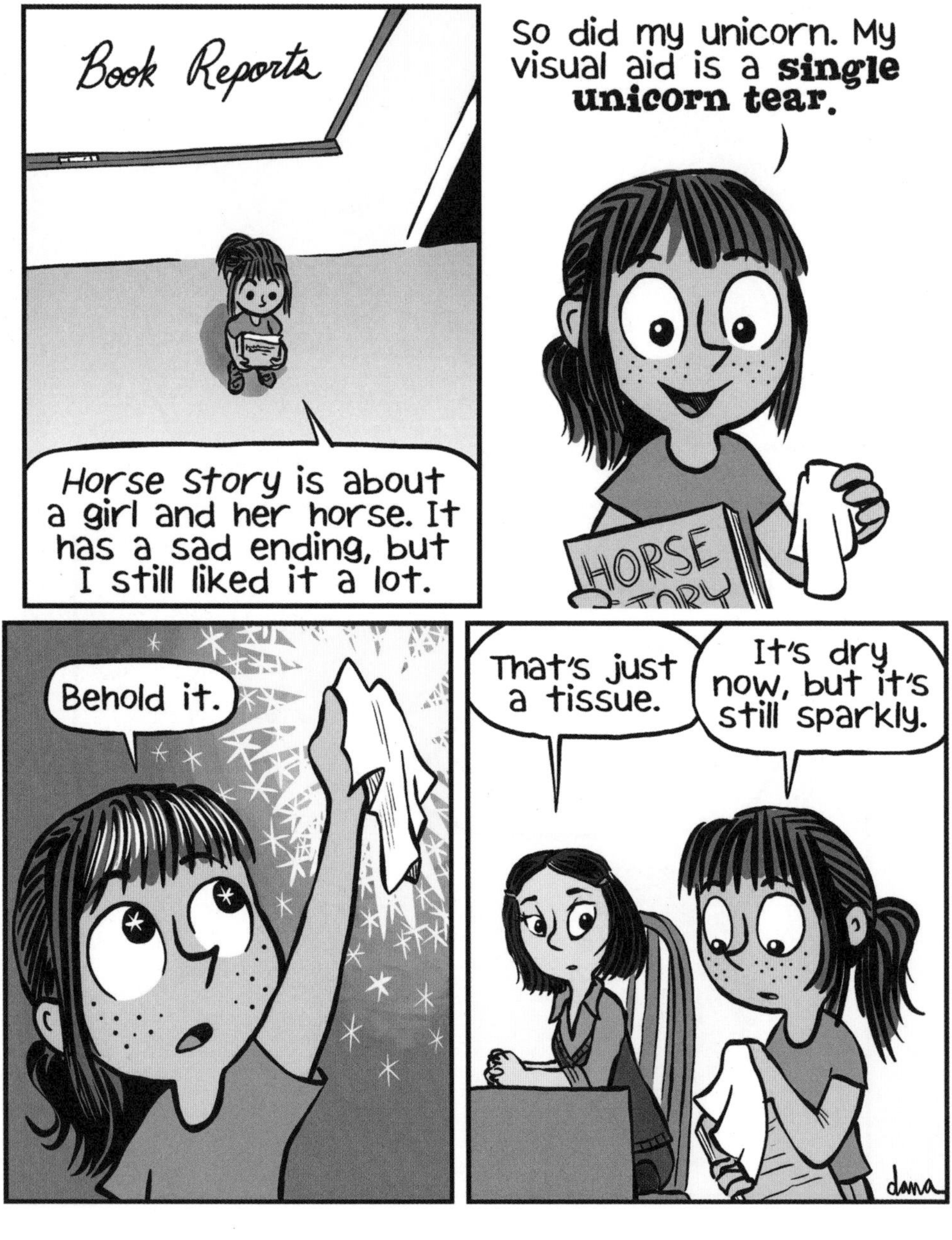
Book Reports
Horse Story is about a girl and her horse. It has a sad ending, but I still liked it a lot.
So did my unicorn. My visual aid is a **single unicorn tear.**
HORSE STORY
Behold it.
That's just a tissue.
It's dry now, but it's still sparkly.
dana

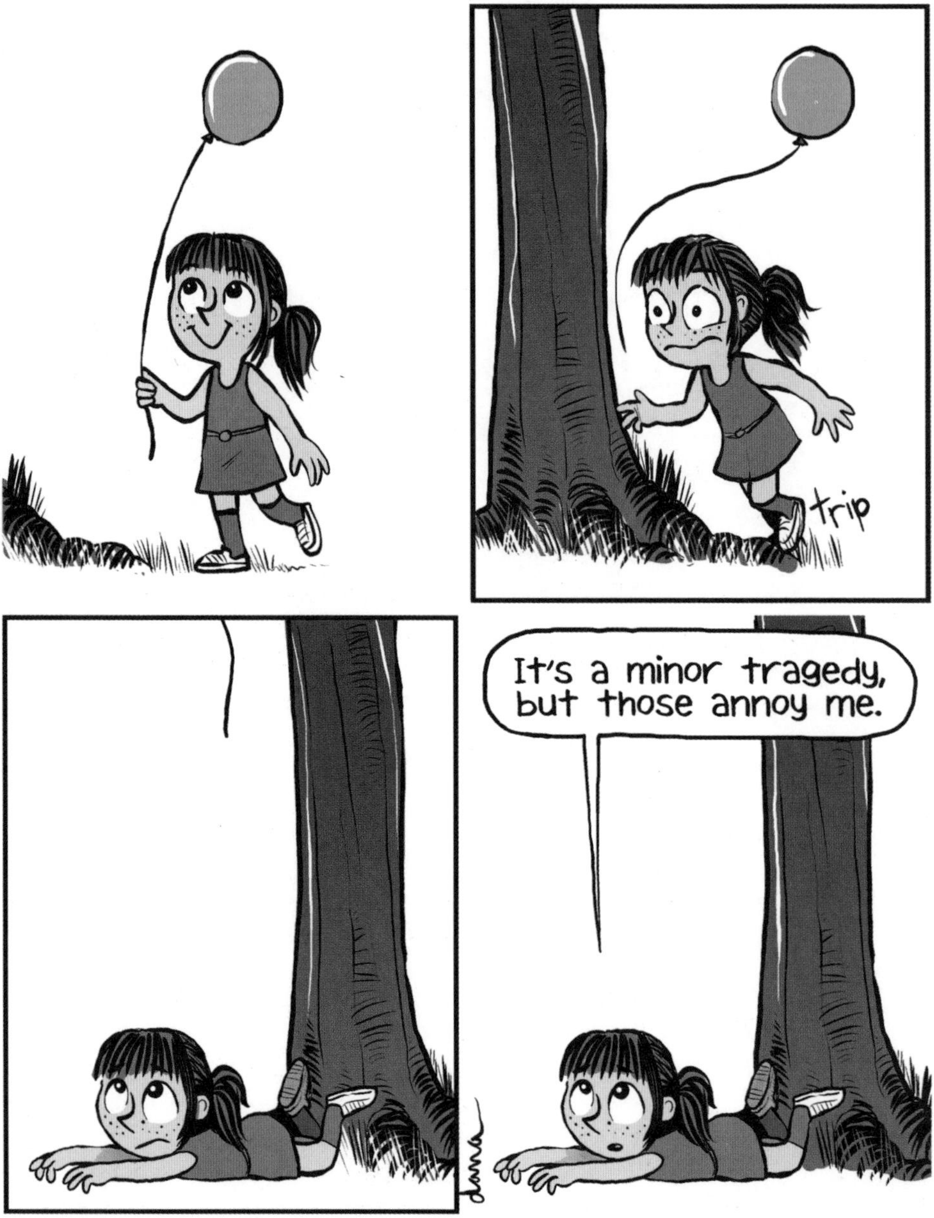
trip
It's a minor tragedy, but those annoy me.

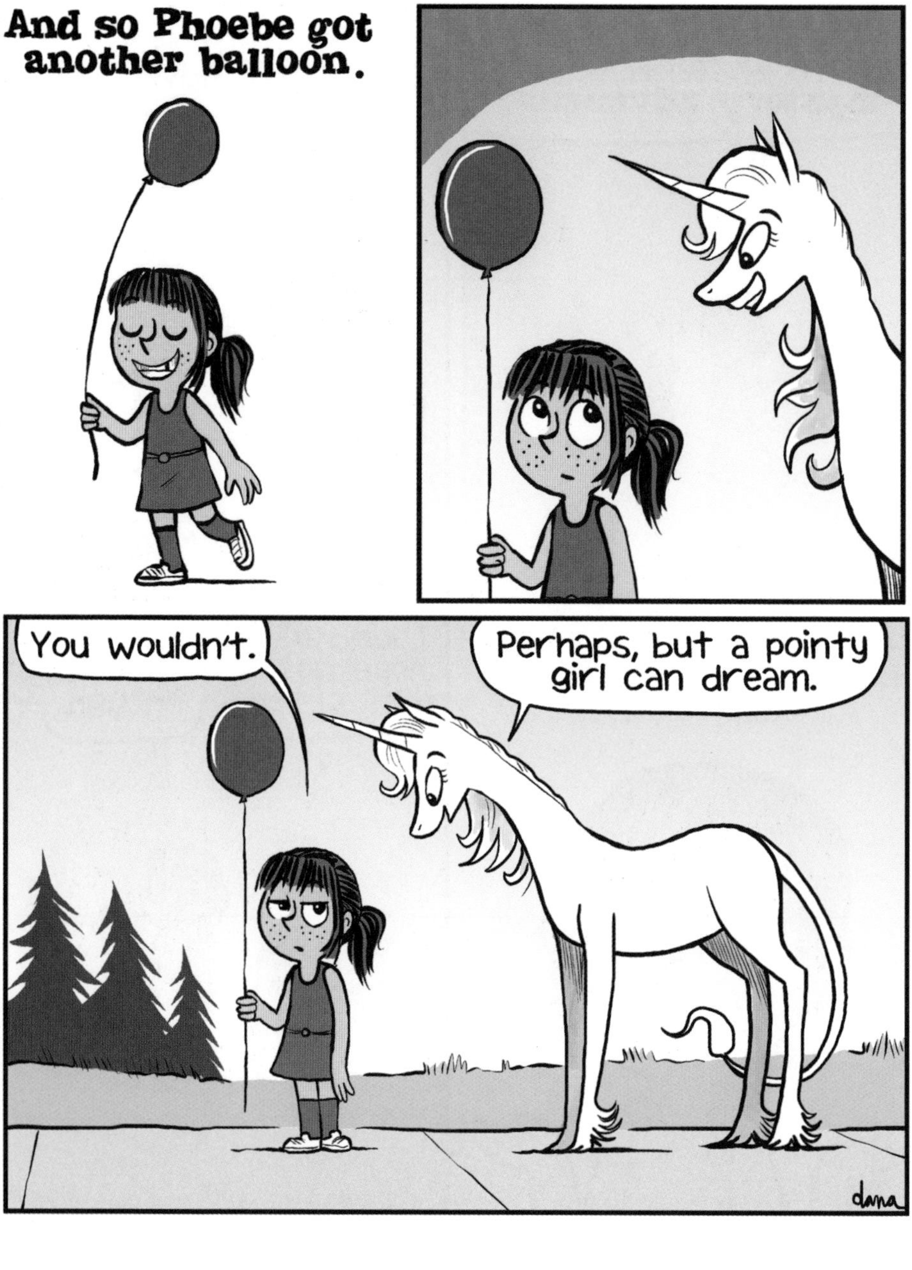
And so Phoebe got another balloon.
You wouldn't.
Perhaps, but a pointy girl can dream.
dana

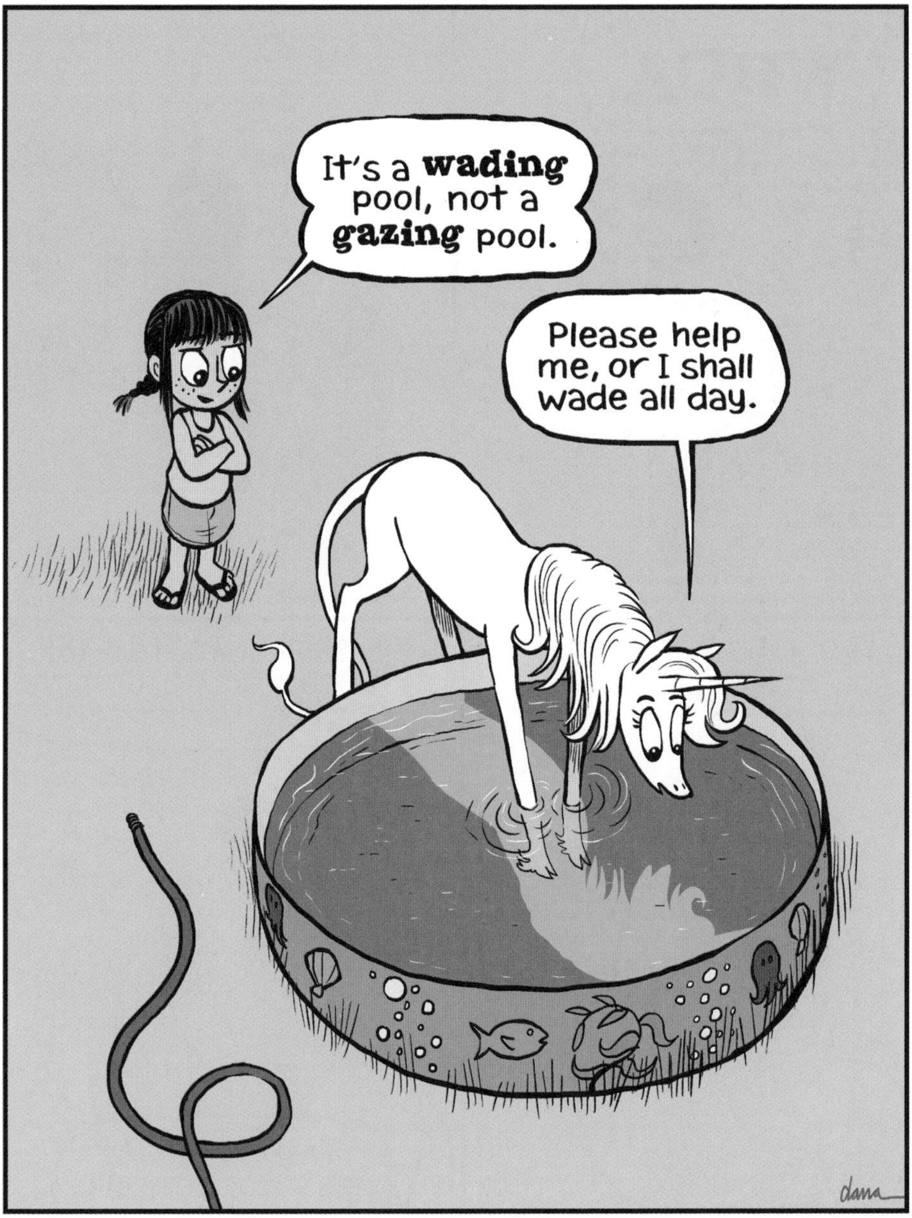
It's a **wading** pool, not a **gazing** pool.
Please help me, or I shall wade all day.
dana

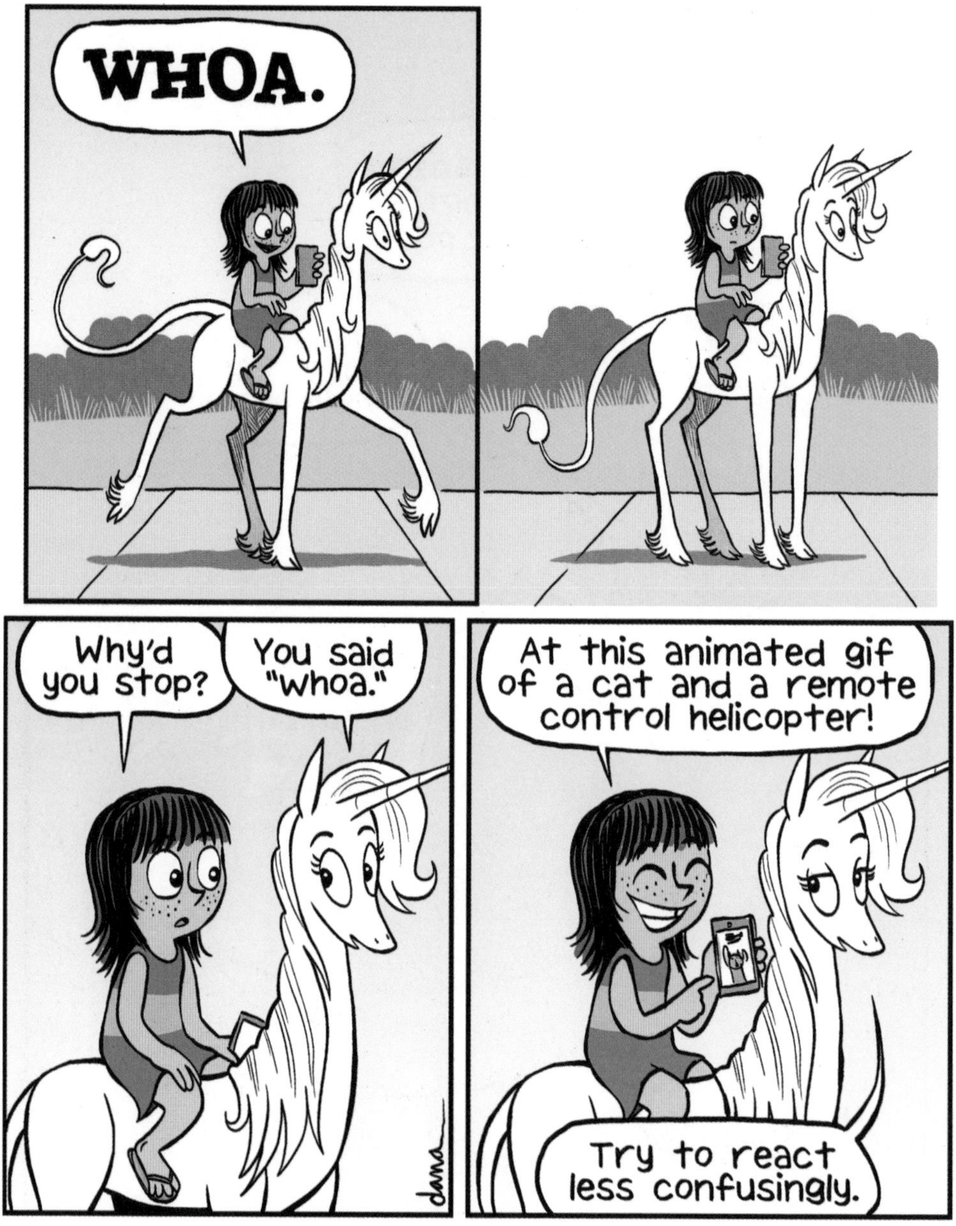
WHOA.
Why'd you stop?
You said "whoa."
At this animated gif of a cat and a remote control helicopter!
Try to react less confusingly.
dana

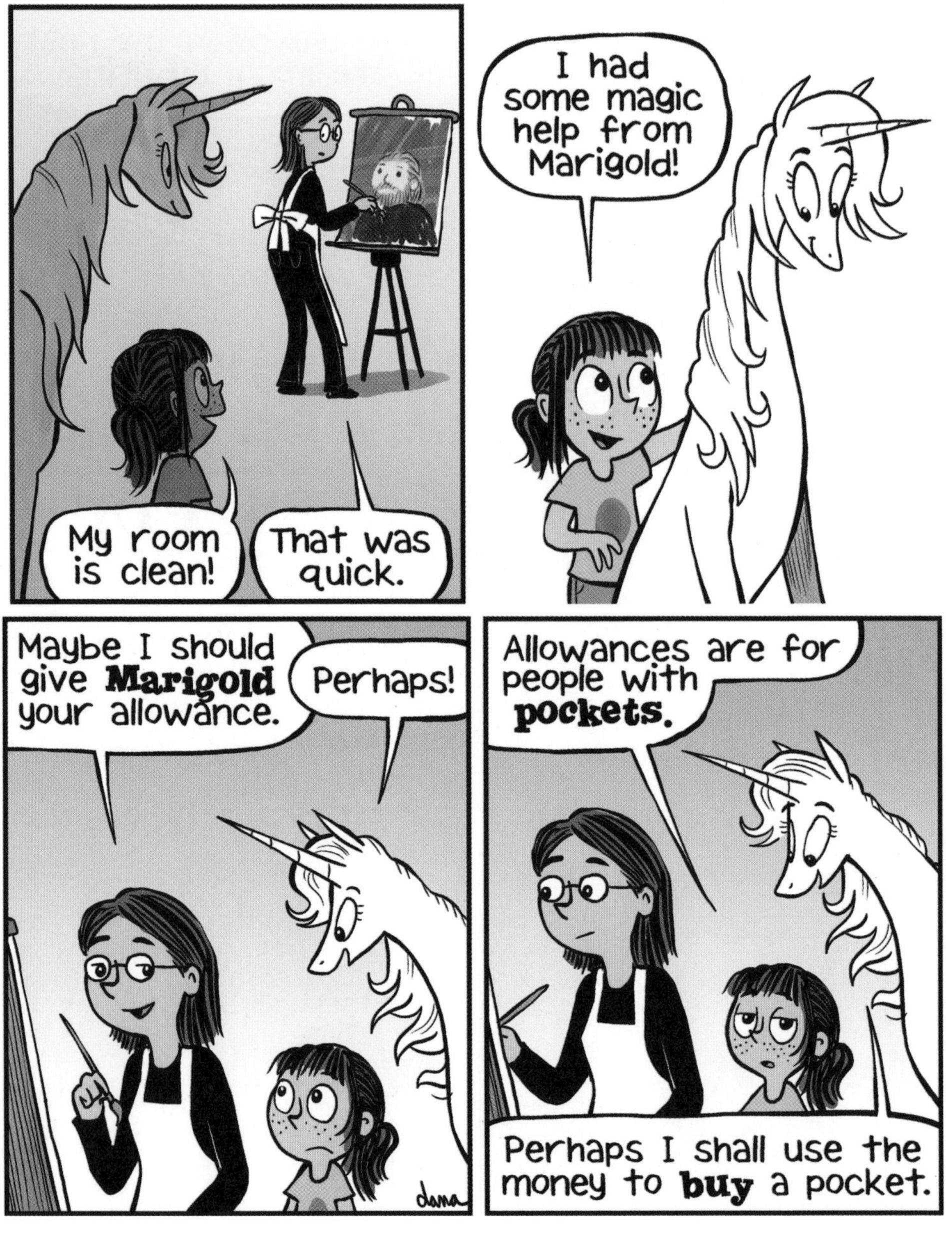
My room is clean!
That was quick.
I had some magic help from Marigold!
Maybe I should give **Marigold** your allowance.
Perhaps!
Allowances are for people with **pockets**.
Perhaps I shall use the money to **buy** a pocket.
dana

133

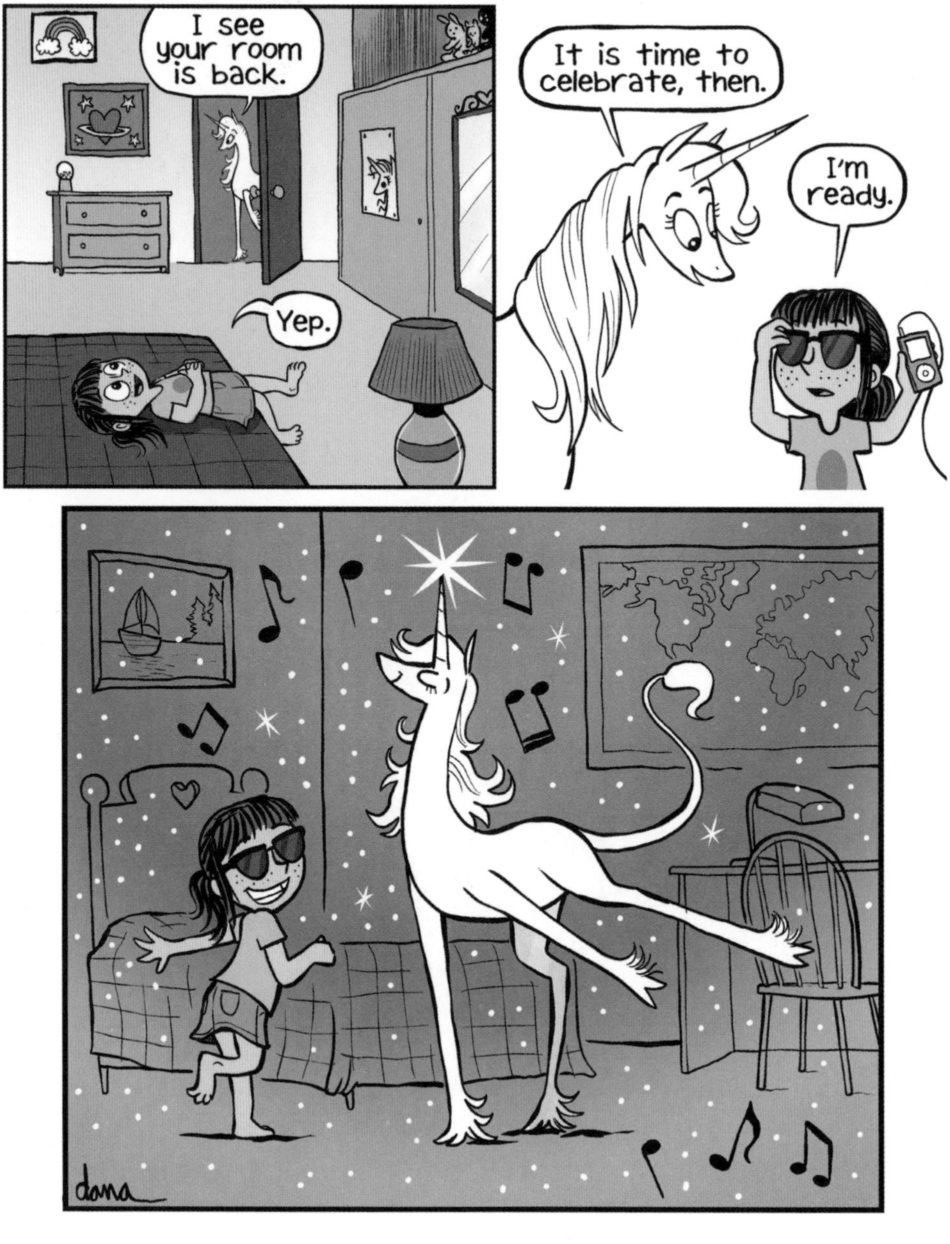
I see your room is back.
Yep.
It is time to celebrate, then.
I'm ready.
dana

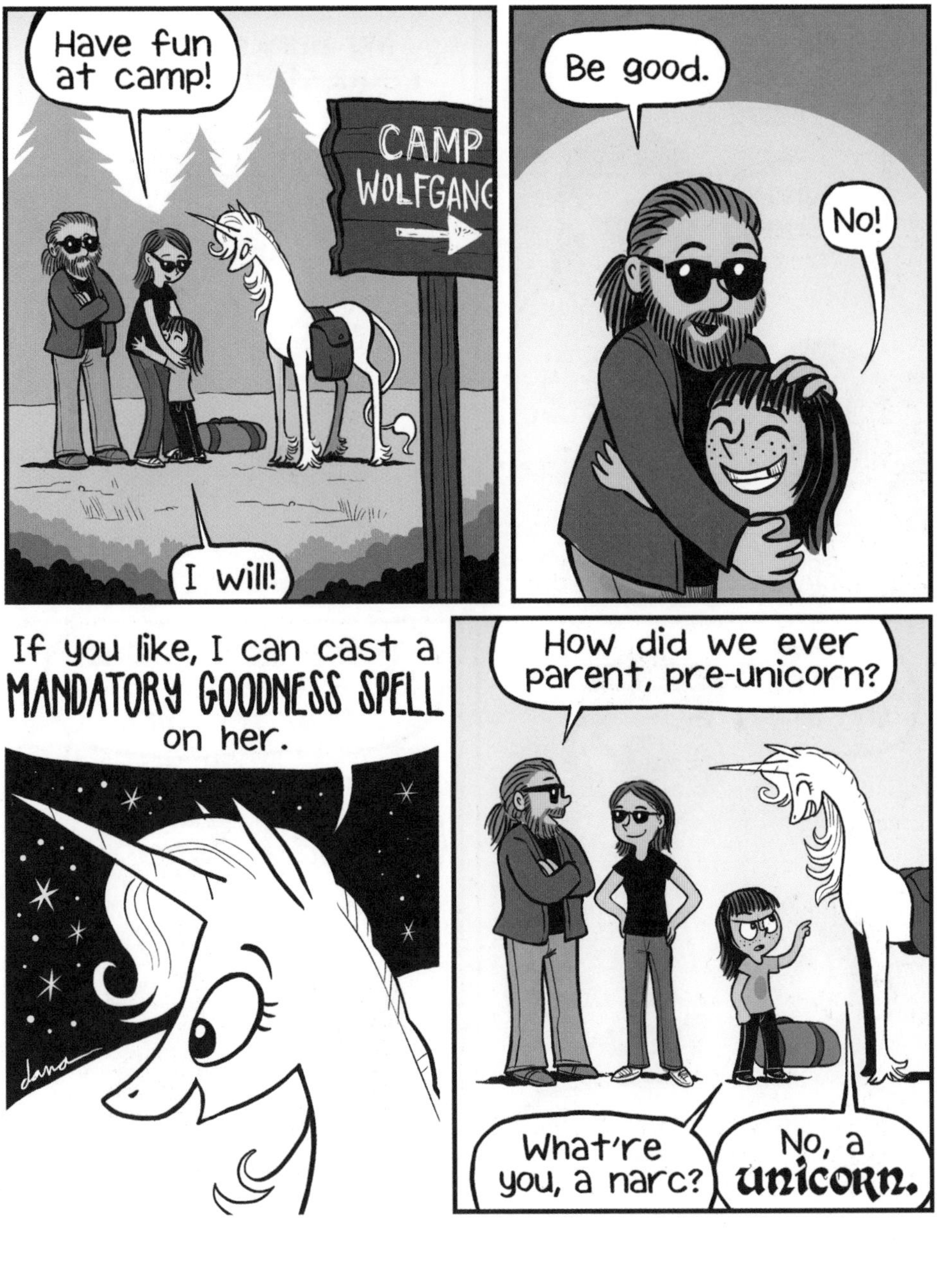
Have fun at camp!
CAMP WOLFGANG
I will!
Be good.
No!
If you like, I can cast a MANDATORY GOODNESS SPELL on her.
How did we ever parent, pre-unicorn?
What're you, a narc?
No, a unicorn.

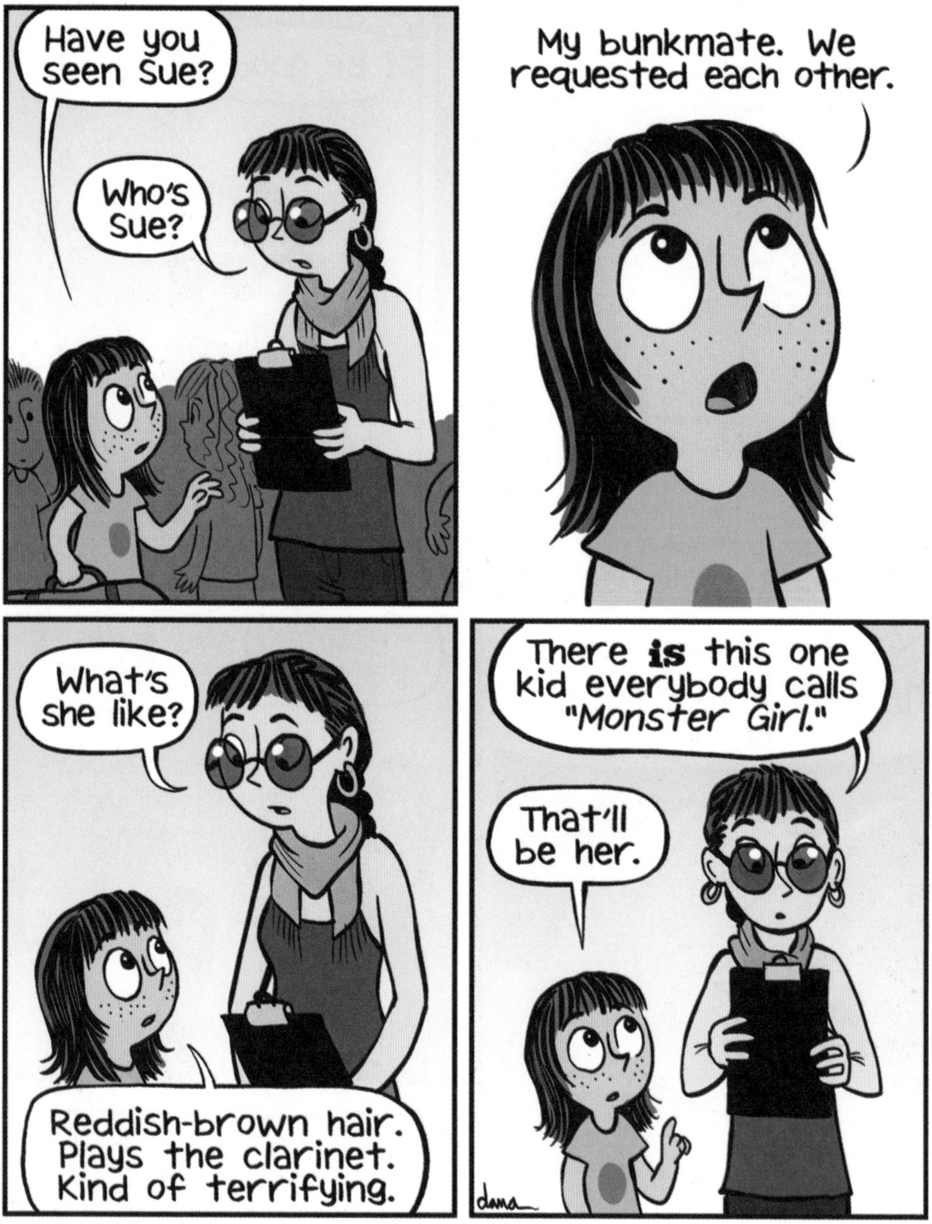
Have you seen Sue?
Who's Sue?
My bunkmate. We requested each other.
What's she like?
Reddish-brown hair. Plays the clarinet. Kind of terrifying.
There **is** this one kid everybody calls *"Monster Girl."*
That'll be her.
dana

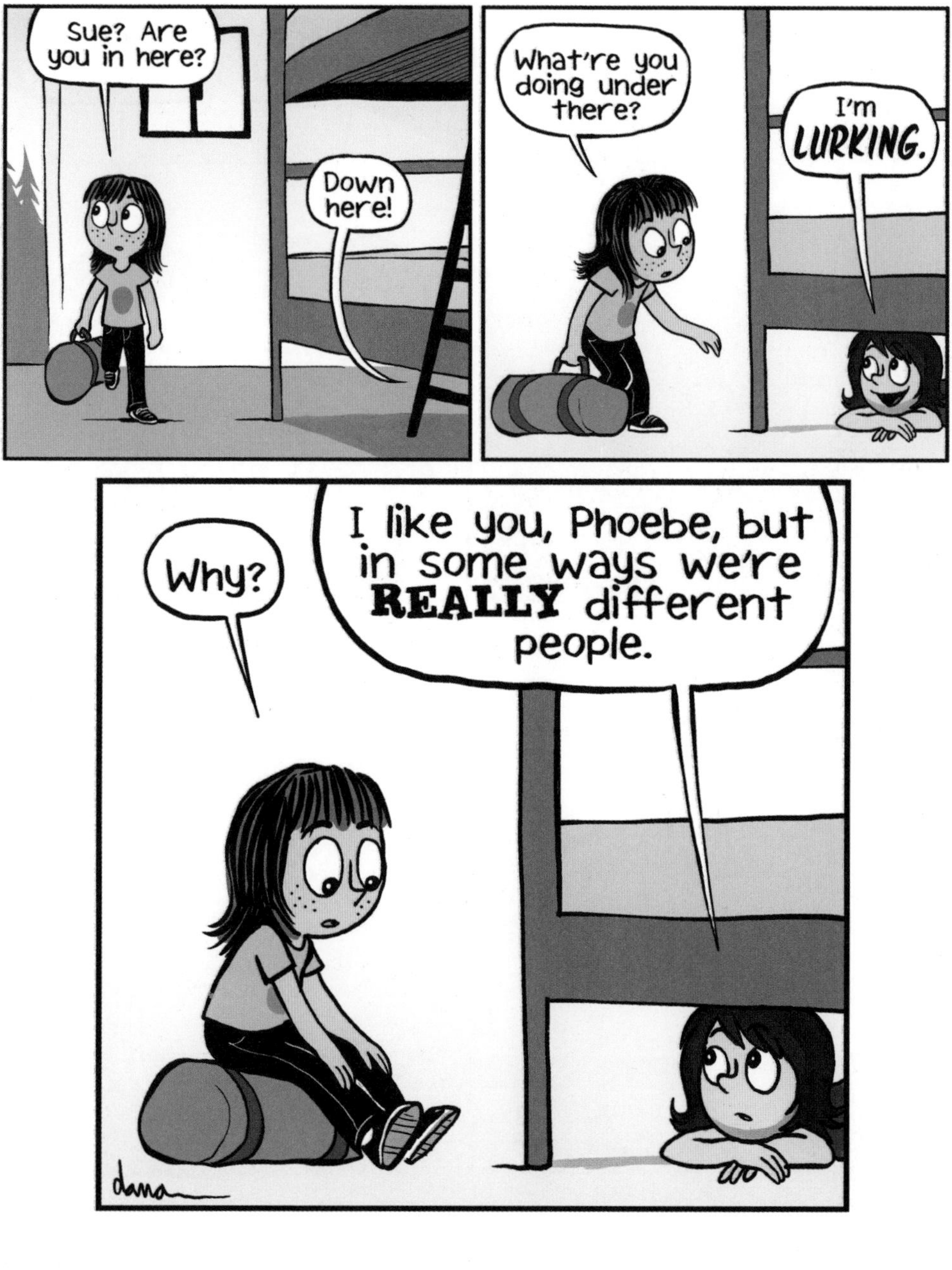
Sue? Are you in here?
Down here!
What're you doing under there?
I'm LURKING.
Why?
I like you, Phoebe, but in some ways we're REALLY different people.
dana

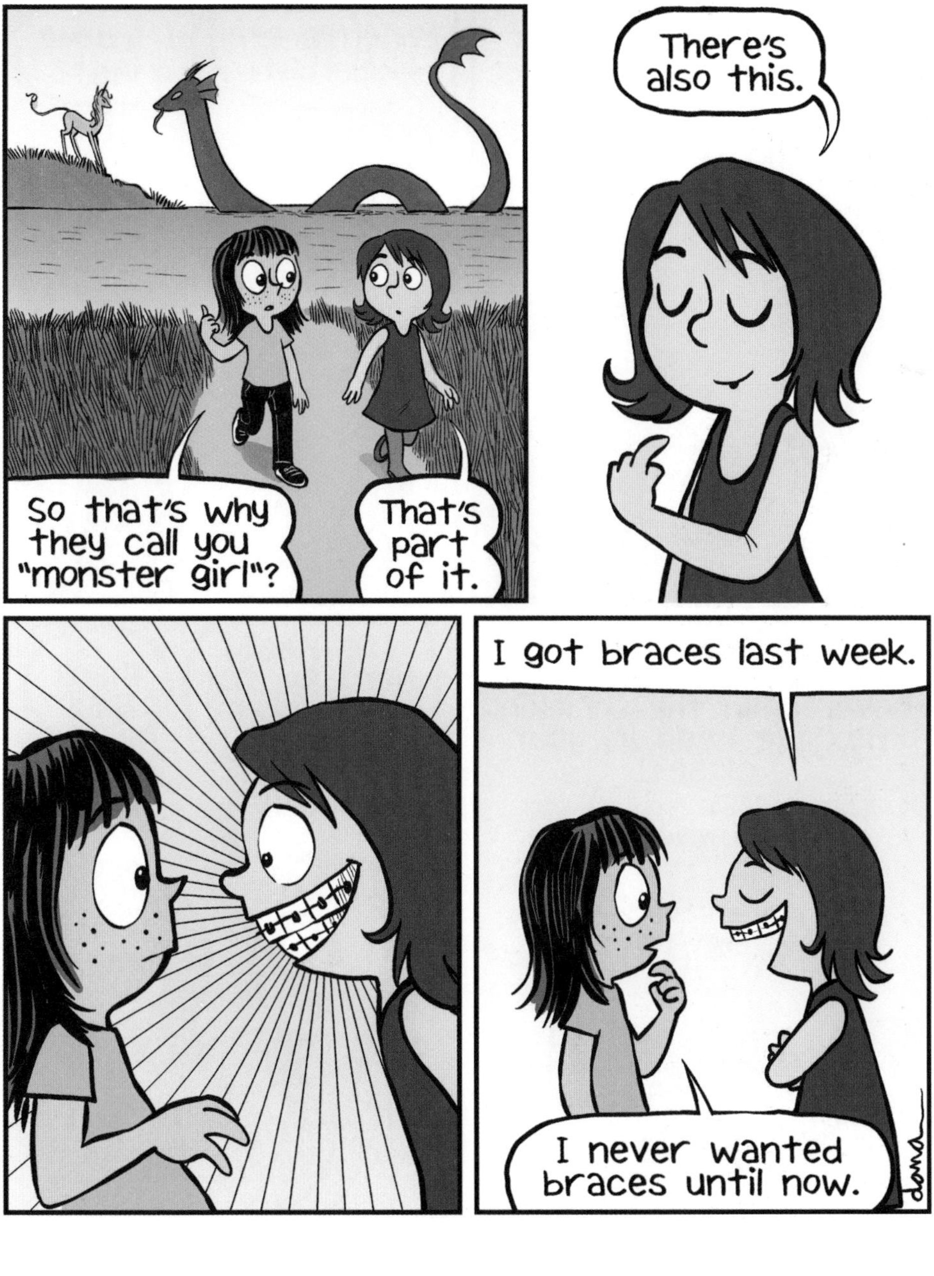
So that's why they call you "monster girl"?
That's part of it.
There's also this.
I got braces last week.
I never wanted braces until now.
dana

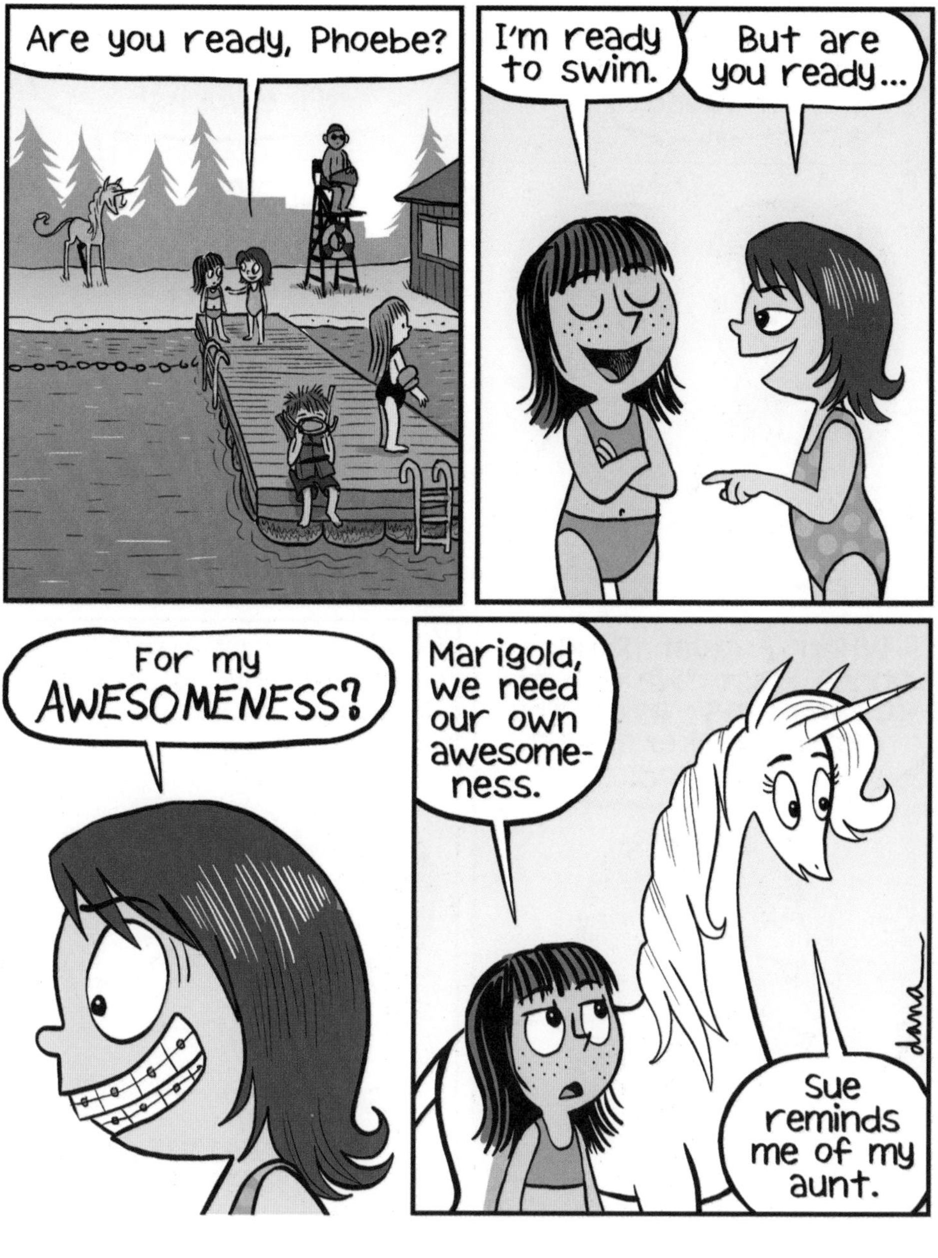
Are you ready, Phoebe?
I'm ready to swim.
But are you ready...
For my AWESOMENESS?
Marigold, we need our own awesomeness.
Sue reminds me of my aunt.
dana

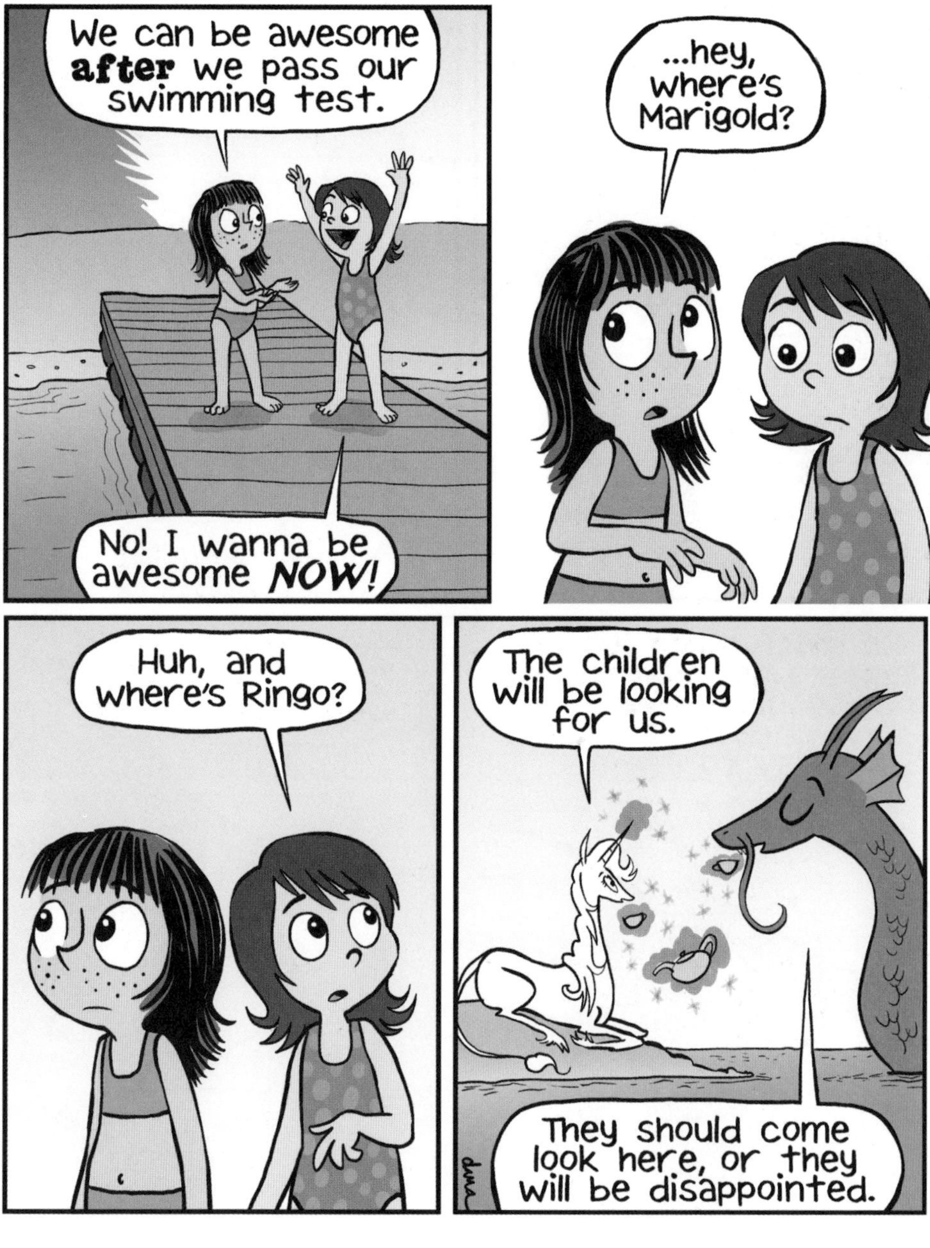
We can be awesome **after** we pass our swimming test.
No! I wanna be awesome *NOW*!
...hey, where's Marigold?
Huh, and where's Ringo?
The children will be looking for us.
They should come look here, or they will be disappointed.
dana

158

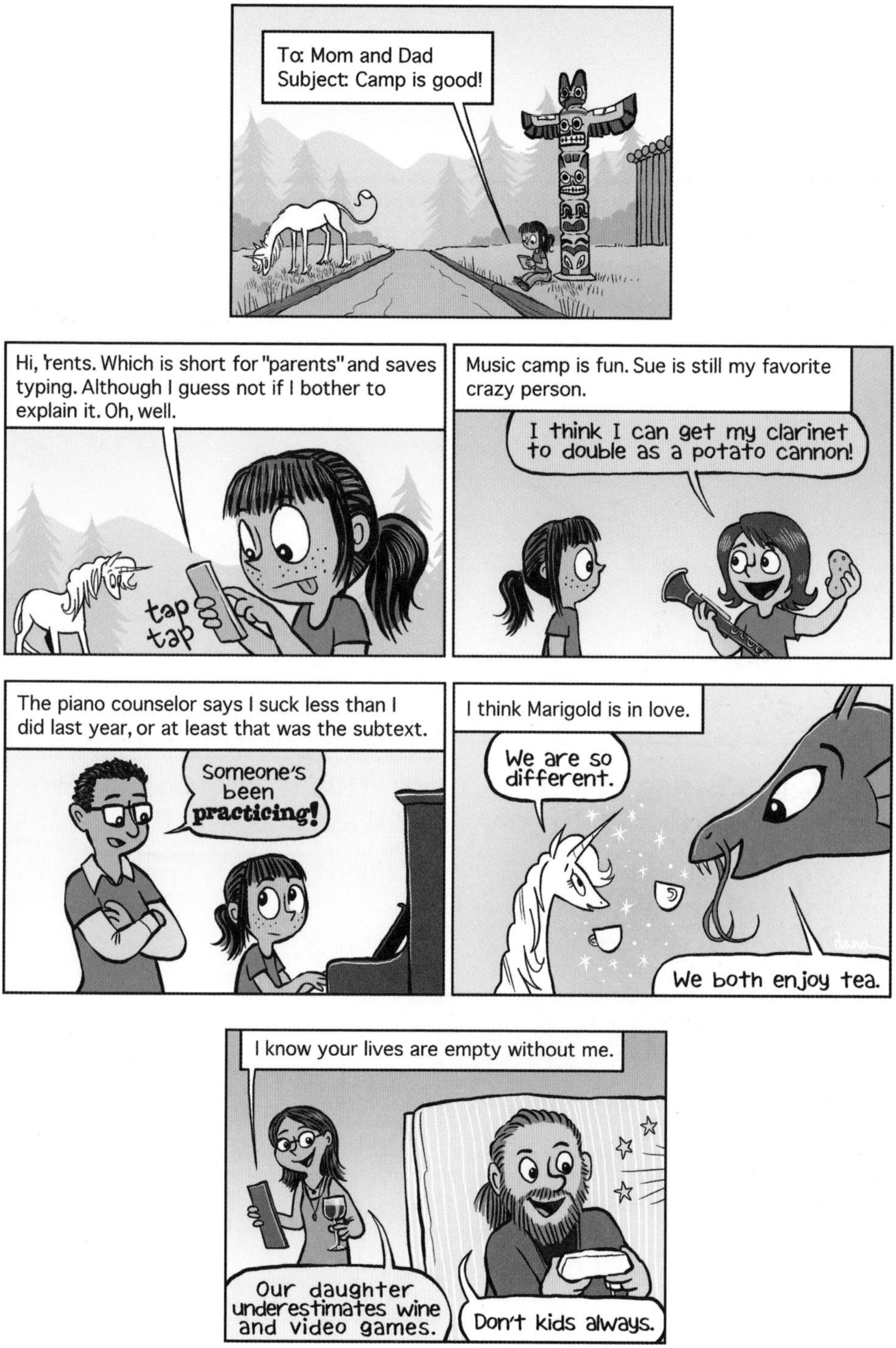
To: Mom and Dad
Subject: Camp is good!
Hi, 'rents. Which is short for "parents" and saves typing. Although I guess not if I bother to explain it. Oh, well.
tap tap
Music camp is fun. Sue is still my favorite crazy person.
I think I can get my clarinet to double as a potato cannon!
The piano counselor says I suck less than I did last year, or at least that was the subtext.
Someone's been practicing!
I think Marigold is in love.
We are so different.
We both enjoy tea.
I know your lives are empty without me.
Our daughter underestimates wine and video games.
Don't kids always.

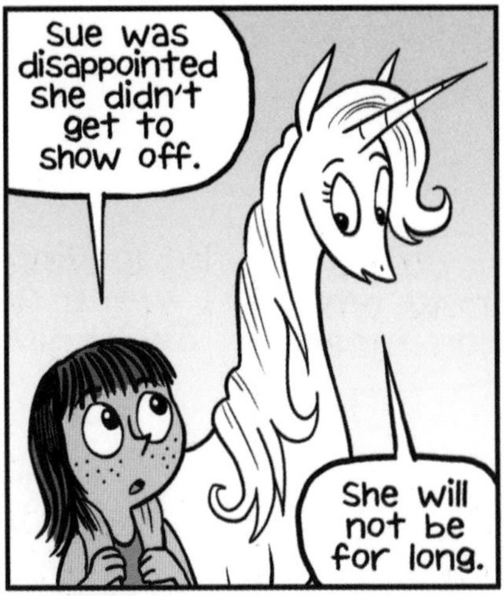
Sue was disappointed she didn't get to show off.
She will not be for long.

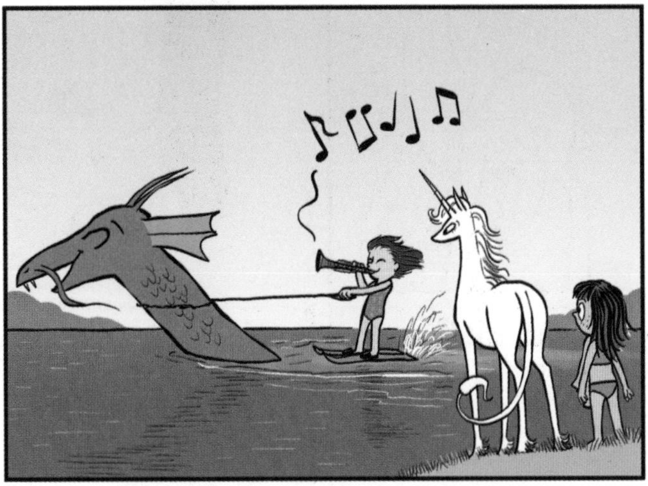

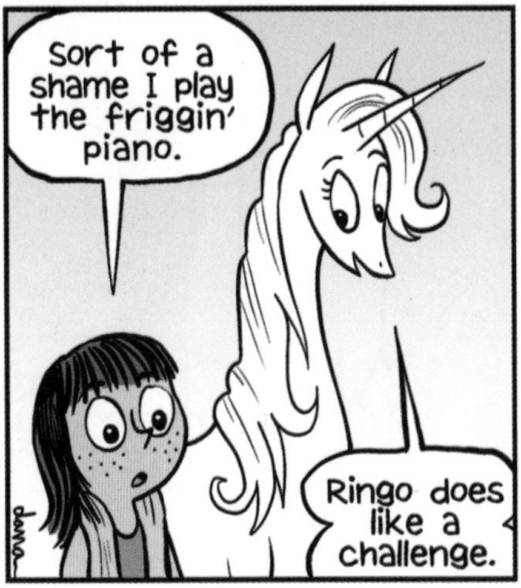
Sort of a shame I play the friggin' piano.
Ringo does like a challenge.

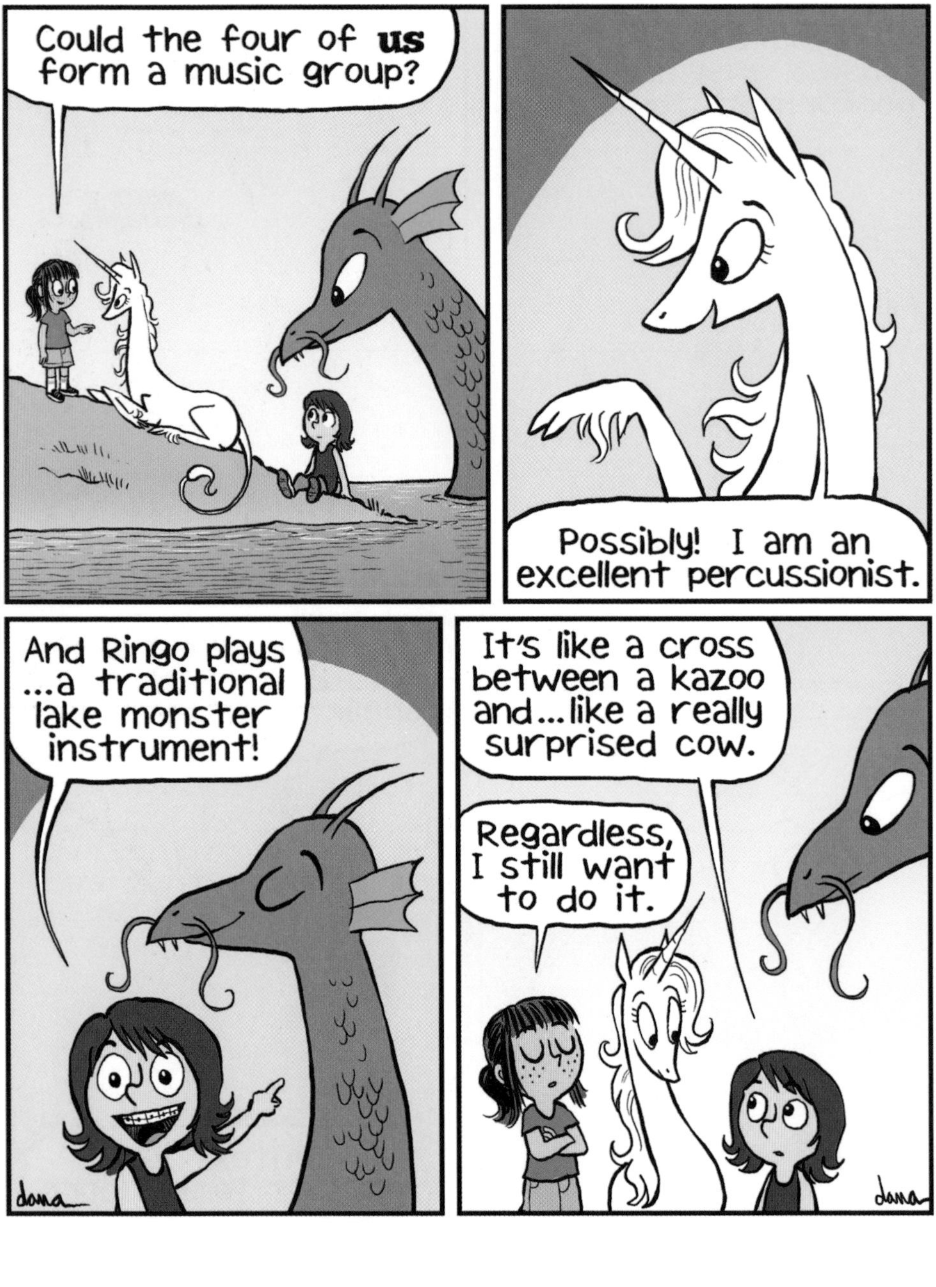
Could the four of **us** form a music group?
Possibly! I am an excellent percussionist.
And Ringo plays ...a traditional lake monster instrument!
It's like a cross between a kazoo and...like a really surprised cow.
Regardless, I still want to do it.
dana
dana

165

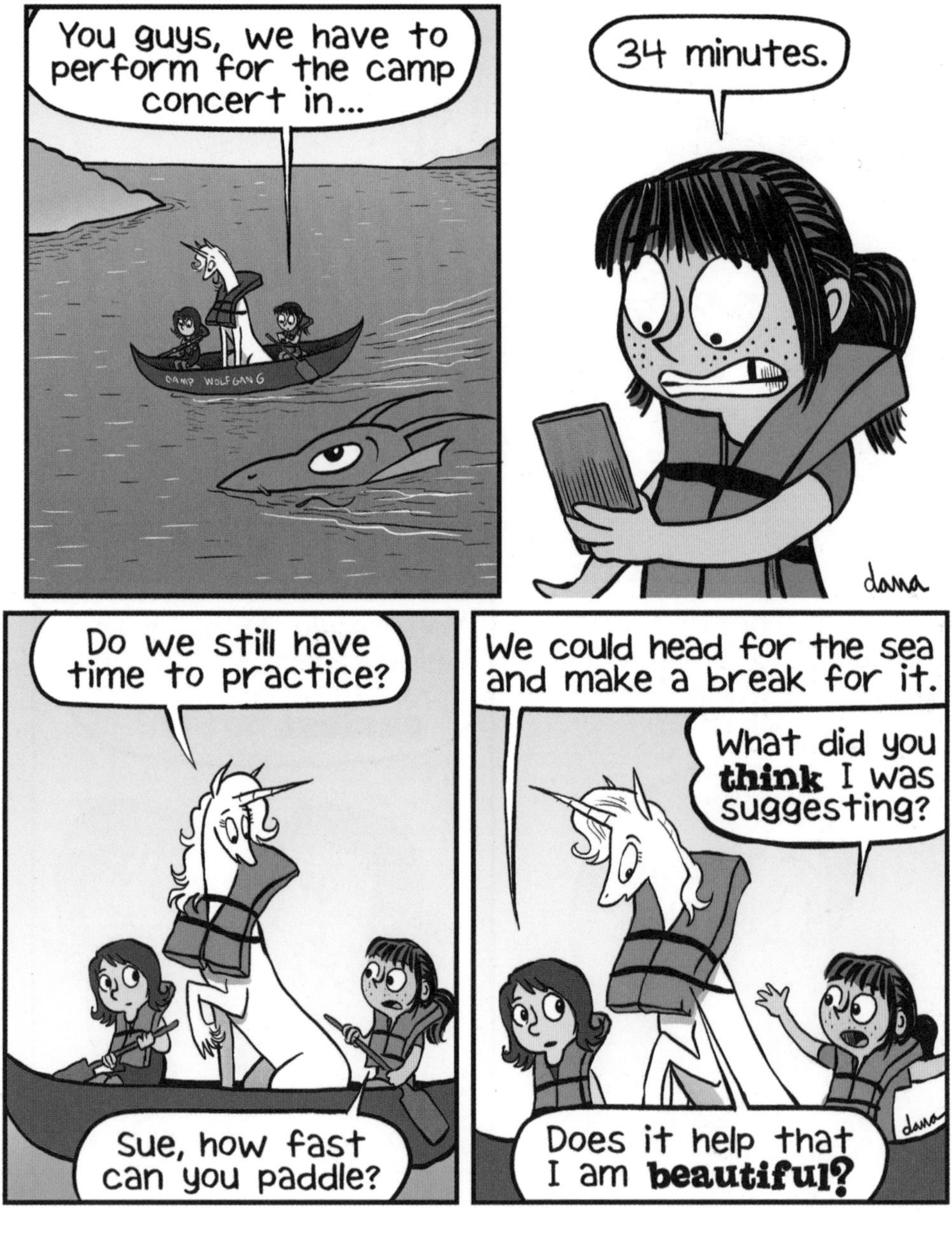
You guys, we have to perform for the camp concert in...
CAMP WOLFGANG
34 minutes.
dana
Do we still have time to practice?
Sue, how fast can you paddle?
We could head for the sea and make a break for it.
What did you **think** I was suggesting?
Does it help that I am **beautiful?**
dana

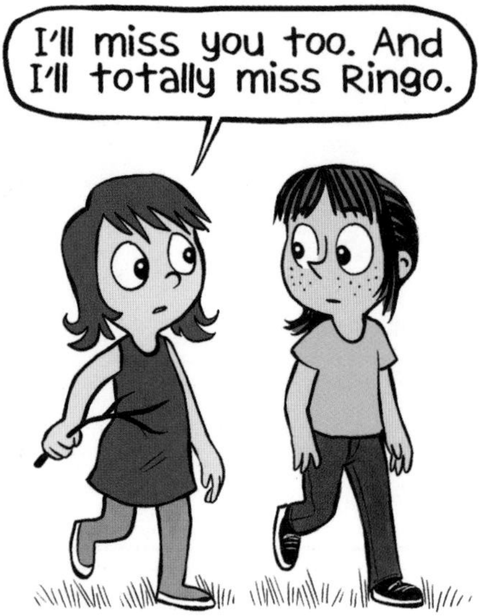
I'll miss you too. And I'll totally miss Ringo.

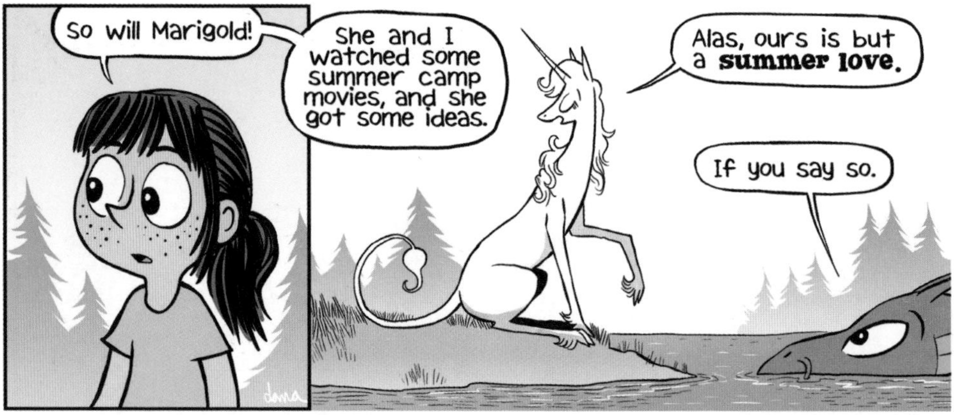
So will Marigold!
She and I watched some summer camp movies, and she got some ideas.
Alas, ours is but a **summer love.**
If you say so.

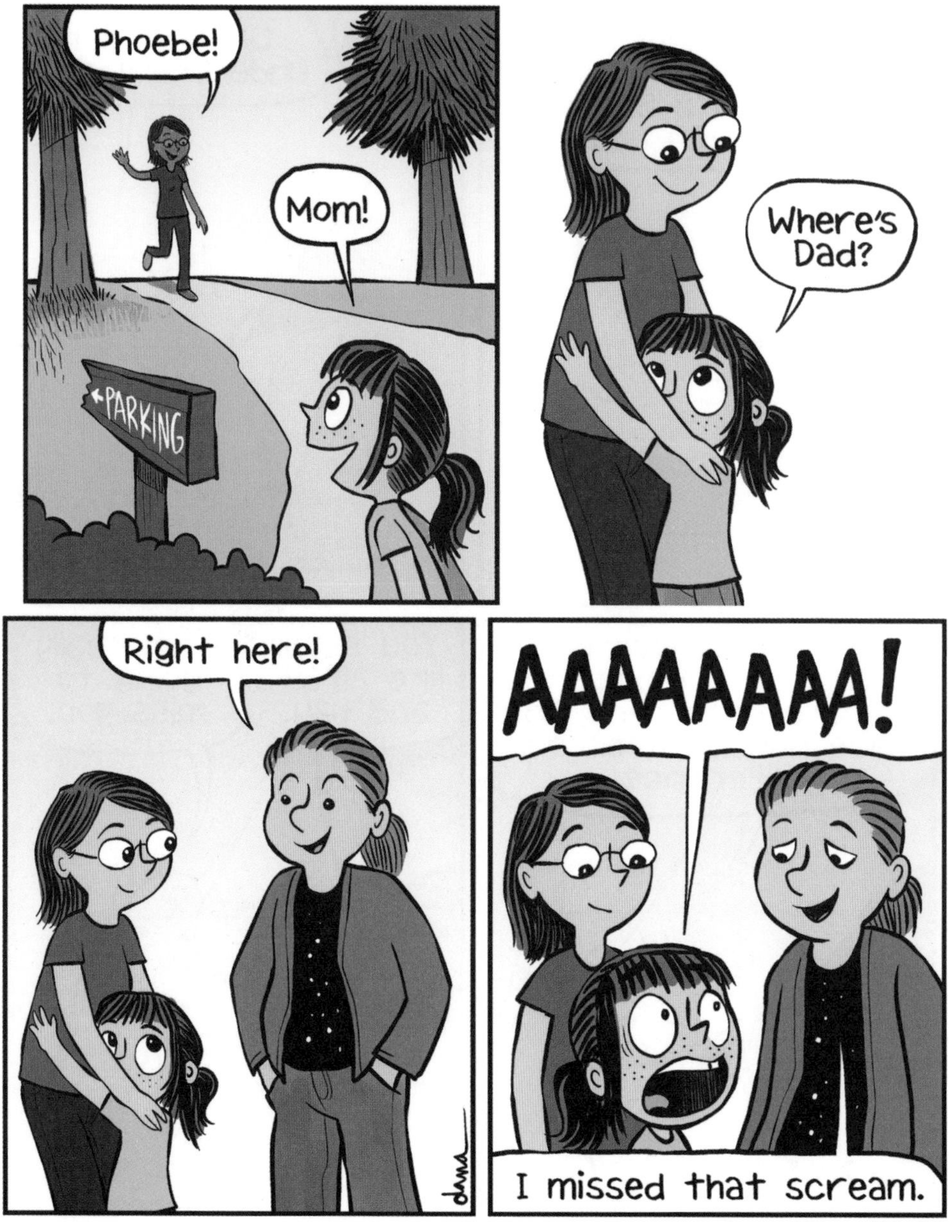
Phoebe!
Mom!
PARKING
Where's Dad?
Right here!
dana
AAAAAAAA!
I missed that scream.

Learn the Creative Process

In the earlier books, I showed you some of how I draw Phoebe, Marigold, and friends.

Now, let's look at how I make comics.

For example, the one where Phoebe asked Marigold about her New Year's resolutions. (It's on page 34 of this book.)

First, I have to come up with ideas.

I like to leave my house to do that. My house is full of distractions.

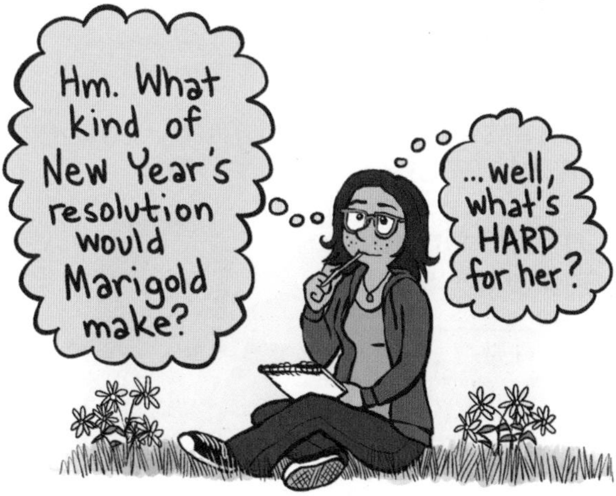
Hm. What kind of New Year's resolution would Marigold make?
...well, what's HARD for her?

When I draw them in my notebook, they look like this:

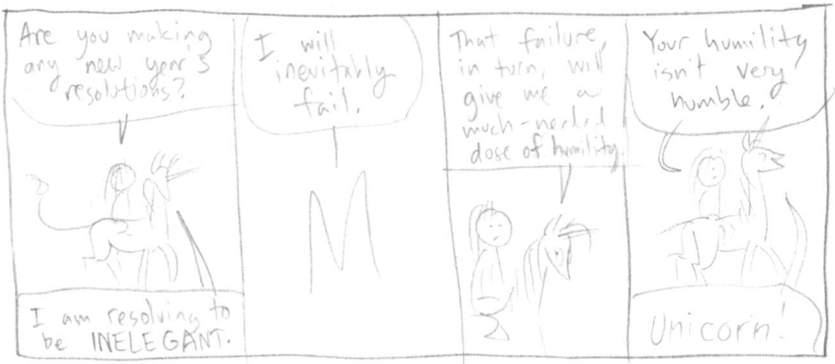
Are you making any new year's resolutions?
I am resolving to be INELEGANT.
I will inevitably fail.
That failure, in turn, will give me a much-needed dose of humility.
Your humility isn't very humble.
Unicorn!

It doesn't have to be much, just enough to show who's talking and what they're doing. (Sometimes, Marigold is just an M, or Phoebe is just a P.)

I take a picture of it on my phone and send it to my editor, so she can tell me what she thinks.

Sometimes she thinks something could be clearer, or funnier.

Other times, she just says:

Once she approves, I get to work on the finished artwork. I do all that on my computer.

First, I add the lettering, so I know how much space I have for the artwork.

Then, I add the rough "pencil" lines, usually in light blue.

Next, I add the black "ink" lines...

Finally, I add in various shades of gray.

(A colorist who works for my publisher does most of the coloring, and as you can see throughout this book, he does a pretty amazing job!)

Glossary

calibrate (cal-li-brate): pg. 35 — verb / to plan carefully

context (con-text): pg. 163 — noun / the set of circumstances that surrounds an event

ensemble (on-som-ble): pg. 163 — noun / a group of musicians

exoskeleton (exo-skel-le-ton): pg. 82 — noun / a hard, external covering

feign (fain): pg. 98 — verb / to imitate or pretend

hallucination (ha-loo-sin-ay-shun): pg. 166 — noun / a vision of something that does not exist

incoherence (in-co-here-ence): pg. 150 — noun / a state of not making sense

percussionist (per-cuh-shun-ist): pg. 164 — noun / a drummer or any musician who plays an instrument by striking or beating it

prescient (pre-shunt): pg. 60 — adjective / having foresight

proximity (prox-im-it-ee): pg. 175 — noun / nearness

schism (si-zem): pg. 98 — noun / a division into two opposing groups

scintillating (sin-till-ate-ing): pg. 57 — adjective / brilliant or exciting

victuals (vitt-tles): pg. 26 — noun / food or provisions

vortex (vor-tex): pg. 173 — noun / a whirling mass that draws things into its current

whippersnapper (whip-per-snap-per): pg. 37 — noun / an offensively bold young person

Andrews McMeel Publishing
a division of Andrews McMeel Universal
1130 Walnut Street, Kansas City, Missouri 64106

www.andrewsmcmeel.com

18 19 20 21 22 SDB 11 10 9 8 7 6 5 4

ISBN: 978-1-4494-7791-2

Library of Congress Control Number: 2016931068

Made by:
Shenzhen Donnelley Printing Company Ltd.
Address and location of manufacturer:
No. 47, Wuhe Nan Road, Bantian Ind. Zone,
Shenzhen China, 518129
4th Printing—1/29/18

ATTENTION: SCHOOLS AND BUSINESSES

Andrews McMeel books are available at quantity discounts with bulk purchase for educational, business, or sales promotional use. For information, please e-mail the Andrews McMeel Publishing Special Sales Department: specialsales@amuniversal.com.

Check out more *Phoebe and Her Unicorn*

Phoebe and Her Unicorn
Dana Simpson

Unicorn on a Roll
Another Phoebe and Her Unicorn Adventure
Dana Simpson

Unicorn vs. Goblins
Another Phoebe and Her Unicorn Adventure
Dana Simpson

Unicorn Crossing
Another Phoebe and Her Unicorn Adventure
Dana Simpson

Phoebe and Her Unicorn in
The Magic Storm
Dana Simpson

Rainy Day Unicorn Fun
140 Magical Puzzles
A Phoebe and Her Unicorn Activity Book
Dana Simpson

If you like Phoebe, look for these books!

Anne of Green Gables
a graphic novel

the Pinkaboos
BITTERLY AND THE GIANT PROBLEM
FRIGHT SCHOOL
Jake and Laura Gosselin

Wallace the Brave
Will Henry

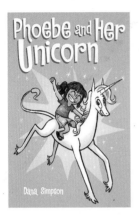

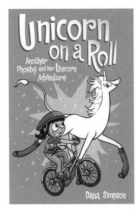

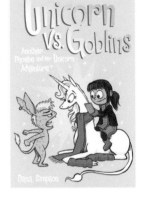

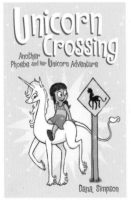

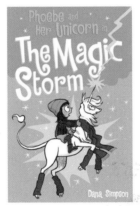

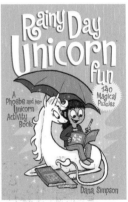

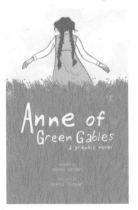

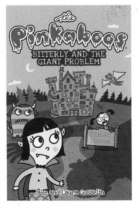

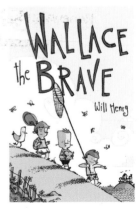